THE
HEALING
QUILT

Return of the

Half-Stitched *Amish* Quilting Club

THE
HEALING
QUILT

WANDA &
BRUNSTETTER

New York Times Bestselling Author

SHILOH RUN PRESS

CHAPTER I

Sarasota, Florida

Seating herself on a weathered, wooden bench, Emma Miller gazed at the waves lapping gently against the shore. The soothing scene almost lulled her to sleep. Lido Beach was peaceful on this early January morning, and there weren't many people milling about yet. It almost felt as if she and Lamar had the whole beach to themselves. This morning after breakfast, Lamar had talked her into catching the bus and coming here so they could enjoy the beach before it got too crowded.

Wiggling her bare toes in the sand, Emma watched as her husband rolled his trousers up to his knees and waded into the crystal-clear, turquoise water. Lamar seemed happy and contented, and thanks to the balmy weather, his arthritis didn't bother him nearly so much.

Lamar was definitely getting around more easily, and that made it worth moving down here for the winter.

Unfortunately, after only two weeks of living in their newly purchased vacation home inside the village of Pinecraft, Emma was bored. Sure, there was plenty to do. They could visit other Amish and Mennonites; spend time on the beach looking for shells; or ride their three-wheeler bikes to the park or one of the many stores and restaurants in the area, since horse and buggies were not allowed. But Emma wanted more. She needed something meaningful and constructive to do.

"Come join me," Lamar called, looking eagerly at Emma. "The water's warm, and there are lots of shells!" His thick gray hair and matching beard stood in stark contrast to the turquoise-blue water behind him.

Emma smiled and waved in response. She wasn't in the mood to get her dress wet this morning. For that matter, she wasn't in the mood for much of anything just now. Emma missed her family and friends in Shipshewana, Indiana. She even missed the cold, wintry days, sitting by the fire with a cup of hot coffee while she worked on one of her quilting projects. Fortunately, Emma's daughter, Mary, and her family lived next door and were keeping an eye on Emma and Lamar's Indiana home, as well as feeding and caring for Emma's goats.

Emma's sister, Rachel, had planned to come down for a few weeks, but one of Rachel's daughters was sick, and she'd gone to her house to help out while she recuperated, so she might not make it, after all. Emma couldn't help feeling disappointed.

Maybe I should call Mary and ask her to send me some of my quilting supplies, Emma thought. *It would be good to have something productive to do while we are here.*

"Emma, aren't you going to join me?" Lamar hollered, holding up a large shell he'd found. "You oughta come and take a look at this one. It's the best shell yet!"

"Maybe later," she called in response.

Lamar waded out of the water and plodded across the white sand, stopping in front of Emma. "Is something wrong? You usually enjoy looking for shells with me."

Making circles in the sand with her big toe, Emma sighed. "I do, Lamar, and don't take this wrong, but I wish there was more for me to do than come here to the beach or bike around Pinecraft, where I end up talking to people about family back home. I need something meaningful to do with my time."

He took a seat on the bench beside her and placed the colorful shell in her lap. "Why don't you teach some quilting classes? We talked about that before we left Indiana."

She gave a slow nod. "*Jah*, that idea was mentioned, but I'm not sure there would be enough interest in quilting here in Florida. At home where so many tourists come to learn about the Amish, people are eager to learn how to quilt. Here where it's warm and sunny most of the winter, people are probably more interested in spending time on the beach and being involved in other outdoor activities."

"You won't know if you don't try." He patted her arm affectionately. "Why don't we run an ad in the local newspaper and put some flyers up around the area? Maybe you could talk to the owner of the quilt shop on Bahia Vista Street and see if you could teach your classes there."

Emma shook her head. "If I'm going to teach quilting, I prefer that it be done in our own home, where it's less formal and people will feel more relaxed."

"I understand," Lamar said. "And if it's meant for you to have another six-week quilting class, then people will come."

Emma pursed her lips as she mulled over the idea. "If I did hold some quilting classes, would you be willing to help me again?"

"Of course. I can explain the history of quilts at the introductory class and be there to help out whenever I'm needed. It'll be a little different in our new surroundings. I'm sure I'll enjoy it as much as I have all the other times I've helped you teach back home." Lamar smiled, his green eyes twinkling like fireflies on a summer's night. "It will be interesting to see who God sends to our classes this time around."

Emma nodded, anticipation welling in her soul. "Okay then. Let's start advertising right away."

Chicago, Illinois

Bruce "B.J." Jensen stood in front of the easel he'd set up near the window in his studio. He tipped his head, scrutinizing his most recent painting— ocean waves lapping against the shore as the sun began to set.

B.J. frowned. He hadn't been to the ocean since his wife, Brenda, died five years ago. For that matter, he hadn't been anywhere outside of Chicago since then. At first his responsibilities as an art teacher had kept him tied to home. After he retired a year ago, freelance jobs kept him too busy to travel. But he was running out of time. Pretty soon, if he didn't see some of the things he'd been wanting to, it would be too late.

He stared out the window at the fresh-fallen snow. B.J. had always loved winter and appreciated that he lived where all four seasons could be enjoyed. But this year for the first time, the snow and bitter cold winds Chicago was known for really bothered B.J., and he was ready for a change.

If only I had more time, he thought with regret. *Time to see all the things I've missed and time to spend with my family and friends.*

B.J. had been diagnosed with cancer two years ago—just a few days after his sixtieth birthday. Recently, he'd found out that the cancer had spread from his throat to other parts of his body. But he hadn't told his daughters, Robyn and Jill; they both had busy lives of their own, and he didn't want them to worry. They thought the cancer surgery had been successful and that he was in remission. He didn't have the heart to tell them the truth. Knowing his daughters, they'd set everything aside to take care of him. B.J. didn't want that. He didn't want their sympathy, either. Maybe when he reached the final stages he would tell them. Until then, he planned to live each day to its fullest, while seeing and doing some of the things he'd always wanted to do. First off would be a trip to Sarasota, Florida, to see the Gulf of Mexico and paint some beautiful scenes on the beach.

Sarasota

Kyle Wilson stopped near the living-room couch. His fifteen-year-old daughter, Erika, sat in her wheelchair in front of the window facing the bay. She seemed so forlorn, with head down and shoulders slumped. But then, that was nothing new for her these days. Once full of life and unafraid, Erika was a different person now. She'd been despondent for more than a year—ever since her accident.

Kyle reflected on the event that had left his only child paralyzed from the waist down. Erika had invited two of her friends over to swim in their pool. They'd had a great time, laughing, splashing each other, and taking turns competing on the diving board.

Erika had learned to swim when she was a young girl. Kyle and his wife, Gayle, had nicknamed her "tadpole" because she loved the water so much. Last year when Erika turned fourteen, her interest turned to diving and trying different techniques off the springboard. Kyle was truly amazed at how fearless his daughter had been. She'd seemed to be good at everything, no matter what she attempted.

Kyle's throat constricted as he recalled how the accident happened. . . .

"Come on, Erika, it's getting late, and you're tired. I think you'd better get out of the pool."

"In a few minutes, Dad. I just wanna do one more dive," Erika protested. "It's called a 'forward reverse.'"

Kyle could almost feel her eagerness as she climbed out of the pool and clambered up the diving-board ladder, so he let it go. He watched as Erika stood forward on the board, staring down at the pool's blue depth, her honey-blond hair pulled back in a ponytail, with water still dripping off the ends. As she leaped into the air, her body arching backward, it was like watching in slow-motion as her head and shoulders cleared the board.

Kyle held his breath. His daughter's fluid motion seemed to go perfectly. But instead of Erika's body straightening out after clearing the board, she made a wrong move. Her body came out of the arc at an odd angle, throwing her off-balance.

Kyle stared in horror as Erika's back and legs hit the board with a terrible crack. He watched helplessly as she bounced off the board and let out a scream as she fell into the water. Something had gone terribly wrong.

He leaped out of his chair, knowing he had to get his precious daughter help as quickly as possible.

Sweat beaded on Kyle's forehead as his mind snapped back to the present. *It's my fault she's crippled,* he berated himself for the umpteenth time. *If only I'd insisted she quit for the day, before she did that stupid dive. If I'd known what Erika had in mind, I would have stopped her before it was too late. I'm a doctor who treats many children every year, but I couldn't help my own daughter because the damage to her spine could not be fixed.*

Kyle clenched his fingers until his nails dug into the palms of his hands. Erika's accident had been the second traumatic event he'd faced in a relatively short time. Kyle's beautiful wife had died a year earlier from injuries she'd sustained when her car was broadsided by a truck. Truth was, Kyle felt guilty about Gayle's accident, too. She'd asked him to run to the store that rainy evening to pick up some baking soda she'd forgotten when she'd gone shopping earlier in the day. Gayle had all the other ingredients she needed to make a batch of chocolate chip cookies, Kyle's favorite. But Kyle had said he was too tired after a long day at the hospital to run to the store. So Gayle had gone out on her own. If Kyle had been driving the car, he might have avoided the accident. Even if he'd been the one killed, Erika would at least still have her mother.

Kyle rubbed a pulsating spot on his forehead. He knew all the *if onlys* and *what ifs* wouldn't change the facts, but it was hard not to be consumed by guilt—especially when he'd had to watch his daughter struggle with her disability. Erika needed something to look forward to each day—something meaningful to do with her time. He'd tried to interest her in some creative projects she could do from her wheelchair—like making beaded jewelry and painting—but she'd flatly refused. She wasn't even interested in playing her violin anymore. Gone was her dream of becoming a high school cheerleader, swimming, and going to dances. Erika seemed to think her life was over, and that grieved him immensely.

Should I force the issue and hire someone to come in and teach Erika something despite her objections? he wondered. *Would she cooperate if I did?*

The phone rang, startling Kyle out of his musings.

"I'll get it, Dad," Erika said, seeming to notice him for the first time. "At least answering the phone is something I can manage."

Kyle couldn't help noticing her sarcastic tone. Did she really feel that she wasn't capable of doing anything more than answering the telephone?

Dear Lord, he silently prayed. *Please help me find something beneficial for my daughter to do.*

———

"Come here, girl!" Kim Morris called as her dog frolicked on the beach, kicking up sand. The black-and-tan German shepherd ignored her and chased after a seagull.

Kim clapped her hands. "Stop that, Maddie, right now!"

Apparently tired of chasing the gull, Maddie darted in the direction of a young boy playing in the sand with his bucket and shovel. Thinking the child might be frightened by the dog, Kim picked up a stick and called Maddie again. "Come on, girl, let's play fetch!"

Woof! Woof! Maddie raced to Kim's side, eagerly wagging her tail.

Kim flung the stick into the water and laughed as Maddie darted in after it. The dog might be six years old, but she had the energy of a pup.

Coming out of the water and bounding across the sand, Maddie dropped the stick a few inches from Kim's bare toes. Kim grunted and picked it up. She would toss it a few more times, and then it would be time to get off the beach. It wouldn't be good if she were late to work her first day on the job. Being fairly new to the area, Kim was glad she'd been hired as a waitress at a restaurant a short distance from the small community known as Pinecraft. A lot of Amish and Mennonites lived in Pinecraft, either full- or part-time, and she'd been told that the restaurant business during the winter months was always the best because of so many visitors.

I just hope I don't lose this job because of my klutziness, Kim thought as she gave the stick another good toss, and Maddie tore after it. *I can't live on unemployment forever, and I need this job if I'm gonna start a new life for myself.*

Kim had moved from her home state of North Carolina to Sarasota a few months ago, hoping to start a new life with her boyfriend, Darrell. But things hadn't worked out, and they'd broken up. Rather than moving back home and admitting to her folks that she'd lost another boyfriend, Kim had decided to stay in Florida and make the best of the situation.

Since she loved the beach and enjoyed year-round warmer weather, she thought she could be happy living here, even without Darrell. Kim's track record with men wasn't that good, and she was beginning to doubt whether she'd ever find the right one. For now, though, she needed to settle into her new job, make a few friends, and find something creative to do in her spare time. Hopefully, this would give her life more meaning. Making friends shouldn't be that difficult, as she'd always been a people person. Finding something creative to do shouldn't be that hard, either. The thing Kim worried about most was keeping her job, but with determination to do her best, she was sure that would work out, too. At least she hoped it would. If it didn't, she might be forced to return to North Carolina, and that would mean admitting to her folks that she'd failed again.

CHAPTER 2

Phyllis Barstow smiled across the dinner table at her husband, Mike. "How'd it go on the boat today?" she questioned.

"The fishing went fine, but my boat started acting up. If it keeps on, I'll have to take it in for an evaluation. Things are busy right now, with all the visitors in town, and I can't afford to lose any business." He took a drink of his lemonade.

"Well, don't take any chances with the boat," Phyllis cautioned. "I don't want you getting stranded in the middle of the gulf or the bay—especially with a boat full of people."

Mike pulled his fingers through the ends of his dark, wavy hair. "You worry too much, Phyllis. I'm not gonna get stranded." He finished his pancakes, pushed away from the table, and stood. "I need to get going. See you this evening, hon." He gave Phyllis a quick peck on the cheek, grabbed the lunch she'd packed for him, and raced out the back door.

Phyllis sighed. Mike had become a workaholic. His charter fishing boat seemed to be his life these days, and his relationship with her was no longer at the top of his list. Even though she went on the boat with him sometimes to help out, it wasn't the same as spending time alone with her husband, since Mike was busy with the people who paid him to take them fishing.

Ever since their twin girls, Elaine and Elizabeth, had gone off to college, Phyllis had been trying to get Mike to pay more attention to her. But work always came first. She was forty-five and he was forty-six, and since they weren't getting any younger, she hated to see him pulling away from her—especially when a boat and fish were what seemed to be coming between them.

Phyllis reached for her cup of coffee and drank the last of it. *What I need is something fun and creative to do that won't leave me smelling like fish.* She tapped her fingers along the edge of the table. *Maybe I should take that quilting class I read about on the bulletin board at the supermarket the other day. At least it would be something to look forward to, and it would give me the opportunity to be creative.*

She reached for the phone. *Think I'll give the teacher a call and see if she has room in her class for one more student. This will certainly be an adventure. . .something I've never done before.*

———◦———

As Noreen Webber drove home from her hair appointment, a sense of satisfaction welled in her soul. She had wanted a red sports car since she was eighteen years old and had finally purchased one last week, on her sixty-fifth birthday. The car not only looked cute, but it had all the bells and whistles. She'd waited a long time to have the car of her dreams, and just sitting in the vehicle, not to mention driving it, caused her to feel like a teenager again. So much so, that it made her wish she was young again and could flirt the next time she saw a good-looking guy.

Better get my head out of the clouds and come down to earth, because I think my flirting days are over. Noreen glanced in her rearview mirror to see if her hair looked as good as she hoped. Yes, every hair was in place, and Noreen's stylist had done a good job with the new cut and style. She knew it was vain, but if she was going to drive a sports car, then she wanted to look as young as possible.

At least I can enjoy driving it for a few good years—until I'm either too old, or the desire to own a sporty-looking car passes, she told herself. *In the meantime, I'm going to dress and think as young as I can. Who knows, maybe some nice-looking man will ask me out. I'm not looking to get married again, but it might be kind of fun to start dating. If I were to find the right man, I might even consider marriage again.*

Noreen, a widow for the last five years, had retired from teaching high school English two years ago. She'd been married to her husband, Ben, for forty years, until he died unexpectedly from a heart attack. The first couple of years after his death had been hard, but Noreen's job kept her going. Now that she was retired, she felt like a fish out of water, and always seemed to be searching for something meaningful to do. Her only child, Todd, whom she and Ben had adopted, was married and lived in Texas, so Noreen only saw him a few times a year. Todd's wife, Kara, had been previously married and had two young boys, whom Todd was helping her raise. They'd invited Noreen to move to Texas, but she liked the warmer weather in Florida and preferred not to move.

Noreen often filled her lonely hours walking on the beach. She also volunteered a few days a week at a local children's hospital and took as many creative classes as she could, just to have something fun to do, and so she could be around people. This morning, Noreen had seen an ad in the local newspaper about a six-week quilting class being offered by a woman who lived in the village of Pinecraft. She was seriously considering signing up for it. Quilting was one thing Noreen hadn't tried yet, and she was sure it would be interesting.

A horn honked from behind, pulling Noreen out of her musings. "Don't be in such a hurry," she mumbled. "The light hasn't been green that long. People shouldn't be so impatient."

The car behind her sped up, and as it came alongside her on the right, the horn tooted again.

"What is your problem?" Noreen glanced over at the driver, and her face warmed when she realized it was Tina, one of the nurses at the hospital where she volunteered. Tina pointed at Noreen's car and mouthed, "Nice. Is it new?"

Noreen smiled and nodded. She'd obviously misjudged the horn honking. Tina had simply been trying to get Noreen's attention.

Tina waved and moved on up the street in her minivan. Noreen looked forward to telling Tina, as well as the other nurses, about her new car when she went to the hospital next Monday morning. At least it would give her something exciting to talk about. Maybe she would mention the quilt class she was thinking about taking, too.

———

As Jennifer Owen sat on a wooden bench, waiting for the bus, she watched the traffic go by and thought about the situation she and her husband, Randy, were in. They'd been having a tough time since Randy lost his job, and she worried that if he didn't find something soon they wouldn't be able to keep up with their monthly bills. And in nine weeks, their first baby was due, but they didn't have any health insurance.

Jennifer, a hairdresser, had wanted to find a job at one of the local hair salons, but she'd had morning sickness during the first half of her pregnancy and knew she'd never make it through a workday without getting sick, so Randy had insisted she not work at this time. That had been before he'd lost his job working as a cook in a local Italian restaurant. It wasn't that the owner was displeased with Randy's cooking; the business was struggling and had to close. So for the last two months, they'd been living on Randy's unemployment checks and what little they'd managed to put away in their savings.

Jennifer tried to remain positive for Randy's sake, but she was scared. If Randy didn't find a position in one of the local restaurants soon, they might not be able to continue paying the rent on their small, two-bedroom home.

Today, like every other day since Randy lost his job, he'd scoured the want-ads and checked at the local unemployment office for a cook's position. Then he'd gone out looking for work. Since Randy's older model pickup was in for some repairs, he'd taken Jennifer's car. That left her to take the bus to the nearest pharmacy and pick up a few necessary things.

Jennifer felt fortunate to have a husband like Randy, who wanted to provide for his family. Her sister, Maggie, wasn't that lucky. Maggie's husband, Brad, sat around the house all day, drinking beer and smoking cigarettes, while his wife went to work cleaning people's houses. Well, at least Maggie wasn't expecting a baby, and they only had two mouths to feed.

"Would you mind if I sit here?" a young Amish woman asked as she approached.

Jennifer smiled. "No, not at all."

"Have you been waiting long?"

Jennifer looked at her watch. "Oh, five minutes or so."

They sat silently for a while; then Jennifer asked, "Do you live around here?"

"No, I live in Pinecraft, but I came over to this area early this morning to do some shopping. How about you? Do you live close by?"

Jennifer nodded. "Our house is right there—the white one with blue trim across the street. I don't normally take the bus, but my husband needed my car today so he could look for a job."

"What kind of work does your husband do?" the young woman questioned.

"He's a cook."

"It must be kind of scary to be unemployed, especially when you're expecting a baby," she said, glancing at Jennifer's stomach.

"Yes," Jennifer admitted. "We have some money saved up, but it won't last long if he doesn't find a job soon." She folded her hands across her stomach and gave it a gentle pat. "I saw an ad in the paper this morning, placed by a woman who lives in Pinecraft. She'll be teaching some quilting classes in a few weeks, and if I had extra money right now, I'd take the classes. It would nice to make a special quilt for our baby." She sighed. "Unless Randy gets a job in the next week, I can't even think about taking that class."

The bus pulled up. Jennifer thought she might continue talking with the Amish woman once they got on the bus, but there were no seats together. So she made her way down the aisle and took a seat beside an elderly woman, eager to get off her feet. She was glad she didn't have to take the bus on a regular basis, but if things didn't change, she and Randy might have to sell one of their vehicles.

CHAPTER 3

Two weeks later

T here's something I forgot to tell you," Lamar said as he and Emma sat across from each other at the kitchen table Saturday morning.

"What's that?" she asked, reaching for her cup of tea.

"Yesterday, when I met Amos Troyer for coffee at the restaurant up the street, Anna Lambright was our waitress."

"Oh? How's she doing?"

"Seems fine. Said she really likes it here." Lamar added a spoonful of sugar to his coffee and stirred it around. "It's good that she's keeping in contact with her folks, though. I hope they've finally accepted the fact that she wants to try living in Sarasota."

Tapping her fingers absently against her chin, Emma stared out the kitchen window, gazing at the oranges hanging on the tree in their small backyard. "Looks like the Honeybells are about ready to be picked," she mentioned. "Maybe we can offer some to those who attend our quilt class."

"That's a good idea, Emma," Lamar said. "The neighbor next door said those oranges are good eating in January, and I'm sure we'll have more than enough to share with our students."

Emma nodded as she continued to stare absently out the window, tapping her fingers.

"Are you *naerfich* about today's quilting class? You seem kind of stressed this morning," Lamar commented.

"I'm not really nervous," she replied. "Just a little concerned."

"About what?"

"Whether teaching quilting classes here in Pinecraft is a good idea."

Lamar's thick gray eyebrows lifted high on his forehead. "Why wouldn't it be? It didn't take long for six people to sign up for the class, so there must be some interest."

"I suppose that's true," Emma agreed, "but our home here is much smaller than our place in Shipshewana, so we'll be a bit cramped. We barely have room for the table our students will sit at, and the two sewing machines we bought, plus the one I borrowed, take up even more space in our small dining room."

"It'll all work out, you'll see." Lamar left his seat and patted Emma's shoulder affectionately. "I have a feeling that, just like all our other classes, God has directed these six new students to our home for a special reason."

She smiled and relaxed a bit. "You're probably right, Lamar. I hope and pray we will not only be able to teach each of our new students how to quilt, but that God will give us the wisdom to meet their needs."

———

Erika Wilson folded her arms and stared out the side window of her father's van. She couldn't believe he had signed her up to take a quilting class, and without even asking if she wanted to go. Now they were heading across town to Pinecraft, and she had no say in it. Truth was, Erika hadn't had much say about anything since her accident. Dad made all the decisions, and she was stuck in her wheelchair, forced to do whatever he said. It wasn't fair! Life wasn't fair—at least her life.

If her legs weren't paralyzed, she would be able to do all sorts of fun things with her friends. Now, whenever Lynne and Becky came over to see her, all they could do was sit and talk, watch TV, or play a computer game. No more swimming, bike riding, water skiing, dancing, roller boarding, or cheerleading—all the things Erika used to love to do. She'd practiced so diligently, hoping it would help when the time came for cheerleader tryouts. But that, as well as everything else, had been squashed from her life. She'd tried to be happy for her friends when they told her they had been picked for the squad, but that made it even harder to be around them lately. Erika's fun, teenaged years had been stolen from her, and there was no way to get them back.

How does Dad think me learning to quilt can make up for all the things I can't do? I hate the idea of quilting. It's for old ladies, not someone like me. Erika swiped at her cheeks, her fingers wet with salty tears. *I feel like an old lady, stuck in this chair. Dad may as well put me away in a nursing home, because I'm not good for much of anything but sitting around, staring out the window, and wishing I could turn back the clock to the minutes before I stupidly got on that diving board.*

"You're awfully quiet back there," Dad called from the front seat of their van.

Erika continued to stare out the window, feeling sorry for herself. She noticed some birds fly past the van and was envious because they were free.

"I know you're not thrilled about going to the quilting class, Erika, but I think if you give it a chance, you'll have a good time."

"I doubt it," she muttered.

"Don't be so negative."

"Kids my age don't learn how to quilt."

"I'll bet Amish girls do," he countered.

Erika grunted. "I'm not Amish."

"Well, just give it a try, okay?"

"Do I have a choice? You're the one in control these days."

Dad thumped the steering wheel with the palm of his hand. "I don't like your attitude, Erika, or your tone of voice. Now I want you to go to that class this morning with a smile on your face. Is that understood?"

Erika frowned. "Don't see why I have to smile about something I don't wanna do."

"I'm not asking you to smile about the quilting class. I just want you to be pleasant and try to have a positive attitude. Can you do that for me, Erika?"

"I–I'll try," she murmured. *But I don't have to like it.*

B.J. felt a sense of apprehension as he drove along Bahia Vista Street in the convertible he'd rented, following his GPS to the address of the quilting class he'd signed up for after arriving in Sarasota. Although he was interested in the design of Amish quilts and thought he'd like to create a painting of one, he was sure he'd be the only man in the class and would probably feel foolish.

Well, what does it matter? he asked himself. *I don't have long to live, so I may as well enjoy whatever time I have left and do the things I want to do, no matter how ridiculous I may look or feel.*

B.J.'s thoughts turned to his daughters back home. They knew he was here, but he'd only told them that he was going to Florida to enjoy the beach and warm weather and hoped to get some painting done.

Neither Jill nor Robyn had any idea he was taking a quilt class. He still felt guilty for not telling them his cancer had returned, but he'd convinced himself that for now, at least, it was for the best.

As B.J. turned up the street leading to Emma and Lamar Miller's house, he made a decision. If he was able to learn how to quilt, he would make Diane, his ten-year-old granddaughter, a quilted wall hanging so she could remember him after he was gone.

When Noreen pulled her sports car in front of the house where the quilt class was supposed to take place, she spotted a silver convertible with the top up, parked in the driveway. *Well, someone here has good taste in vehicles,* she thought.

She'd just opened her car door when a baldheaded man, who looked to be in his early sixties, got out of the convertible. He glanced her way and nodded. "Are you here for the quilting classes?"

"Yes, I am, and I'm really looking forward to it," she responded.

"Same here."

Her eyebrows lifted. "You want to learn how to quilt?"

"That's right; I'm an artist, and because of all the unusual designs in the quilts I've seen, I'm hoping to paint a picture of one." The man's voice was deep and sounded a bit gravely, but he had a pleasant smile.

Noreen still thought it was a bit strange that a man would want to learn how to quilt, even if he was an artist, but she figured, *Each to his own.*

"Shall we go inside and meet the teacher?" he asked, moving toward the house.

She gave a nod. *Having a man in the class should make things interesting.*

CHAPTER 4

Phyllis Barstow had just stepped onto the porch of a small Amish home in Pinecraft, when a noisy motorcycle pulled up to the curb. She frowned. *What's a biker doing in a place like this? I'm sure he's not planning to take the quilting class.*

Phyllis shook her head, glancing at the other cars parked in the driveway. *There won't be any men in this class—just a bunch of women like me, looking for something fun and creative to do. The biker's probably lost and asking for directions.*

Watching as the biker climbed off the cycle and removed his helmet, Phyllis was surprised to see that it wasn't a man at all. The thirty-something woman pulled her fingers through the ends of her wavy blond hair, grabbed a satchel from the back of the bike, and started up the walk leading to the house. Removing the elastic band that held the rest of her hair back, she gave her head a good shake, and more waves fell into place. When the young woman reached the porch, she smiled at Phyllis. "You here for the quilt class?"

Phyllis nodded. "Are you?"

"Sure am, and I'm glad the classes are being held on Saturdays, 'cause right now I have the weekends off."

"Where do you work?" Phyllis asked.

"At the restaurant a few blocks up on Bahia Vista Street." The young woman extended her hand. "I'm Kim Morris."

"Phyllis Barstow. It's nice to meet you. Shall we go inside and see who else came?"

"Hello everyone," Emma said as she and Lamar stood in front of the table where their six students sat—five in the folding chairs she'd provided, and the teenage girl in her wheelchair. "I'm Emma Miller, and this is my husband, Lamar."

Lamar stepped forward and smiled. "It's nice to have all of you here."

Everyone nodded—everyone but the teenage girl, that is.

"Why don't you take turns introducing yourself?" Emma suggested. "Oh, and please tell us the reason you signed up for this class. We can start with you," she said, smiling at the petite blond-haired woman sporting a nice suntan.

"My name is Kim Morris, and I'm taking this class to make some new friends and do something creative."

"Thank you, Kim." Emma motioned to the next person, who happened to be the only man. In the past, there had been at least two men in Emma's classes.

The man, looking more than a bit uncomfortable, said in a gravelly sounding voice, "My name is B.J. I'm an artist, and I thought it'd be fun to learn about the color and design of quilts. I may try to paint a picture of one as well."

"Lamar is an artist, too," Emma said. "He's designed a good many quilts."

Lamar's cheeks reddened. "I don't really consider myself an artist. I just enjoy coming up with various designs that depict many things." He motioned to the older woman who sat next to B.J. "Now it's your turn."

She rubbed her hands briskly together, as though eager to speak. "My name is Noreen Webber, and like Kim, I'm taking this class to make some new friends."

Emma was surprised that the woman made no mention of wanting to learn how to quilt. If she came here only to make friends, then she probably wouldn't get much out of the class. She could have made friends just as easily by doing something else.

"Guess I'm next," the young pregnant woman with long black hair and dark brown eyes, spoke up. "My name is Jennifer Owen, and I'm here because someone graciously paid for me to take this class."

"That was nice. Was it a friend or relative?" Kim asked.

Jennifer shrugged. "I don't know. My husband's a cook, but he lost his job awhile back, so I'd given up on the idea of taking this class. Then, two days ago I found an anonymous note in my mailbox, saying I was signed up to take the quilt classes and that they had been paid for." Jennifer paused and rubbed her stomach. "I'm expecting our first child in seven weeks, and I would love to know how to make a quilt for the baby."

Emma smiled and nodded. "Lamar and I are glad you're here." Then she motioned to the middle-aged woman with shoulder-length auburn hair, sitting across the table. "Would you please tell us your name and why you signed up for this class?"

"I'm Phyllis Barstow, and I'm eager to learn something new. My husband has a charter fishing boat service, and since he's out on the water so much, it leaves me a lot of time to explore some creative things. I've done some sewing and several craft projects over the years, so I'm looking forward to learning how to quilt."

Emma glanced at the teenage girl in the wheelchair. "What is your name, dear?"

The girl mumbled something in a voice barely above a whisper.

Emma leaned closer. "What was that?"

"I said my name's Erika. Erika Wilson."

"And what brings you here?" Lamar questioned.

She turned her head to look at him. "I don't wanna be here, but my dad made me come."

Emma cringed, remembering how Anna Lambright's mother had forced her to take Emma's quilting classes last fall. The young Amish woman had made it clear from the start that she didn't want to learn how to quilt. If Erika was here against her will, she might not learn a thing.

Perhaps I should speak to her father when he comes to pick Erika up after class, Emma thought. *If I'm unable to find a way to make Erika enjoy the class, maybe she shouldn't be here. But it's not my decision to make. Her father paid for the class, and he obviously thinks this is something his daughter needs, so I'll do my best to teach her.*

"Should I go ahead and explain about the history of Amish quilts now?" Lamar asked, breaking into Emma's thoughts.

"What? Oh yes, why don't you do that?" Emma's face heated, and she took a seat beside Kim as Lamar began to talk.

"The existence of quilts among the Amish began as early as the 1830s, although the quilts back then were much plainer than those being made now," he explained. "During that time the Amish used quilts as simple coverings for their beds."

"That's right," Emma agreed. "In the early days, most Amish made their quilts using simple materials from one color. Later, they began sewing several colored pieces of cloth into a variety of patterns."

"The earlier designs were basic rectangles and squares, but as time went on, more colorful, bold patterns were used," Lamar put in. "An older Amish quilt can be identified by its simple design, with less decoration than the Amish quilts that are made today." He continued to talk about the variety of colors and numerous designs in Amish quilts, and ended his talk by saying, "The Amish not only make quilts for their homes, to give others, or to sell, but they often donate quilts to be auctioned at local benefit events to help those in need. It's a gift of their time, and by giving, a demonstration of their love for others is shown. Owning an Amish quilt has a special meaning, reminding us that since the beginning of our church, we've been taught the same priorities: God first and family second."

Lamar picked up one of the quilts on display. "This one I designed myself. I call it, 'Pebbles on the beach.'"

"That's beautiful," Phyllis said as Lamar brought it closer to the table. "I've always enjoyed living near the water, and I guess that's a good thing, since my husband fishes for a living."

"My wife has a few other quilts she'd like to show you," Lamar said.

Emma stood, and with Lamar's help, held up the first quilt. "Here's another pattern that reflects the beauty of the ocean. It's called, 'Ocean Waves,'" she explained.

"I really like that one." Kim smiled. "My dog, Maddie, loves to frolic in the waves."

"What kind of dog do you have?" B.J. questioned.

"Maddie is a German shepherd, and I think she loves the beach as much as I do." Kim chuckled, her laugh lines deepening. "Her favorite thing is chasing seagulls, but she also enjoys prancing through the waves and playing fetch with whatever I throw her."

Everyone smiled. Everyone but Erika, that is. She just sat with her arms folded, looking bored with it all.

"What's that pattern called?" Jennifer asked, pointing to a quilt Emma had draped over a wooden rack.

Emma smiled. It was good to see her students taking an interest in the quilts. "That one is the dahlia pattern. As you can see, it has a three-dimensional effect from the gathered petals surrounding the center of each star-shaped flower."

"I think I'd like to try painting that quilt," B.J. said. "I like the unusual design and muted fall colors."

"Now that Lamar has explained the history of Amish quilts, and we've shown you several quilt designs, I'll explain what we're going to do with the quilted wall hangings you'll be learning to make." Emma motioned to the bolts of material stacked on the table. "As you can see, I have lots of fabric to choose from, and I always ask my students to begin with a simple star pattern for their first project."

Noreen frowned. "I thought we were going to learn how to make a full-sized quilt. I want one to put on my bed."

"You need to become well-acquainted with the basics of quilting first," Lamar said.

"That's right," Emma agreed. "By the time you finish these classes, you'll know the basics of quilting, so you should be able to make a larger quilt if you want. Of course, you may use whatever colored material you like for your wall hangings, which will make each of them distinct." She held up a smaller quilt with various shades of green. "I wanted to show you what your quilted wall hangings will look like when they're done. You'll begin today by choosing the colors you want and then cutting out the log cabin squares and the points for the star."

"Before we do that, why don't we take a break for some of the tasty cookies Emma made this morning?" Lamar suggested. "When we're finishing eating, everyone can choose their material and cut out the patterned pieces."

Kim smacked her lips, while patting her stomach. "That sounds good to me. I'm always ready for a snack."

Everyone but Erika nodded. The girl sat with a scowl on her face.

Dear Lord, please show me how to get through to her, Emma prayed. *I believe this young girl needs to know how much You love and care for her, and maybe that will be revealed to her during one of our classes.*

CHAPTER 5

When Emma and Lamar returned from the kitchen with a plate of cookies and a pot of coffee, B.J.'s stomach growled. He hadn't felt up to eating breakfast, but now he was actually hungry.

When he'd been taking chemo, he'd had no appetite, and often got sick to his stomach. Then there was the hair loss and the unrelenting fatigue. He could handle being bald, since many men his age shared that condition. But between being nauseous and feeling so tired he could barely cross a room, he had concluded that the treatments were worse than the cancer itself.

Then B.J. had been told that his cancer was beginning to spread. He'd decided to quit chemo and live out the rest of his life trying natural alternative treatments that would hopefully strengthen his immune system. He knew taking supplements and eating right probably wouldn't cure his illness, but they might make him feel better and possibly give him a little more time on earth. Even if they didn't, it was his body and his life, and he planned to die *his* way, without family members or doctors telling him what to do.

"These are really good cookies. What do you call them?" Kim asked, bumping B.J.'s arm as she reached for another one from the plate in the center of the table. "Oops! Sorry about that."

"It's okay. No harm done," he replied.

"They're raisin molasses," Emma said, pushing a stray piece of gray hair back under her head covering. "They were my favorite cookies when I was a girl, and my mother taught me to make them as soon as I was old enough to learn how to cook."

"Well, they get my vote," B.J. said, licking his lips. "Haven't had cookies this good since my wife died five years ago."

"So you're a widower?" Noreen's question sounded more like a statement. Then she quickly added, "Isn't that a coincidence? I lost my husband five years ago, too."

"Sorry for your loss," B.J. mumbled around another cookie.

"What did your wife die from?" Jennifer asked.

B.J. clenched his fingers. He didn't want to talk about this, especially with people he'd only met. "She had a heart attack a few days after her fifty-fifth birthday."

"My husband, Ben, died on the operating table," Noreen said, dropping her gaze to the table. "He, too, had a heart attack, but the doctors couldn't save him."

Feeling the need for a change of subject, and realizing that all eyes and ears seemed to be focused on him, B.J. looked at Lamar and said, "Would you mind if I stayed a few minutes after class and photographed some of your quilts?"

"The Amish don't like people to take their picture," Erika spoke up, glaring at B.J. as though he had said something horrible.

"I wouldn't be taking their picture," B.J. countered. "Only the quilts."

"I have no problem with that," Lamar said. "And just to be clear, here in Pinecraft some Amish, especially the younger ones who haven't joined the church, don't seem to mind if someone snaps their picture, although most won't actually pose for a photo."

Erika folded her arms. "Well, I think it's rude to take pictures of people who are different than you."

"We're not really so different," Emma spoke up. "We just dress modestly and live a different lifestyle than some people." She motioned to her plain green dress.

B.J. wondered if Erika's remark had more to do with herself than Emma or Lamar. He had a feeling the young woman felt self-conscious about being in that wheelchair. He was tempted to ask how she'd lost the use of her legs but thought better of it. Just as he didn't want to talk about his cancer or his wife's death, Erika might not like talking about her disability.

"If everyone has finished their refreshments, I think we should get back to our quilting lesson," Emma said. "I'll demonstrate how to use a template, and you can begin by marking the design on your pieces of fabric, using dressmaker's chalk or a pencil. When that's done, you'll need to cut out your patterns."

"What will we do after that?" Phyllis questioned.

"In the next step, called piecing, you will stitch the patterned pieces together onto the quilt top, which will also need to be cut," Emma explained. "Now, the quilt top is usually pieced by machine. Then later, the backing, batting, and quilt top will be layered, put into a frame, and quilted by hand. Of course, we won't do all that in one day. It will be spread out over the course of six weeks."

"Now using the templates," Emma continued, "I'd like you to begin marking the patterned pieces on the back of your fabric. When you're done, you'll need to cut out the pieces of material you'll be working with." Emma smiled. "Next week, you can sew the pieces you've cut."

Perspiration beaded on B.J.'s forehead. Maybe he was in over his head. If he tried using one of the sewing machines, he'd probably end up making a fool of himself.

"What will we do during our last class?" Kim asked.

B.J. rolled his eyes. Talk about skipping ahead! Couldn't the little blond take the classes one at a time without having to know what was coming next?

"You'll put the binding on, and then your wall hangings will be done," Lamar responded.

Everyone worked silently until it was time to go home. When Erika's father came to pick her up, he asked how things had gone, and B.J. overheard Erika whisper, "I'm not coming back next week."

It's just as well, B.J. thought. *She obviously doesn't want to learn how to quilt.* B.J. reached for his camera bag. *I, on the other hand, want to know everything I can about quilts.*

————

When Phyllis arrived home that afternoon, she was surprised to see her husband lying in the hammock on their porch.

"What are you doing home so early?" she asked, taking a seat in the wicker chair across from him.

"The motor on my boat gave out. Had to have the boat towed to shore, and now it's outta commission till the motor can either be fixed or replaced." Mike groaned. "This is not what I need right now."

Phyllis's eyebrows shot up. "Oh Mike, if it can't be repaired, can we afford a new motor?"

"Doesn't matter. I need the motor to run the boat, and I need the boat to take people out fishing. The boat will be dry-docked for several weeks, so I may as well make the best of it." He yawned and stretched his arms over his head. "Haven't you been saying I work too hard and you wanted us to take a vacation?"

She pursed her lips. "If you're out of work, we can't afford a vacation. Besides, I've already paid for the quilting class, and I'm committed to finishing it."

"If we're not gonna take a vacation, then I guess I'll get caught up on my sleep, 'cause I've been pretty tired lately." Mike closed his eyes and clasped his hands behind his head. "Wake me when supper's ready."

Phyllis groaned inwardly. Mike finally had some time off, and now they couldn't afford to go anywhere. She wished she hadn't signed up for the quilting classes. *Well, I've already paid for the class, and it'll only tie me up one day a week,* she reminded herself. *Maybe the rest of the week Mike and I can find something enjoyable to do that doesn't cost any money. If nothing else, we can spend some time on the beach.*

"How'd the job hunting go?" Jennifer asked just as her husband, Randy, said, "How'd the quilting class go?"

She giggled. "Should I answer your question, or do you want to go first?"

Randy bent to kiss her, his light brown hair falling forward and brushing her cheek. "Your face is glowing, Jen. Does that mean you had a good time today?"

"Oh yes," she said sincerely. "Emma and Lamar Miller are the nicest couple, and they have the cutest little house. I even saw an orange tree in their backyard." She touched his arm. "Oh, and I learned a lot about the history of Amish quilts."

"Is that all? I thought you went there to make a quilt."

"We did begin working on our wall hangings, but Lamar thought it would be good if we understood a bit about the background of Amish quilts." Jennifer flipped the ends of her hair over her shoulder and started pulling it up to make a ponytail. "It was really quite interesting—almost as intriguing as the people who are taking the class with me."

"What do you mean?" Randy asked, taking a seat on the couch.

She tucked in beside him, securing the rubber band around her ponytail. "Well, besides me, there were three other women: Kim, Phyllis, and Noreen. Then there was a teenage girl in a wheelchair. Her name is Erika, and she had a negative attitude. There was also a man who's an artist. I'm not sure what his real name is, but he introduced himself as B.J."

Randy's mouth opened slightly. "I'm surprised a guy would want to learn how to quilt."

"He said he's interested in painting a picture of a quilt, and he even stayed after class to photograph a few that Emma and Lamar had on display."

"What about the girl in the wheelchair?" Randy questioned. "What was she doin' there?"

"She said her dad made her come, and it was obvious that she didn't want to be there."

"That doesn't surprise me." Randy shook his head. "Most teenagers have other things they'd rather be doin' besides sitting in a room with a bunch of women and one weird man, listening to the history of quilts."

"B.J. isn't weird," Jennifer said protectively, although she had no idea why she felt the need to defend a man she barely knew. "If I had to wager a guess, I'd say that the reason Erika's dad made her take the class is because he wants her to learn something creative."

"Maybe you're right." Randy reached for Jennifer's hand. "Now, in answer to your question about the job hunting, I had no luck at all today. None of the restaurants in Sarasota need a cook right now. I'm thinkin' I may have to start looking in Bradenton or one of the other towns nearby."

"Maybe we should go back to Pennsylvania and move in with one of our folks," she suggested.

He shook his head vigorously. "No way! I like the warm weather here, and I sure don't miss those January temperatures in Pennsylvania. Besides, we moved to Sarasota for a new start and to be on our own, and one way or the other, we're gonna make it work."

CHAPTER 6

Monday evening, B.J. sat in the living room of the small cottage he'd rented near the beach, looking at the pictures he'd taken of Lamar and Emma's quilts after class on Saturday. He was pleased with how the photos had turned out and was even more impressed with the vivid shades and unusual designs. After B.J had taken the photos, he'd stayed awhile longer, visiting with Lamar and Emma. They'd even invited him to stay for lunch.

What a nice couple, B.J. thought. They had a welcoming home that reminded him of his grandparent's house, where tempting aromas used to drift from the kitchen whenever Grandma had spent the day baking.

B.J. had considered sharing his health situation with the Millers during lunch but decided there wasn't much point to that, since they couldn't do anything to change his situation. They'd probably pity him, and B.J. didn't want that. Sympathy wouldn't change the fact that he was dying, nor would it make him feel better. He just wanted to make whatever time he had left seem as normal as possible.

B.J.'s cell phone rang, pulling his thoughts aside. He checked the caller ID. It was one of his daughters. "Hey, Jill. What's up?"

"Hi, Dad. I'm calling to see how you're doing."

"I'm fine. How are you and the family?"

"We're all good. Kenny and Diane miss their grandpa, though. When are you coming home?"

B.J. chuckled. "I've only been here a few days, and the quilt class I'm taking is for six weeks, so. . ."

"You're taking a quilt class?"

"Yeah, I know. It's not the kind of thing you'd expect me to do, huh?"

"It sure isn't. What made you decide to take up quilting, Dad?"

He laughed again, hoping it didn't sound forced. "I'm not planning to become a quilter, if that's what you're thinking. I just thought it would be interesting to learn how they're made. I'm also hoping to do a few paintings of Amish quilts. Oh, and I took some pictures the other day after my first lesson. I'm using them as my guide while I paint."

"Oh, I see. Well, the quilts I saw when we visited Arthur, Illinois, were beautiful, so I'm sure your paintings will be, too."

"I hope so." B.J. drew in a quick breath as he sank into a chair. Right about now, he felt as if he could use a nap.

"Are you sure you're feeling okay?" Jill asked. "You sound tired, Dad."

"Guess I am a little," B.J. admitted, picking up the picture of Jill and her sister, Robyn, that he'd brought along. *How much more time do I have to spend with them?* he wondered. *Should I have come here to Florida, knowing my time could be short?*

Shaking his thoughts aside, B.J. said, "I got up early this morning to walk on the beach, and I've spent the rest of the day painting a seascape. I want to finish that before I get started on a quilt painting."

"Sounds like you're having fun."

"Sure am. That's why I came down here—to have fun and enjoy the sun." B.J. stifled a yawn and put the framed picture back on the table.

"I'll let you go, Dad, so you can rest. Talk to you again soon."

"Okay, Jill. Tell the kids and your sister I said hello." B.J. clicked off the phone and dropped his head forward into his hands. He felt like a heel keeping the truth from his daughters, but he wasn't ready to tell them just yet.

"Hi, I'm Anna Lambright," a young Amish woman with auburn hair peeking out from under her white head covering said to Kim.

Kim slipped on her work apron and extended her hand. She had the dinner shift this evening and had arrived at the restaurant a short time ago. "It's nice to meet you, Anna. I'm Kim Morris. I assume you're a waitress here, too?"

Anna nodded. "I've been working here for the last couple of months. I moved down from Middlebury, Indiana, with my friend Mandy Zimmerman."

"Does Mandy work here, too?" Kim asked.

"Yes, but she worked the morning shift today."

Kim smiled. "Maybe I'll get the chance to meet her sometime."

"I'm sure you will. We often have our shifts switched around, so one of these days you and Mandy will probably work the same hours."

"Did your whole family move to Sarasota?" Kim questioned.

"No, they live in Middlebury, and I doubt that any of them would ever move here," Anna replied. "My folks didn't want me to move, but a woman I took quilting lessons from talked to them about it. After she explained that she and her husband were coming down here for the winter and would keep an eye on me, they finally agreed that I could

43

go." Anna's eyebrows lowered. "I really don't need anyone watching out for me. I'm nineteen years old, and I can take care of myself."

"You took quilting lessons?" Kim asked.

"Yeah, but not 'cause I wanted to. My mom signed me up for the class."

"I'm taking quilting lessons, too," Kim said enthusiastically. "From an Amish lady who lives in Pinecraft."

"Her name wouldn't be Emma Miller, would it?"

"As a matter of fact, it is."

"Emma's the one who taught me how to quilt—only it was at her home in Shipshewana, Indiana," Anna said. "She and her husband, Lamar, bought a place down here because Lamar has arthritis and needed to get out of the cold winter weather."

"That makes good sense." Kim glanced at her watch. "It's been nice talking to you, Anna, but I'd better get to work."

"Same here." Anna gave Kim's arm a tap. "See you around."

Kim gave a nod, then moved into the dining room. Anna seemed nice. She hoped she would have the opportunity to get to know her better.

———————

Noreen tapped her foot impatiently, glancing around the room and then back at her watch. She'd come to this Amish-style restaurant for supper and had been sitting at a table for ten minutes, waiting for a waitress. The place was crowded, and maybe they were short-handed, but that was no excuse for poor service. If someone didn't come to her table in the next five minutes, she was leaving.

Finally, a young woman with short blond hair stepped up to her and said, "Have you had a chance to look over the menu?"

"Yes, I certainly have." Noreen studied the woman's face. "Say, didn't

I meet you at the quilt class last Saturday?"

"Yes, I'm Kim, and your name is Noreen, right?"

Noreen nodded. "I didn't realize you worked at this restaurant. I've been here several times and never saw you waiting tables before."

Kim smiled cheerfully. "I started a few weeks ago." She motioned to the menu. "Have you decided what you want to eat or drink?"

"I'd like the chicken pot pie with a dinner salad. Oh, and a glass of unsweetened iced tea with a slice of lemon."

"Okay, I'll put your order in right away," Kim said before hurrying away.

Noreen sighed. She hoped Kim didn't take as long to bring her meal as she had to wait on her. She may have said something to her about it if it hadn't been for the fact that she and Kim were taking the same quilting class. Kim seemed like a nice person, and there was no point in causing dissension between them, especially since they'd be spending the next five Saturdays together.

Noreen glanced around the dining room again, wondering if she knew anyone else here. She didn't recognize anyone in the sea of faces.

A short time later, Kim returned with a glass of iced tea, which she placed on the table.

Noreen picked it up and took a drink. "Eww. . .there's sweetener in this. If you'll recall, I asked for unsweetened tea."

Kim's cheeks reddened. "I am so sorry about that. I must have written it wrong on the order pad. I'll get you another one right away." She picked up the glass and hurried away.

Noreen crossed her arms and stared at the table. At this rate she'd never get anything.

Finally Kim showed up again. "Here you are, Noreen." When she reached over to set the glass down, it wobbled and tipped, spilling some of the iced tea onto the table. The next thing Noreen knew, the icy cold liquid had dribbled onto her beige-colored slacks. "Oh no," she groaned, heat rising to her cheeks. "This is probably going to leave a nasty stain!"

"I'm sorry again." Kim grabbed some napkins and began wiping up the tea on the table, as Noreen blotted her slacks. "If you can't get the stain out, I'll buy you a new pair of slacks. Just please don't say anything to my boss."

Noreen could tell from the way Kim glanced over her shoulder that she was fearful of losing her job. "I won't say anything," Noreen promised. "Just relax. If I can't get the stain out, I'll let you know when we meet at the quilt class this Saturday."

"Oh, thank you. I don't know what I'd do if I lost this job." Kim blew out her breath with obvious relief.

"Would you please pass the parmesan cheese?" Phyllis asked her husband as they sat on their deck together, eating supper.

Mike stared absently at his plate of spaghetti.

"Did you hear what I said, Mike? I asked you to pass the cheese."

"Oh yeah, sure." He handed her the jar and leaned back in his chair with a groan. "I know you worked hard making supper, honey, but I'm not really hungry tonight."

"I've noticed you've been tossing and turning in your sleep lately. Are you still stressing over your boat?" Phyllis questioned.

Mike grunted. "How can I not be stressed? There's more wrong with it than I was originally told, and now it looks like it's gonna be out of commission for at least five weeks. Maybe longer."

"Try not to worry," she said. "We have enough in our savings to get us by till you're able to start working again."

"It's not just the money, Phyllis. I'm bored out of mind. All this sitting around doing nothing is making me feel like a slug." He thumped his stomach. "Think I'm gaining weight, too. All I seem to want to do is nibble. Then I'm not hungry at mealtime."

The phone rang, interrupting their conversation. "Want me to get it?" Phyllis asked, rising from her seat.

Mike nodded. "I don't feel like talking to anyone right now."

Phyllis hurried into the other room. When she returned several minutes later, her brows were furrowed.

"What's wrong, honey?" Mike asked. "You look upset."

"It's my sister, Penny. She slipped on the wet grass when she went out to get the mail this morning and broke her leg."

"That's too bad." Mike reached for his glass of water and took a drink. "Is she gonna be okay?"

"I'm sure her leg will heal, but she'll be wearing a cast for six weeks and could really use some assistance." Phyllis placed her hand on Mike's shoulder. "Would you mind very much if I went there to help out?"

"How long would you be gone?" he asked.

"Until she's out of her cast and able to get around on her own. Would you like to go with me, Mike? It might be a good time for you to get away while your boat is being fixed."

He shook his head. "Think I need to stick around here in case the boat gets fixed sooner than expected."

"Do you have any objections if I go? Penny said she'd pay for my plane ticket to North Dakota, but I'd be there for several weeks. Do you think you can survive without me for that long?"

"You go ahead and take care of your sister; that's important—especially since she lives alone. I'll miss you, of course, but I think I can manage okay while you're gone."

Phyllis smiled. "Great. I'll call Penny back and let her know." She started for the door but turned back around. "Oh. I forgot about the quilting class."

"Just call the teacher and tell her something's come up and you can't finish the class."

"But I paid for it already, Mike." Phyllis moved back to the table. "Would you go in my place?"

"To the quilt class?"

"Of course. That's what I was talking about. Weren't you listening, Mike?"

"Yeah, I was listening."

"Then would you finish the classes for me?"

His eyebrows shot up. "You're kidding, right?"

"No, I'm not. You don't have much else to do while you're waiting for the boat to be fixed, so I thought—"

Mike held up his hand. "Well, you thought wrong. I don't know a thing about quilting, Phyllis."

"Neither do I, but I was planning to learn, and if you go in my place, you can show me what you've learned after I get home. Just think, Mike, we could quilt together and maybe make one for each of our daughters for Christmas next year." She leaned over and kissed his neck. "If you do this for me, when your boat gets fixed and you get your next paying customer, I'll go out with you and act as your bait boy."

He hesitated but finally nodded. "All right then, it's a deal. After all, how hard can quilting be?"

Chapter 7

Emma had just taken a seat at her sewing machine to begin work on a quilt, when Lamar came into the room. "I know you're busy, but could I talk to you for a minute, Emma?" he asked.

"Of course." She set her sewing aside and turned to face him. "I wanted to ask you something, too, but you go first."

He shifted his weight a couple of times, like he did whenever he was nervous or unsure of something.

Emma felt immediate concern. "What is it, Lamar? Is something wrong?"

He shook his head. "Not wrong; I just have a favor to ask."

"What's that?"

"My friend Melvin Weaver wants to hire a driver and go down to Venice tomorrow to look for sharks' teeth, and he invited me to go along."

"But tomorrow is Saturday—our second quilt class, remember?" Emma reminded.

"I haven't forgotten," he said, scrubbing his hand down the side of his bearded face. "I just thought. . . . Well, if you think you can get along without me tomorrow, I'd like to go with Melvin. If not, then I'll go some other time. Maybe you and I can hire a driver and look for sharks' teeth together. Doesn't that sound like fun to you?"

"It's okay, Lamar. You go ahead. I'll manage without your help on Saturday. After all, before I married you, I used to teach the classes on my own. And as far as me hunting for sharks' teeth. . . Well, I've heard how it's done, and the idea of standing in the surf, sifting through the sand with a bulky scoop, seems like hard work to me. Think I'd rather stay here and quilt." Emma pursed her lips. "My only concern about you being gone this Saturday is that it'll mean B.J. will be the only man in class. He might feel uncomfortable with that."

Lamar's forehead wrinkled. "I never thought of that. Maybe it would be better if I stayed here to help you. I can go hunting for sharks' teeth some other time."

"Are you sure about that?" Emma asked. "I don't like to disappoint you."

"It's okay, really," he said with a nod of his head. "I promised to help you teach this group of quilters, and that's what I'm gonna do. I'll get in touch with Melvin and take a rain check with him on that."

Emma smiled. Like her first husband, Ivan, Lamar was a kind, caring man. She felt fortunate to have found love a second time.

"Now what was it you were going to ask me?" Lamar questioned, turning to look out the window.

"I was going to ask if you could pick some of the oranges from our tree later today or even tomorrow morning. I thought it would be nice to share some of them with everyone at the quilt class."

"Sure thing. I was just about ready to pick us each one for a snack later on. If they're ripe enough, I'll pick some in the morning for everyone." Lamar rubbed his hands briskly together. "Weren't we lucky that this house had an orange tree in the backyard?"

Emma nodded. "It'll be nice to send a healthy snack home with everyone tomorrow after class."

———

Mike groaned as he rolled out of bed on Saturday morning, rubbing his eyes to clear his vision. He couldn't believe he'd agreed to take Phyllis's place at the quilt class in Pinecraft. "I must have been out of mind," he muttered. The only good thing was that Phyllis had told him one of the teachers was a man and that another man was also taking the class, so Mike figured that might help him feel less out of place. Of course, he didn't know a thing about sewing, nor did he want to know how to quilt. No matter what Phyllis thought, as far as Mike was concerned, anything that involved a needle and thread was for women, not a man who felt more at home on his boat than anywhere else.

Mike's cell phone rang, and he picked it up off the dresser. After checking the caller ID, and realizing it was Phyllis, he answered. "Hi, honey. How's your sister doing?"

"Penny's still in a lot of pain, but she's so appreciative that I'm here to help out. Thanks for allowing me to do this, Mike."

"Sure, no problem."

"I called to remind you about the quilt class," she said. "It starts at ten this morning."

"Yeah, yeah, I know, and don't worry, I won't be late. Wouldn't wanna miss one minute of that exciting class."

"Are you being sarcastic?"

" 'Course not," Mike lied. "I'm looking forward to learning how to quilt." *In a "dreading it more than coming down with the flu" kind of way,* he mentally added.

"When I get home I'll be anxious to hear about everything you've learned."

"Let's hope I'm able to learn anything at all," he muttered.

"What was that?"

"Oh, nothing. Listen, Phyllis, I'd better get going or I *will* be late for the class."

"Okay. Talk to you again soon, Mike."

"Bye, hon." Mike clicked off his phone and sank to the edge of the bed. *Sure hope my boat's up and running soon. That'll give me a good excuse to quit going to the quilt classes.*

Goshen, Indiana

"Guess who I talked to last night," Jan Sweet said to his twenty-one-year-old daughter, Star. He'd just arrived at Star's house to pick her up for a motorcycle ride. They'd be meeting his buddy Terry and Terry's girlfriend, Cheryl, later on this morning. First, though, Star had offered to fix Jan breakfast.

"Who'd you talk to?" Star asked, motioning for Jan to take a seat at the table.

"Emma Miller. She and Lamar are spending the winter in Sarasota, you know."

Star smiled, pushing her long dark hair away from her eyes. "That's nice. Are they enjoying the warm weather down there?"

"I think so, but Emma said she misses her friends and family here in Indiana." Jan flopped into a chair. "I miss Emma and Lamar, too. Miss stopping by their place for a visit and some of Emma's tasty homemade treats." He smacked his lips. "That angel cream pie she made for our quilting class was the best. You oughta get the recipe from her and make it for your old dad sometime."

Star rolled her coffee-colored eyes. "You're not old, but I'm not really into baking pies. Just wait until Emma gets home and then you can ask her to make you one."

"But that won't be till spring," Jan complained. "Don't think I can wait that long."

"Well, you don't have much choice." Star handed him a cup of coffee, then went to the stove to begin cooking their eggs.

"I don't know about that. Thought it might be fun to take a run down to Florida sometime soon. Would you like to go with me, Star?"

She looked at him over her shoulder. "Are you serious, Dad?"

Jan nodded. "We could head down to Sarasota to see the Millers and enjoy some time on the beach." He winked at Star. "It might be more fun if we just drop in and surprise them, though."

"Do you think they'd appreciate that?"

"Ah, sure. Emma and Lamar are good sports. I'm sure they'd be happy to see us."

"When were you thinking of going?" Star asked.

"I can't go right away 'cause I'm in the middle of a roofing job, and I need to get it done soon, before we get snow or heavy rain. It's been a fairly mild winter so far, which has been good for business, but I'm sure it won't last forever." Jan paused. "I should get the job finished up in a day or two though."

"So when did you want to go?" she persisted.

"I could wait a few weeks. Would you be able to get time off from your job by then?" he asked. "I'll leave Brutus with Terry, so the dog won't be a problem."

"I do have a couple weeks' vacation coming," she said. "When I go to work Monday morning, should I put in for the time off?"

"Yeah, why don't you?" Jan leaned back in his chair, locking his fingers behind his head. "This will be great, kiddo. I can hardly wait to go."

"Will we ride down there on our motorcycles, or did you plan to take your truck?" Star asked.

"If the weather cooperates, I think we oughta ride our bikes. It'll be more fun that way, and I can hardly wait to see the look on Emma and Lamar's faces when we show up."

Sarasota

Lamar whistled as he headed out the back door to pick some oranges. It was a beautiful Saturday morning—the kind of day that made a person feel alive and raring to go. He paused in the yard a few minutes, breathing in the fresh clean air.

On a morning like this, it's hard to imagine bad things going on in the world, he thought. Lamar hadn't told Emma, because he didn't want her to worry, but earlier in the week when he'd gone to the store to pick up a few things, he'd overhead someone say there had been some robberies in a neighborhood not far from where they lived. A few people had been robbed in broad daylight, right in their own backyard. After hearing that, Lamar had been keeping his wallet in the house whenever he went into the yard.

Lamar reflected on the economy, and how so many folks were struggling to find good ways to make it through life's hardships, while others, like this group of thieves, had turned to crime and stealing from others, perhaps to survive. He sent up a silent prayer as he gazed into the deep blue sky, then headed toward the orange tree.

Lamar remembered how he and Emma had enjoyed their juicy oranges for a snack yesterday. There was nothing like eating fresh fruit picked right off the tree. The oranges were so sweet, and he was happy they could share some with their quilting students.

Continuing to whistle, Lamar started putting oranges, still wet from the morning's dew, into his basket. *It doesn't get any better than this,* he thought, lifting his face to the sun.

Suddenly, he realized that the birds were silent. That seemed a bit odd. Usually, the yard was full of birds chirping out a chorus of welcome to Lamar as soon as he stepped into the yard.

"Stay where you are, and don't move a muscle!" a male voice said sternly.

Lamar froze in his tracks, watching a drop of dew fall from one of the oranges, as if in slow motion, and then splatter on top of his shoe.

Another male voice said firmly, "Don't turn around; just stay where you are."

Lamar's heartbeat picked up speed. All he could think about was his dear wife, Emma. *Am I about to be robbed? What should I do? I don't want to do or say anything to anger these men. The back door's not even locked. What if they barge inside and hurt Emma?*

As if to send his wife a silent message that only she could hear, Lamar whispered, "Please, Emma, stay in the house and lock the door."

CHAPTER 8

Emma hummed softly as she removed a coffee cake from the oven. She planned to serve it to her students during the quilting class. Last week, she'd served cookies, and everyone seemed to enjoy them, so she hoped the cake would be just as well received.

Squinting over the top of her metal-framed glasses as she placed the cake on a cooling rack, Emma wondered what was taking Lamar so long to pick the basket of oranges. He'd been out there at least half an hour already. Maybe she should check on him. First, though, she would get out the plates and forks and put them on the counter for when dessert would be served. Once Lamar brought the oranges in, she would peel a few to serve with the cake.

Emma took a platter from the cupboard and placed it on the table. Then, remembering that she had some grapes in the refrigerator, she got them out as well. She stood there a moment, tapping her finger against her lips, while looking around the kitchen. There really wasn't much else to do, so she decided to peek out the window to check on Lamar, knowing he should have that basket pretty much filled with oranges by now. She was almost to the slightly open window, when she heard someone outside speaking rather loudly.

"I'll walk to him slowly from behind," a stranger's voice hollered.

"Okay. I'll approach him from the front," a second man said.

What's going on out there? Emma wondered. When she reached the window, she gasped. Emma could not believe the scene unfolding right there in their own backyard.

"Okay, I got him!" the man yelled. "Quick, bring me the electrical tape."

Lamar had been standing there, still as a statue and struggling not to turn around to get a good look at the person who'd told him to remain where he was, while waiting for "who knew what" to happen. Were these men going to tie him up, tape his mouth shut, and then go into the house and rob them? *But wait a minute,* he thought. *That guy just said, "I got him," yet I'm still standing here untouched.*

Lamar couldn't take it any longer. It seemed like forever that he'd been standing in the same position, unmoving like the men had told him. He was getting a cramp in his leg, and just as he was about to turn around, someone tapped his shoulder and said, "Okay, sir, it's safe now."

Safe? Lamar whirled around, and was about to demand that the young man wearing a white T-shirt and blue jeans tell him what was going on. Instead, he froze, staring in disbelief at the sight in front of him.

"Sorry if I scared you, sir, but I didn't want anything to happen to you," the man said in a soothing voice. "My partner and I have been lookin' for this fella since yesterday, when a call came in that he was spotted in your neighborhood."

Lamar blinked a couple of times, unable to believe his eyes. Was he

WANDA &. BRUNSTETTER

really seeing what he thought he was? Just then, he saw Emma coming out the back door, then running toward him with eyes wide, looking as astonished as he felt. There, by the side of the house was another man wearing jeans and a T-shirt, hunkered down and sitting on top of a large alligator, of all things.

"I wanted to get his mouth taped shut before I felt it was safe enough for you to move," the first man said to Lamar. Then glancing at Emma, he added, "We have a truck parked around the corner that we'll put the gator in to relocate it to another area." He extended his hand. "By the way, the name's Jack, and that's Rusty over there, sittin' on the gator. We do this for a living, capturing and relocating wild animals. Bet you never expected to see one of those creatures in your backyard this morning, did you?"

"No, I sure didn't," Lamar said, slowly letting out some air as he put his arm around Emma's waist. It felt like he'd been holding his breath for hours instead of minutes. He could feel his limbs finally relaxing, relieved that it wasn't a robbery after all.

"Oh Lamar," Emma cried, her cheeks turning pink, "you could have been hurt! What if that alligator had attacked you?"

"The good Lord was with me, that's for sure," Lamar answered, looking at the eight-foot gator and shaking his head. "Guess he blended in so well with all the greenery by the house that I never even saw him lying there. When I came outside, he didn't make a sound. Of course," Lamar continued with a nervous laugh, "I had my mind on those oranges getting picked."

"Where did that alligator come from?" Emma asked Jack.

"We got a report there'd been one seen over in the pond by the golf course not far from here, and when we went to capture it, the gator was nowhere to be found."

58

"Oh my! I guess he decided to do some exploring." Emma looked up at Lamar with a wide-eyed expression.

Lamar nodded, while gently patting her arm.

"Come on, Jack. It's time to get this guy moved. You better go get the truck," Rusty said, still sitting on top of the gator.

"Sorry I had to meet you folks this way, but I'm glad everything went good with no mishaps," Jack said. "Have a good day, and if you see some of your neighbors, let 'em know the creature was captured. This morning we were going door to door, letting people know a gator was roaming about, and just as we were coming to notify you, Rusty and I spotted the creature in your yard."

"I'm glad you did, 'cause I sure wouldn't have known what to do," Lamar replied, swiping at the trickle of sweat above his brows as he and Emma stood there watching. "You take care now, and thanks." It was amazing how big that alligator was, yet it lay there, fairly calm, letting Rusty hold it down.

"Don't worry, folks; I've done this hundreds of times," Rusty assured them. "Once you tape their mouth shut, they remain pretty quiet."

"Please be careful anyway," Lamar said to Rusty as he and Emma started walking toward the house.

"Wait. Aren't you forgetting something?" Emma asked, brushing his arm with her hand.

Lamar laughed as he went back to get the basket of oranges. "Just wait till our quilters hear about this." He stopped walking and sniffed the air. "By the way, Emma, do I smell the aroma of coffee cake coming through the open window?"

She smiled and nodded. "But you can't have any till it's time to serve refreshments."

"That's okay," Lamar said, looking down at the basket he held. "I can always have one of these juicy oranges if I get a craving for something sweet before then."

———◆———

"I guess we need to remind ourselves that we're in Florida, not Indiana, and there are a few critters here that we don't have back home," Emma said as they entered the house.

Lamar nodded. "I thought of that the other day, when I spotted a gecko crawling along the windowsill outside our bedroom. We need to make sure we keep the screens in place on all the doors and windows so none of the outdoor critters can make their way inside."

"That's a good idea," Emma agreed. "If I found a gecko crawling around in here, I'd probably fall on my face trying to catch the little creature."

Lamar chuckled. "They do move quite fast."

"And I don't move like I used to, either," Emma said as they made their way into the dining room, where the quilt class would be held.

"Do you need my help with anything before our students arrive?" Lamar asked.

"No, I think everything's pretty much ready." A knock sounded on the front door. "Now I wonder who that could be," Emma said. "It's too early for any of our students to be here."

"Well, there's only one way to find out." Lamar went to the door and opened it.

Anna Lambright stepped in with red cheeks and tears in her eyes. "Anna, what's wrong?" Emma asked, rushing to the young woman's side.

"My folks are pressuring me again to move back home. I thought they understood why I wanted to live here, but now they've started badgering me." Anna sniffed. "I know you spoke to them before I left Indiana, but will you talk to them again, Emma? Please make them see that I'm a grown woman with a life of my own."

Emma put her arm around Anna's trembling shoulders. "I'm so sorry, Anna. I thought your parents were fine with the idea of you being in Sarasota. They know Lamar and I are here to help with anything you might need, but perhaps it would be good if I remind them of that."

Anna bobbed her head. "I think the thing that set them off was when they read an article in the paper about some robberies that had been going on down here. They're worried I might not be safe." She paused to blow her nose on the tissue Emma handed her. "They don't realize I'm not a little girl anymore. Besides, robberies can happen anywhere."

"That's true. It seems like no one is safe these days," Lamar put in. "However, we can't hide out in our homes or stop living. We need to use caution and ask God to keep His protecting hand upon us." He looked over at Emma. "We can certainly attest to that, right, Emma?"

She nodded, and was about to tell Anna what had just happened in their backyard, when another knock sounded on the door. While Lamar went to answer it, Emma motioned for Anna to take a seat. "Our quilt class doesn't start for another forty-five minutes, so why don't we visit awhile? I'm anxious to hear how your job at the restaurant is going."

Anna smiled and took a seat at the table. "For me it's going good, but not so much for one of the other waitresses."

"Oh, why is that?"

Before Anna could respond, Lamar entered the room, pushing Erika in her wheelchair.

"Sorry for showing up early," the young girl mumbled. "There was an emergency at the hospital, and my dad had to go, so the woman who Dad hired as my caregiver dropped me off now 'cause she has a hair appointment. I hope that's okay."

"It's not a problem at all," Emma said. She was pleased to see that

Erika had come back. After last week, she'd half expected a call from Erika's dad saying Erika had dropped out of the class. "Since you're here early, you can join us and our Amish friend for a glass of freshly squeezed lemonade before the others in our class arrive. It'll give us a chance to get better acquainted."

Erika glanced at Anna, then back at Emma. "Something cold does sound good."

Emma introduced Anna and Erika; then she excused herself to get the lemonade. Lamar went with her, and as they left the room, Emma said a silent prayer for both young women, asking God to show them the path He wanted them to take. She felt certain that each of these young women had a special purpose in life.

CHAPTER 9

Erika knew it was rude, but she couldn't help staring at Anna. Not only was she dressed in Amish clothes, like Emma, but she was young and had two good legs. As far as Erika could tell, Anna might be a little older than her, but not by much.

Anna didn't know how lucky she was. Erika envied people, especially those who were close to her age and weren't bound to a wheelchair. They didn't have to worry about the rest of their lives; they still had dreams they could live out, that would hopefully come true. Erika wondered, in her condition, if she was destined to be alone for the rest of her life. Who would want to be strapped down by someone in a wheelchair? And what would she do if she did fall in love with a man someday? Could she expect him to commit to a relationship, knowing he would always have to do certain things for her? That was the burden she'd placed on her dad, as well as the woman he'd hired as Erika's caregiver.

The silence in the room was thick, as neither Erika nor Anna spoke to each other, while waiting on Emma's return.

A short time later, Emma came back with glasses of lemonade for them. She placed them on the table and was about to sit down, when Anna suddenly stood, gave Emma a hug, and said she needed to go.

Is Anna as uncomfortable around me as I am her? Erika wondered. *Does she feel sorry for me, sitting here in my wheelchair, not saying a word?* She grasped the armrests on her chair tightly and clenched her teeth. *Well, I don't need her pity.*

Anna started for the door, hesitated, then glanced quickly at Erika. "It was nice meeting you. I'm sure you'll enjoy the quilting classes, 'cause Emma and Lamar are good teachers." Then she turned and rushed out the door.

Emma stood several seconds, watching out the window as Anna made her way out of the yard. Then she turned to Erika and said, "How was your week?"

Erika shrugged, running her finger down the side of the wet, cold glass of lemonade. "Same as usual. I wake up in the morning, and whether I'm at school or home, I sit in my wheelchair the rest of the day. Dad and my caregiver, Mrs. Drew, take care of most of my needs, so I've pretty much got it made, wouldn't you say?"

Emma, as though sensing Erika's frustration, gently touched her shoulders and said, "I'm sure it must be hard for you, and I'm hoping that by taking this class. . ."

"As I've said before, I really don't care about learning how to quilt. I'm only here because my dad insisted I come." Erika gulped down some of her drink, thinking how good the lemonade tasted. *I bet Emma made this herself. It sure doesn't taste like the store-bought kind.*

"You know," Emma said, motioning to the front door, "when Anna took my class up in Shipshewana last year, she didn't want to learn how to quilt, either."

"Then why'd she come?" Erika asked, after taking another swallow of lemonade

"Her mother signed her up for the class." Emma's glasses slipped to the end of her nose, and she paused to push them in place. "Anna wasn't interested in sewing at home, and her mother hoped I could teach her."

"That's interesting, but what's that got to do with me?"

"Take this napkin and wrap it around your glass. It will soak up some of the moisture." Emma smiled and then continued. "Even though Anna didn't want to come to the class at first, eventually she liked it, and she learned to quilt."

Erika didn't respond, just wrapped the napkin around the glass and finished her drink. She hoped the others would get here soon so they could get on with the class, because the sooner it was done, the sooner she could go home to the solitude of her room, which was fast becoming her only safe place.

Maybe I've said enough, Emma thought. *It might be better to just show Erika kindness and do the best I can at teaching her to quilt. Once she discovers that she can do it, she might find it enjoyable and realize she can do something useful.*

"If you'll excuse me a minute, Erika, I need to go back to the kitchen," Emma said. "Lamar's still in there, and I need to make sure he isn't sampling the snack I prepared for our quilt class today."

"Go right ahead," Erika responded in a sullen tone.

Emma hurried to the kitchen, where she found Lamar at the table, peeling an orange. "I was hoping you weren't testing the coffee cake," she said, taking a scat beside him.

He wrinkled his nose. "Nope. I knew better than that. Don't want to do anything to get my *fraa* riled at me."

"It would take a lot more than you eating a piece of my coffee cake to get your wife riled," Emma said. "Now, if you ate the whole thing that would be an entirely different matter."

"Figured, to play it safe, I couldn't get into much trouble if I just had an orange." He glanced at the doorway leading to the other room. "Is everything okay with Erika? She seems pretty down-in-the-mouth today."

"I'm afraid you're right," Emma agreed. "She doesn't want to be here, but I think the real problem may lie in the fact that she has no self-esteem."

"Guess that might be the case, all right." Lamar bit into a piece of orange, sending a spray of juice in Emma's direction. "Oops! Sorry about that."

"No harm done." Emma grabbed a napkin and blotted the juice that had sprayed her apron. "Getting back to Erika, I can understand why she'd be depressed and feel as though she has no self-worth, but there are other people in the world who are worse off than her."

"That's true," Lamar agreed.

"I feel as though Erika has come to us for a reason, and I hope there's something we can do to help her."

"God will give us the right words at the right time; He always has," Lamar said. "And who knows, Emma, a breakthrough for Erika might come about because of something that someone else says or does, rather than through one of us."

Emma nodded. "I'm fortunate to have married a man as *schmaert* as you."

Lamar grinned, bouncing his bushy eyebrows up and down. "Well, I did convince you to marry me, so I must be fairly smart."

———

"It's nice to see you this morning," Kim said as she and Noreen stepped onto the Millers' front porch.

"Same here," Noreen said with a nod.

"I've been wondering if you were able to get that tea stain out of your slacks," Kim said.

"As a matter of fact, I was," Noreen replied. "I used cold water and some Stain Stick, and it came right out."

Kim blew out her breath. "That's a relief."

"Would you like a friendly piece of advice?" Noreen asked.

"Sure."

"During my college days, I worked as a waitress for a while, and one thing I tried to remember was to be careful with the food and beverages I carried to and from the table. Some customers wouldn't be as nice as I was about a waitress spilling something on their clothes, and if you want to keep your job, you have to be on your toes."

"Yes, I know, but accidents can happen."

"And it's your job to make sure that they don't." Noreen pursed her lips. "Otherwise, you could end up getting fired. In my day, I saw that happen more than once."

Kim cringed. While Noreen had kept quiet about her spilling the tea, she figured if something like that should happen to Noreen again while Kim was waiting on her, she would tell Kim's boss. Kim had a hunch that Noreen wasn't one who gave people a second chance.

Kim wasn't normally so klutzy—only when she got nervous or overly stressed. Hopefully things would go better for her at the restaurant once she relaxed and felt more comfortable with her new job.

"Guess we'd better get inside," Kim said, knocking on the front door. "I don't know if everyone else is here or not, but we don't want to hold up the quilting class."

Soon after Kim and Noreen showed up, Jennifer arrived.

"Are you feeling all right? You look tired today," Emma said, feeling concern when she noticed the dark circles beneath the young woman's brown eyes.

"I didn't sleep well last night," Jennifer said. "The baby kept kicking, and I couldn't seem to find a comfortable position."

"I remember when I was carrying my youngest daughter, Mary," Emma said. "She used to get the hiccups, and that would wake me out of a sound sleep." She gave Jennifer's arm a tender squeeze. "Once that *boppli* comes, you'll forget about any discomforts you had before she was born."

Jennifer tipped her head curiously. "Boppli? Is that another name for baby?"

Emma's face heated as she slowly nodded. "It's Pennsylvania Dutch, and even when I'm talking English I sometimes forget and say something in our traditional Amish language."

"It'd be fun to learn a few Pennsylvania Dutch words," Kim spoke up. "Would you teach us, Emma?"

"I'd be happy to," Emma replied. "Maybe I can do that during our refreshment time. Right now, though, I think we need to get started with our quilting lesson."

"But B.J. and Phyllis aren't here yet," Lamar said. "Don't you think we should wait for them?"

Emma touched her hot cheeks. "Of course. How silly of me." She didn't know why she felt so flustered this morning. Maybe it was because of the scare they'd had earlier with the alligator in their yard. That was enough to put anyone's nerves on edge.

Emma glanced at the clock, and noticed that it was almost ten. She hoped her last two students weren't going to be late. If they didn't get started soon, they would fall behind schedule, and she wanted everyone to finish their quilted wall hanging by the end of the sixth lesson. "I guess we can wait a few more minutes to get started," she said, "but if B.J. and Phyllis aren't here by ten fifteen, we'll need to begin without them."

"While we're waiting, Emma, why don't we tell these ladies about our exciting morning?" Lamar said.

"Since it actually happened to you, I'll let you tell them," Emma replied.

Everyone, even Erika this time, focused on Lamar as he proceeded to share the story about the alligator that had entered their yard and been captured by the two men. When he got to the part about Rusty sitting on the gator, Erika's eyes widened. "That guy must have been very brave or incredibly stupid," she said. "Even when I had two good legs, I would never have done anything like that."

"Each of us has different fears and things we feel brave about," Lamar said. "It's just a matter of what we're willing to do."

"That's right," Kim agreed. "Some people are afraid to ride a motorcycle, but I'm not the least bit scared when I'm riding mine."

"Two of our previous quilters from Indiana own cycles," Lamar interjected. "I don't think they're afraid to ride, but they do use caution."

Kim bobbed her head. "Same here. One thing I always remember is to wear my helmet. I've seen some bikers go without it, but in my opinion, that's just asking for trouble."

"Is there anything you've ever done that others might be afraid to try?" Emma asked, looking at Jennifer.

A wide smile spread across the young woman's face. "Before Randy and I got married, I loved to water-ski. Of course, I'd never try that now. It wouldn't be safe for the boppli." Jennifer patted her stomach, and looking at Emma, she grinned. "Did I pronounce that word right?"

Emma smiled and nodded.

"Why don't you go next?" Lamar said, motioning to Noreen. "Is there something you do that others might be afraid to try?"

"Not unless you count teaching high school English. Some people might be afraid of that." Noreen paused, snickering quietly. "Now I recently did something that surprised even me. Imagine a sixty-five-year-old woman like myself buying a sports car. But I did, even though I'm still trying to figure out why." She lifted her gaze to the ceiling, rolling her hazel-colored eyes.

Everyone laughed. Everyone but Erika, who sat staring at her hands, clasped firmly in her lap. Emma thought about asking the girl if there was anything she'd ever done that would seem frightening to others, but decided against it. If Erika wanted to open up, she would.

As if she were able to read Emma's thoughts, Erika suddenly blurted, "I was never afraid of anything till I tried a new dive. It went horribly wrong, and I ended up with a spinal cord injury." She lifted her chin in a defiant pose, although Emma noticed tears glistening in the girl's pretty blue eyes. "Guess that's what I get for showin' off when I should have listened to my dad when he said I should get out of the pool. Some people might believe I got just what I deserved for doing the dive, and they'd probably be right about that."

"Blaming yourself is not the answer," Emma said. "In the Bible we are told to forgive others, and I believe that means we need to forgive ourselves as well."

"I know what the Bible says; my dad and I go to church every Sunday," Erika said with a huff. "So you don't need to preach at me."

Emma's heart went out to Erika. It was obvious that she held herself accountable for the accident that had left her legs paralyzed. Worse than that, Erika thought she deserved her physical limitations. She saw them as a punishment for disobeying her dad. No doubt that was the reason for her negative attitude and cutting remarks.

I won't say anything more to her about this right now, Emma thought, *but I can certainly pray for Erika and ask God to bring healing to her young heart.*

CHAPTER 10

Emma was about to have the class begin sewing their quilt squares, when she heard footsteps on the porch. "That must be B.J. or Phyllis," she said to Lamar.

"Whoever it is, I'll let them in." He moved toward the door.

When Lamar returned a few minutes later, B.J. was at his side.

"Sorry I'm late," B.J. apologized. "Guess I was more tired than I thought last night, because I slept right through the alarm this morning."

Seeing the look of exhaustion on the man's face, Emma became concerned. "Are you feeling alright?" she questioned.

"I'm fine. Just tired is all." B.J. took a seat at the table, next to Noreen. "Did I miss anything?" he asked.

"Not really. Emma was waiting until you and Phyllis got here," Noreen replied. "I wonder what her excuse is for being late."

"Maybe something unexpected came up," Emma was quick to say in

Phyllis's defense. "I'm sure if she wasn't able to be here she would have called."

Noreen shook her head with a look of disgust. "In the world we live in today, it seems that many people aren't dependable and only live for themselves. Why, the other day my neighbor's teenage son was supposed to mow my lawn, but he never showed up."

"Did you call to see what happened?" Kim asked.

"Of course I called. His mother said he'd gone off with his friends to watch a ball game." Noreen's forehead wrinkled. "That's just one example of the lack of dependability I was talking about."

Emma tapped her hand gently against the table. "Once Phyllis gets here, I'll explain what she needs to do with her quilt squares, but I think the rest of you should get started now." She hoped Noreen wouldn't make any negative comments when Phyllis arrived. Noreen and Erika's catty remarks brought tension into the room.

Noreen's face tightened as she looked at her watch. "We're already fifteen minutes behind, so we may end up needing to stay longer today."

"If that turns out to be the case, then any of you who wish to, can stay as long as you need to after class." Emma motioned to the three sewing machines on the other side of the room. "You'll have to take turns using the machines."

"What should we do while we're waiting our turn?" Jennifer questioned.

"You can either visit with the others who are waiting or start cutting out your batting, which is what I had planned for you to do next Saturday."

"We don't want to get ahead of things," Noreen said with a click of her tongue. "But then there's not really much for us to visit about, since we barely know one another."

"That's how you'll get to know each other," Lamar spoke up. "All of our students in the past became well acquainted by the end of six weeks. In fact, some even became close friends, and last fall one of our students' friendships turned to romance."

"How interesting." Noreen glanced quickly at B.J. and smiled.

Emma wondered if Noreen thought there might be a chance for her to find romance in this class. *Now wouldn't that be something?* she thought, smiling to herself.

"Actually one of our students signed up for the class just so he could get to know a pretty young woman who'd come to learn how to quilt," Lamar interjected.

"How'd it work out?" Kim asked, leaning slightly forward in her seat.

"It didn't start out too well," Lamar said. "Terry was a bit overbearing at first, and Cheryl didn't want anything to do with him." He looked over at Emma and grinned. "Eventually, Terry won Cheryl's heart."

"I didn't come here for love or romance," Noreen said, "but if by chance it were to happen, I wouldn't turn it down." She gave B.J. another quick glance, but he wasn't looking her way.

Is something going on here? Emma wondered. *Could Noreen be interested in B.J.? Or maybe it's just my imagination, because they barely know each other.*

"I'm definitely not interested in romance," Kim said. "With romance comes heartache, and I've had my share of that already."

"Are we done with all this silly talk about love and romance?" Erika asked, frowning. "I thought we came here to learn how to quilt."

"And so we shall," Emma said. "Why don't I get Jennifer, Noreen, and Erika started on the sewing machines, and the rest of you can visit with Lamar? I'm sure he'd be happy to tell you more about the quilts he's designed."

Lamar gave a nod. "I'm always eager to talk about quilts."

Erika groaned. "I'd like to know how you think I'm supposed to use one of the sewing machines when they all have foot pedals to make the machine go. In case you've forgotten, my legs are paralyzed."

Emma's face warmed, and quickly spread to her neck. "Oh dear, I hadn't thought about that. Perhaps Kim would be willing sit beside you and operate the pedals while you guide the material under the pressure foot to sew the seams."

"I'd be happy to do that while we're here," Kim said, "but what will Erika do when she's at home and wants to start another quilt or do some other type of sewing?"

Erika shook her head. "That won't be a problem because after I finish this wall hanging, I don't plan to do any more sewing. As I've said, I'm only doing it to please my dad, and when I'm done, I'm done. In fact, if I never see another needle and thread, it'll be soon enough for me."

Emma cringed. With that negative attitude, Erika might be hard to reach. *But I won't quit trying,* she told herself. *We still have four more classes, and every time Erika comes to our home, I'll make an effort.*

———

"I still can't believe I agreed to do this," Mike grumbled as he parked his car in front of a small cream-colored house in Pinecraft, bearing the address his wife had given him. A few other cars were parked there, along with a motorcycle. *I wonder who rides that,* he thought as he stepped down from his SUV. *I can't believe anyone who rides a bike would be interested in quilts. Maybe it's some poor guy whose wife talked him into coming here like me. Well, here goes nothing.*

Mike tromped up the porch steps and knocked on the door. A few minutes later, an Amish man with a head full of thick, gray hair and a matching beard greeted him. "May I help you?"

"Uh, yeah, I'm here for the quilt class."

The man's bushy eyebrows furrowed. "Excuse me?"

"I'm here for the quilt class. This is the right place, isn't it?" Mike questioned.

"Well, yes, we are holding a quilt class here today, but it's the second class, and we weren't expecting any new students."

"I don't think you understand." Mike tapped his foot impatiently. "I'm here to take my wife's place in the class."

"Who is your wife?"

"Phyllis Barstow. I'm her husband, Mike."

"I'm Lamar Miller." He extended his hand. "My wife, Emma, and I met Phyllis last week when she came for the first lesson."

"Well, she won't be back," Mike said. "Her sister broke her leg, and Phyllis went to Fargo, North Dakota, to take care of her. She asked me to come here in her place and learn how to quilt." *And I stupidly said yes,* he silently added.

"Oh, I see." Lamar opened the door wider. "Come inside, and I'll introduce you to my wife and the others in our class."

As Mike stepped into the house, he caught sight of a small gecko skirting along the baseboard. He didn't pay it much mind, knowing the critter was harmless and good for catching bugs.

Mike's thoughts shifted when he followed Lamar into a room where four women sat at sewing machines, while an Amish woman and a bald, older man were seated at a table in the center of the room.

"Everyone, this is Phyllis Barstow's husband, Mike," Lamar announced. "Phyllis had to go to North Dakota to help her sister who has a broken leg, so Mike's here to take her place."

The Amish woman smiled and rose from her chair. "I'm sorry Phyllis won't be able to complete the class, but it's nice that you can be here to learn how to quilt."

"Yeah, I can hardly wait," Mike muttered under his breath.

"My name is Emma Miller, and these are the quilt squares your wife cut out last week," Emma said, handing Mike a plastic sack. "We are in the process of stitching the squares together now, and I'd be happy to help you with that."

"It's a good thing, too, 'cause I don't know the first thing about sewing," Mike said, wondering once more why he'd agreed to do this. It wasn't likely that he would learn anything he could show Phyllis when she returned. He'd probably make a mess of her wall hanging.

Emma smiled. "It's okay. I'm here to teach you, Mike, and we're glad to have you in our class."

Lamar nodded in agreement.

"I'm not sure I'm even teachable." Mike swiped at the trickle of sweat rolling down the side of his head. "Now give me a fishing pole, some bait, and a hook, and I'm good to go, but I'm not the least bit comfortable with a needle and thread."

The baldheaded man at the table chuckled. "Well, you're in good company then, because other than appreciating the beauty of quilts, I don't know anything about sewing, either."

After Emma introduced each of the students to Mike, he took a seat at the table between her and B.J. He was about to take Phyllis's quilt squares out of the bag he'd been given, when the older woman, Noreen, let out an ear-piercing scream.

"What's wrong?" Emma asked, scrunching her brows.

"Look. . .over there!" Noreen, her eyes wide with obvious fear, pointed to the wall closest to her. "Get it! Get it! I can't stand creepy-crawlies in the house."

"If someone will help me corner the critter, I think we can catch him pretty quick," Lamar said, moving toward the gecko.

Mike, being the sportsman that he was, jumped up right away. "No problem. I bet I can catch him," he hollered as he took up the chase.

After Lamar and Mike pursued the gecko unsuccessfully, B.J. got into the act. "Come back here," he panted, red-faced and gasping for breath as the gecko eluded his grasp and slithered up the wall. The poor man looked exhausted. Winded and coughing, he finally had to quit.

"Are you okay?" Noreen asked, a look of concern etched on her face.

"I—I'm fine. Just a bit winded is all." B.J. flopped into a chair. "Guess that's proof that I'm not as young as I used to be."

Mike made another pass at the gecko, but missed again and fell on his face.

"Maybe I can help." Kim dashed across the room and quickly snagged the critter in the palm of her hand. Everyone but the girl in the wheelchair cheered.

Mike clambered to his feet a bit too quickly and had to steady himself until a wave of dizziness passed. He was embarrassed that he'd made a fool of himself in front of the class, but figured the wooziness had been caused by jerking his head too fast while in hot pursuit of the gecko. Mike had the strength and agility to reel in a big fish when he went out on his boat, but he couldn't even catch a little lizard. And to be shown up by a woman, no less! He really felt like an idiot. This was not a good way to begin his first quilting class, and he could only imagine how the next hour would go.

Chapter 11

After Kim put the gecko outside, the class continued, and the topic of the alligator that had been in the Millers' yard came up again.

"I still can't get over that," Kim said, sitting down at the sewing machine beside Erika once more. "A little gecko is one thing, but I don't know what I would have done if I'd been in your shoes, Lamar. Think I would have run straight for the house, screaming all the way."

"I'd have probably passed out on the lawn," Noreen put in as she finished up with her bit of sewing.

"Back home all we ever had to deal with was my goat, Maggie, getting out of her pen." Emma chuckled. "I guess here we need to be a little more careful when we step into the yard."

"Most gators don't show up in people's backyards unless there's a body of water nearby," Mike said as he laid out the quilt squares his wife had cut the previous week.

That guy seems like a know-it-all to me, Kim thought as she continued

79

helping Erika by pressing on the foot pedal for her. *I don't think he really wants to be here, either. But then neither does Erika, so that has to make it hard on our teachers.*

"I just thought of something," Emma said, coming up beside Erika and Kim. "What if we put the foot pedal for the electric sewing machine up on the cabinet next to the machine? Then, Erika, you can press down on it with your elbow, which would give you both hands free to guide your material under the presser foot."

"That's a good idea," Kim said before Erika could respond. "Don't know why I didn't think of it myself."

"I—I guess I could give it a try," Erika said, with a dubious expression.

As Emma placed the foot pedal on the cabinet and showed Erika what to do, Kim began pinning her own quilt squares together, while glancing over at Jennifer. The young woman seemed nice and was eager to learn how to quilt. Jennifer didn't say a lot, though, and Kim wondered if she was shy or just didn't have much to talk about.

If I was in her place and expecting a baby, that would be all I talked about, Kim mused. At the age of thirty-six, she'd all but given up on marriage and having a family of her own. Oh, she'd dated a few men over the years, but none had been willing to make a commitment, and a few she'd broken up with because she knew they weren't good husband material. Most of the men she'd gone out with were either selfish, had nothing in common with her, or wanted more than she was willing to offer. Kim had made a pledge when she was a teenager to remain pure and give herself only to the man she would marry. But since marriage and children probably weren't in her future, she'd put her focus on other things—riding her motorcycle, walking her dog on the beach, and being cheerful to all her customers at the restaurant.

Kim's thoughts were interrupted when Emma touched her shoulder and asked, "How's it going?"

"Okay, I guess. It just takes awhile to get all the squares pinned in place."

"That's true," Emma agreed, "but once you get the blocks sewn together, your wall hanging will start to take shape."

Kim sighed. "I've been trying to decide what to do with it after I'm done."

"I'm going to hang mine in my living room," Noreen said. "I know just the place for it, too."

"Mine's going in the baby's room," Jennifer spoke up. "That's why I chose pastel colors in shades of pink."

"Does that mean you're having a girl?" Noreen questioned.

"Yes. At least that's what the ultrasound showed." Jennifer's shoulders drooped. "I just hope my husband finds a job before the baby comes."

"What does he do for a living?" This question came from B.J.

"He's a cook, and a mighty fine one, too." Jennifer smiled. "The only good thing about Randy being out of work is that now he cooks most of our meals. I'd gladly take that responsibility over again, though, if he could only find a job."

Kim was glad Jennifer was opening up, but she felt sorry for the young mother-to-be. Maybe there were some benefits in being single. At least she only had to worry about supporting herself and taking care of her dog.

"I'm thankful that someone gave me the gift of this class," Jennifer went on to say. "I just wish I knew who it was so I could thank them for it." She looked over at Emma with a hopeful expression. "Do you know who it was?"

Emma adjusted her head covering, which was slightly askew. "The person who paid for your class wishes to remain anonymous and said they felt it was more of a blessing to keep it that way."

"Someone left a box of food on our front porch the other day, too, and there was no note attached," Jennifer said. "I'm beginning to see that God is providing for Randy and me in many ways."

"We'll be praying for you, dear," Emma said. "Try to keep a positive attitude while waiting for God to provide your husband a job."

As Noreen worked at the sewing machine, she was glad that she had something to do. She'd felt a little foolish, making such a fuss about the lizard—especially after thinking about that big alligator in Emma and Lamar's backyard. She would have had a conniption, seeing such a creature anywhere close to her home.

Noreen's mind drifted to the envelope that had come in this morning's mail. She'd been hoping to hear from her son, Todd, or his wife, Kara, but guessed they were busy with their lives in Texas, because the letter wasn't from them. She understood that Todd and Kara had busy lives of their own, but she missed them and would have gone to visit more often but didn't want to intrude.

Two years after Noreen married her husband, Ben, and they'd found out they couldn't have children of their own, they'd been given the opportunity to adopt Todd. What a wonderful life they'd had raising their boy. All those years when Todd was growing up, they had been a threesome, doing so many things together—simple things like camping, fishing, and going on picnics. They'd also enjoyed going to some of the local festivals every year. Of all the fun things to do at festivals, Todd usually went for the pony rides. In fact, from a very young age, he'd been interested in horses. To follow his dreams, after graduating from high school, he'd gone to Texas to stay with a friend, where he'd learned about ranching. Eventually he'd married Kara, and they'd been living in Texas ever since, working on the ranch where they'd met. In addition to their ranch duties, they had Kara's boys, Nolan, who was ten, and Garrett, age twelve, to raise.

After Ben died, Noreen had felt totally alone, especially given that they had been married for forty years, but she didn't want to burden her son or make him feel obligated to her. She wanted Todd and his wife to pursue their dream of someday owning their own ranch. So Noreen decided to move forward, pushing herself to learn how to cope with living alone. It was hard at first, but she made it a point to get on with her life. She had been a teacher for all those years and used to give her students pep talks when they seemed fearful about their future. Now it was her turn to give herself a pep talk. After all, she wasn't the only woman in the world who'd lost her husband.

Thinking back to the letter she'd received this morning, Noreen was glad it hadn't been a piece of junk mail, like she so often found in her mailbox. Instead, the return address revealed it was from Monica Adams, a former student. Every now and then Noreen received notes from students letting her know what was happening in their lives. She'd put off opening Monica's note until later today so she wouldn't be late to class.

"Is everyone ready to take a break for some refreshments?" Emma's question broke into Noreen's thoughts. She glanced at her watch and realized it was already eleven o'clock.

"I made some coffee cake, and Lamar picked oranges from our tree in the backyard this morning," Emma said, smiling at the class.

"Both sound good to me," Noreen said, putting her sewing away, while several others bobbed their heads in agreement. Not Mike, though. He sat there, wrinkling his nose.

———❦———

"I'm allergic to oranges," Mike informed Emma. "So I'll pass on those.

Sure don't want to break out with a case of hives."

"No, that wouldn't be good," Emma said. "Would you like some of my coffee cake, though?"

Mike nodded eagerly. "That suits me just fine. I didn't have much for breakfast this morning so I'm feelin' kinda hungry right now." He rose from his chair to follow Emma into the kitchen, thinking he might get to taste some of that cake before anyone else. But he'd only taken a few steps when he felt kind of shaky and broke out in a sweat.

"Oh, great, not this again," Mike groaned, grabbing the back of B.J.'s chair as everything blurred before him. He'd felt this way when he'd first woken up this morning and figured he might be coming down with the flu. He'd felt better once he'd had a cup of coffee and a doughnut, however.

"Are you okay?" Lamar asked, taking hold of Mike's arm. "Is it too hot in here? Should I open a window or door?"

"No, I'm fine. Just feeling a little woozy is all."

Lamar quickly pulled out an empty chair and instructed Mike to sit down. "Try to relax and take some deep breaths. I'll open a window to let in some fresh air. Hopefully, that will help you cool down."

Mike did as Lamar suggested. As he sat, fanning his face with his hands, while blinking his eyes to clear them, he could only imagine what Phyllis would say if she knew what was happening to him right now.

What is happening to me? Mike wondered. *I felt fine when I first got here, except for feeling a bit woozy when I got out of the car. Why do I feel so horrible now? Are these spells a warning of some kind?*

CHAPTER 12

"Should we call 911?" Noreen asked, concerned about Mike's strange behavior. "You might be having a heart attack." She remembered too well how her husband had collapsed on the floor of their living room when his heart gave out. And even though she'd called for help, and they'd performed surgery at the hospital, it had been too late for Ben. She hated to think that might be the case with this man, too.

Mike shook his head determinedly. "There's no need for that. I feel a little weak and shaky is all, but I'm sure I'll be okay once I have something to eat."

"It might be a case of low blood sugar," Erika spoke up. "I've heard my dad talk about patients who've actually passed out when their blood sugar dropped, mostly because they hadn't eaten. You oughta make an appointment with your doctor and have it checked out."

Mike flapped his hand. "Don't think there's any need for that. I'm sure it'll pass."

Men can be so stubborn, Noreen thought. *I'll bet if Mike's wife was here, she would insist that he see a doctor today.*

"Erika's right," Lamar said, "but in the meantime, I'll get Emma, and we'll see that you get something to eat." He hurried into the kitchen, as Mike continued to breathe deeply, while keeping his head between his knees.

———

"We have a problem in the other room," Lamar said when he entered the kitchen where Emma stood at the counter cutting the coffee cake.

Emma turned to face him. "What kind of problem? Is someone having trouble with one of the sewing machines?"

Lamar shook his head. "Mike isn't feeling well. Said he felt shaky, and he's sweating profusely. I was afraid he might pass out so I opened some windows and had him sit down to rest."

"Oh dear! We'd better call for help right away." Emma moved quickly across the room, where the telephone sat on the roll-top desk. At a time such as this, she was glad the Amish were allowed to have electricity and telephones in their homes here in Pinecraft.

Lamar stepped between Emma and the desk. "Mike doesn't want us to call for help. He thinks he just needs to eat something, and Erika mentioned, too, that it could be a drop in his blood sugar."

"Well, if that's the case, then some cake might help." Emma handed the platter to Lamar, then she grabbed some paper plates and forks and followed him into the other room. Immediately she cut a piece of cake and offered it to Mike.

"Thanks," he said, quickly wolfing it down. "Boy, that sure tasted good. And you know what? Think I'm feelin' better already. A little food was probably all I needed."

"I'll bet it's your blood sugar, alright," Erika said, nodding her head.

"Eating something sweet brought it up real quick. If you find out you have hypoglycemia it could turn to diabetes, and of course, you'll have to watch what you eat."

"Well now, aren't you just the little doctor?" Mike's eyes narrowed. "I'm sure I don't have that. I just needed to eat something, and I feel fine now, so you can quit badgering me."

"I wasn't." Erika frowned. "Oh, never mind. I'll keep my opinions to myself from now on. It's your health anyway, not mine."

Feeling the need to break the tension, Emma quickly said, "I'll go to the kitchen and get the tray of orange slices now. Then we can sit around the table and eat our snack while we get better acquainted." She rushed back to the kitchen and was surprised when Noreen followed.

"Men can be so pigheaded sometimes," Noreen muttered. "If my husband hadn't been too stubborn to see the doctor for annual checkups, he might still be alive." Her lips compressed, as a frown etched her forehead. "One time I made Ben an appointment, and he got really mad. He even said I was treating him like a little boy."

"That must have been upsetting," Emma acknowledged. "But when a grown person doesn't want to do something, there isn't much anyone can do about it. Sometimes the more we say, the more they refuse to listen."

"I guess that's true. I just wish. . . ." Noreen's voice trailed off, and then she said, "Can I help you with anything, Emma?"

"Well, let's see. . . ." Emma glanced at the refrigerator. "There's a pitcher of iced tea in there, so if you want to bring that in, along with the paper cups on the counter, that would be appreciated."

"I'd be happy to." Noreen smiled as she moved across the room.

Emma was glad Noreen seemed in better spirits. Sometimes rehashing the past, especially something that couldn't be undone, brought a person down. If there was one thing Emma had learned in her sixty-seven years, it was the importance of focusing on the positive and making the most of each day. She hoped by their actions and words that she and Lamar would be able to share that with this group of quilters, just as they had done with all the other classes they'd taught.

When Emma returned to the dining room, she was relieved to see that Mike looked better and was visiting with B.J. as though nothing had happened. It upset her to think that someone in her class wasn't feeling well. Fortunately, it didn't seem to be serious. But if it had been, she would have definitely called for help, despite any objections on Mike's part.

"Those are some really nice shells in that jar over there," Kim mentioned, as everyone enjoyed their refreshments. "Someone must like to comb the beach as much as I do."

Lamar grinned widely. "That would be me. Of course, I think Emma likes beach combing, too. Right, Emma?"

"Yes, it's relaxing; just like working in my flower beds back home." Emma glanced at Erika. "Do you enjoy going to the beach?"

"Not really." Erika frowned. "I mean, what's fun about sitting in a wheelchair staring at the water?"

"I often sit on a bench and watch the waves," Emma said, hoping to bring Erika out of her negativity. "I like that even more than searching for things on the beach. It's also interesting to watch people, especially children when they find something fascinating."

"I do that sometimes, too," Kim interjected. "Of course, if I sit for too long, my dog, Maddie, nudges me with her nose, wanting to play."

"What about the rest of you?" Lamar asked. "Do you all enjoy the beach?"

"I do," B.J. was quick to say. "I like to watch the sunset and try to capture all the vivid colors on canvas."

"Randy and I enjoy the beach," Jennifer said. "It's one of the few things we can do that doesn't cost money."

"Sometimes I think the things that are out there, free to enjoy, are more meaningful than anything else," Emma added. Her heart went out to Jennifer. She remembered back to the days when she and her first husband, Ivan, were newlyweds and struggled financially. If not for the help of their family and friends, some days they might not have had enough money to put food on the table.

Maybe there's something we could do to help Jennifer and Randy, Emma thought. *The very least we can do is give them some food. I hope they won't be too proud to accept it.*

"What about the Amish words you promised to teach us?" Kim asked.

"Oh, that's right. I did say we would do that." Emma looked at Lamar. "Should I share one, or would you like to?"

"You go ahead, Emma."

"Well, the Pennsylvania-Dutch word for children is *kinner*."

"And for *thank you*, we would say *danki*," Lamar interjected.

"That's interesting and all," Noreen spoke up, "but this is taking up time, and I think we should get back to work on our quilts."

"You're right," Emma agreed. "There's more sewing to be done on your quilt squares." She looked over at Mike. "Are you feeling up to trying out one of the sewing machines?"

"Sure. But I'll probably end up stitching my shirt instead of the material," he said with a shrug.

"I'm sure you'll do fine," Emma said, remembering how a couple of her previous students had done that very thing. "I'll show you everything you need to do."

———————

While Jennifer pinned more of her squares together, she visited with Kim. "Are you married?" she asked.

Kim shook her head. "Don't you remember last week when I mentioned that I wasn't looking for love or romance?"

"Oh, that's right. Guess I forgot."

"I don't even have a serious boyfriend right now, but maybe it's better that way," Kim said.

"You have such a nice smile, and you seem so easygoing. I wouldn't have been surprised if you had a husband and a few kids."

Kim leaned her head back and laughed. "I'm so far from that, it's not even funny."

"Do you like kids?"

"Oh sure, but it's not likely that I'll ever have any of my own." Kim picked up another pin and stuck it in place. "It's not that I don't wish for it, but I'm thirty-six years old, and even if I got married in the next few years, I'm too old to start a family."

"My mother was thirty-two when she had me," Jennifer said.

"Are you the youngest child in your family, or did your mother have more kids after you?" Kim questioned.

"I'm the oldest, and I have three younger sisters still living at home."

"Your mom had more courage than me," Kim said. "If I don't get married in the next year or so, I'm giving up on the idea of having any kids."

Jennifer touched Kim's arm. "You never know. Mr. Right could be just around the corner. Or he might be the next customer you wait on at the restaurant. Stranger things have been known to happen."

"My last boyfriend, Darrell. . . Well, let me put it this way—I thought we had a good thing going, and that he was 'the one.' I was so sure of

Darrell's love that I moved from my home in North Carolina to Florida, thinking we could start a new life together." Kim slowly shook her head. "Believe me, I've never done anything that huge before." She paused to pin a few more pieces of her quilt blocks together. "Everything went along smoothly for a while, but then things turned sour and Darrell broke up with me. It only took a few months to know our relationship was going nowhere and that Darrell wasn't the 'Mr. Right' I thought he was."

"Do you have any family here in Florida?" Jennifer asked.

"Nope. My parents are living in North Carolina, and my brother, Jimmy, is in the navy, and currently stationed in Bremerton, Washington. I miss my family, but I stay in touch through phone calls, text messages, and e-mails."

"Have you thought about moving back home?"

"Yeah, many times, but if I did, it'd be like admitting that I failed. I refuse to turn tail and run back home. I want to try and make a go of it here." Kim smiled. "Thank goodness for my dog, Maddie. She and I have fallen into somewhat of a routine, and it's comforting to know she won't desert me."

"I guess sometimes things happen to make us think about what we really want in life," Jennifer said. "Don't give up, Kim. I'm convinced that there's someone in this world for everyone."

Kim snickered. "I don't think it'll be anyone like the crotchety man I waited on yesterday. I wouldn't give him a second glance, even though he was sort of good-looking."

"How come?"

"He got mad because I dribbled some ketchup on his plate when I was handing him the bottle. I don't know why he'd complain about that. He was having eggs and hash browns, and who doesn't like a little ketchup with that?"

"I'm sure you won him over with your winning smile."

"Maybe. At least he didn't say anything to my boss about the incident."

"Did he leave you a tip?"

Kim shook her head. "Guess he thought I oughta pay for my flub-up, so the only thing he left was his dirty napkin, dotted with ketchup."

Jennifer snickered and gently squeezed Kim's arm. "I like you, Kim. You make me laugh."

"Thanks," Kim said. "I enjoy being able to bring humor into people's lives, and I like it when someone makes me laugh, too."

Everyone worked in silence awhile, until Noreen announced that it was time for her to go. "I haven't even read my mail from this morning yet, and I have a hair appointment this afternoon that I don't want to miss." She patted the sides of her hair. "I'm having some color put on to cover my gray, so I don't want to be late."

"I think we're about done for the day anyway," Emma said. "During our next class we'll finish stitching the quilt patches, and then hopefully get the batting cut out."

"Great. I'll see you all next Saturday then," Noreen said, gathering her things and hurrying out the door.

"My ride's here," Erika said when a wheelchair-accessible van pulled up in front of the Millers' house.

Everyone else said their good-byes, and Lamar reminded Mike that if he had another dizzy spell, he should call the doctor.

"Yeah, I'll do that," Mike agreed on his way out the door.

Jennifer had a feeling that he probably wouldn't do it—not unless his wife came home and made the appointment for him. She thought about how Randy relied on her for things like that. He would put off going to the dentist until he had a toothache, unless Jennifer made him an appointment for a cleaning and checkup. *Men are alike in many ways,* she thought, heading for the door.

"Oh, Jennifer, would you wait a minute?" Emma called.

Jennifer halted and turned back around.

"I was wondering if you would like a bag of oranges to take home," Emma said. "We also have some extra lemons we'd be happy to share with you."

"That'd be great. With the way Randy likes to cook, I'm sure he'll put the lemons to good use."

"How about some of those ginger cookies you made the other day?" Lamar said to Emma. "We still have plenty left, and you and I sure aren't going to eat them all."

A lump formed in Jennifer's throat. Emma and her husband were so kind and generous. To show her appreciation, she gave Emma a hug.

"Lamar and I will be praying that your husband finds the right job soon," Emma said. "In the meantime, if there's anything we can do for you, please don't hesitate to ask."

"Thanks, I'm grateful for your concern."

"Now, let me help you carry the fruit and cookies out to your car," Lamar offered.

"See you next week," Emma said. "And don't forget our offer of help."

Jennifer nodded, then hurried out the door. She couldn't believe what a nice couple they were. Too bad everyone didn't have such a generous spirit. If they did, the world would be a better place.

Chapter 13

When Jennifer arrived home from the quilt class, she found Randy sitting on the couch in the living room with his feet propped on the coffee table, staring into space.

"What are you doing here?" she asked, setting her tote bag on the floor. "I thought you had a job interview today."

He grunted. "I did, but when I got to the restaurant I was told that they'd already found a cook, so they didn't ask me one question about my previous experience."

"Then why'd they want to interview you?" Jennifer questioned, taking a seat beside him. She couldn't imagine being called to an interview and then being told that the position had already been filled. That just didn't seem fair!

Randy shrugged like it didn't matter, but Jennifer knew from his dejected expression that it did.

"Guess maybe they interviewed the other cook first, liked what he said, and hired him on the spot." Randy squeezed his hands together. "You'd think they would have at least talked to me first and then decided who was best suited to the job. Whoever heard of doing interviews like that, anyways? And wouldn't you think they'd give everyone a fair chance? They just wasted my time!" He slapped the newspaper lying on the sofa beside him. "I've looked through the want ads till my eyes hurt, and there are no positions for a cook available in this town right now. At the rate things are going, we'll starve to death before I find a job."

Jennifer leaned over and gave him a hug. She felt bad seeing her husband like this, but maybe it was good for him to vent a bit. It wasn't healthy to keep things bottled up. "I know you're upset, and it's understandable, too, but we need to keep a positive attitude and never give up."

"I won't give up," he said, shaking his head, "but I'm not sure I can think positive thoughts right now."

Jennifer sighed, wondering what it would take to get Randy out of his slump.

"How'd it go at the quilt class today?" he asked.

"It went okay. When I got ready to leave, Emma and Lamar Miller gave me a sack of oranges and lemons, as well as a container of cookies. They're out in the car, so if you don't mind getting them. . ."

"Fruit and cookies, huh?" He snorted. "Like we can live on those!"

"We still have some food in the house, Randy." Jennifer took hold of his hand. "I think what the Millers gave us was a nice gesture, don't you?"

"I'm sure they meant well, but we don't need anyone's charity. I accepted it when someone paid for your quilt class, and then when my brother sent us some money so we could get new tires for your car, but now we're accepting food handouts, too? When's it gonna end, Jennifer?

If things get any worse, we may have to sell one of our vehicles."

"I think we should be grateful for whatever help we receive."

"Well, if we're gonna take charity, then I'd at least like to do something nice in return."

"Like what?" she questioned.

"Maybe we could have Emma and Lamar over for dinner some evening. Of course, we can't do that till I've found a job and we can buy a decent cut of meat."

Jennifer sighed. "I don't think the Millers would expect an expensive meal. Maybe you could barbecue some burgers or make a big taco salad."

"I'll give it some thought." Randy rose to his feet. "Guess I'd better get those oranges and lemons brought in before they shrivel up from the heat. It may be the dead of winter and cold as an iceberg in some places, but here in Sarasota, it's hot enough to cook a hot dog on the roof of your car."

Jennifer snickered. She was glad her husband hadn't lost his sense of humor, despite all they'd been going through with the loss of his job.

"Say, Randy, I've been thinking," she said before he headed outside. "Since we still don't have a crib for the baby, why don't we go to one of the thrift stores in the area soon and see if we can find one? They might have some other baby things in good condition, too."

He shook his head. "I don't want our baby girl to have a bunch of used furniture or hand-me-down clothes. She deserves better than that."

"We can't afford to buy anything new right now," Jennifer argued. "Your unemployment check just doesn't go very far."

"How well I know it. Let's wait another week or so and see if I find a job before we look at any of the thrift stores, okay?"

She nodded slowly. "Whatever you think's best."

Noreen entered her house and flopped into the recliner with a moan. She'd gone to the styling salon after the quilt class today, and been told that her stylist had gotten sick and gone home. Noreen could have rescheduled, but since she didn't know how long her stylist would be sick, she decided to stop at a store on the way home and buy a box of hair color. She'd never attempted to color her own hair but figured it couldn't be that difficult. She would fix herself some lunch, read this morning's mail, then do her hair.

Moving to the kitchen, where she'd left the stack of mail, Noreen opened up the letter from her former student Monica:

Dear Mrs. Webber:

I hope this note finds you well. The reason I'm writing is to let you know that the high school class I graduated from is having its twentieth reunion in three weeks and we're inviting many of our teachers to be at the function. I realize this isn't the time of year for most reunions, but we couldn't get the school auditorium when we want it, so the committee decided to have the event this month instead. Please let me know if you'll be able to come.

Sincerely,
Monica Adams

"Of course I'll come," Noreen said aloud. It would be great to see some of her old students again, as well as her teacher friend, Ruth Bates, who would no doubt also get an invitation. Noreen would give Ruth a call later on to see if she was planning to go.

One more reason to get the gray out of my hair so I don't look so old, she thought.

———

After shampooing and towel-drying her hair, Noreen stepped up to the bathroom mirror. She blinked in disbelief, and her mouth dropped open. Her hair was darker, alright, and yes, the gray was gone, but it was darker than it had ever been in her life! The color looked so stark, even against her tanned skin. Had she bought the wrong shade of brown or left it on too long?

Bending over to fish the empty box from the garbage, Noreen gasped. She didn't know how she had missed it before, but the color listed on the box was black, not brown!

Tears pooled in Noreen's eyes. "I look ridiculous like this. What was I thinking? I shouldn't have colored my own hair. I should have waited till Lynn came back to work. How can I go anywhere in public looking like this?" she wailed.

———

Goshen

With a sense of excitement, Jan knocked on Star's door.

"Come in, Dad!" Star hollered from inside the house.

He stepped in and smiled when he found his daughter in the living room, holding her guitar. "Hey, how'd you know it was me at the door?" he asked.

"Are you kidding me?" Star grinned. "I could hear your motorcycle comin' from a block away."

Jan chuckled. "Yeah, I'll bet. If you were playing your guitar you probably couldn't hear much other than that." He winked at her. "More'n likely it was my heavy boots clompin' up your front steps that told you it was me."

She placed the guitar on the sofa and poked his arm. "You got me there, Dad."

Jan draped his leather jacket over the back of a chair and took a seat beside her on the sofa. "So, are you ready to leave this cold weather behind for a few weeks and head to sunny Florida in the morning?"

She drew in her bottom lip. "Uh, I was gonna call you about this, but now that you're here, I can give you the bad news to your face."

His forehead wrinkled. "What bad news?"

"I can't go to Florida with you."

"How come? You're not sick, I hope."

"No, it's nothing like that. I can't get the two weeks off that I have coming right now."

He smacked the side of his head. "Oh great! Why not?"

"When I went to work this morning, the boss informed me that Shawn Prentiss, one of the guys who stocks shelves, had an emergency appendectomy, so that leaves them shorthanded. He asked me to wait a few weeks to take my vacation—until they can hire someone to take Shawn's place, because he probably won't be back for at least six weeks."

"I'm sorry to hear that," Jan said. "Guess we'll put our Florida plans on hold till you're free to go then."

Star shook her head. "Two weeks from now the weather could improve and you might have some roofing jobs. I think you oughta go on the trip without me, and if my boss hires someone to take Shawn's place soon, then I'll hop on a plane and join you in Sarasota. Since I won't be ridin' my bike, we can double up on yours and get around that way. Or maybe I can rent one once I get to Florida."

Jan gave his beard a sharp pull, mulling things over. He really didn't want to go without Star, but she had that look of determination he'd come to know so well, and he figured if he said no, she'd argue with him the rest of the day.

"Well, okay, if you're sure," he finally said.

Star gave a quick nod. "I'm not happy about having to stay behind, or for that matter, even flying down there, but I'd be a little nervous cycling all the way to Florida by myself. Most of all, though, I'd feel worse if you didn't go ahead."

"No, I wouldn't want you comin' all that way alone on your bike." He gave her a hug. "You have a good head on your shoulders, and I'm glad you came back into my life when you did."

"Same here." She hugged him back. "You need to promise me one thing."

"What's that?"

"Don't ride your bike too fast; remember to stop for a break every few hours; and call me every night so I'll know how you're doing."

He tweaked the end of her nose, lightly brushing her gold nose ring with his little finger. "That was three things, and you said one."

She giggled and poked his arm playfully. "Okay, so I lied. Seriously, though, I really do want you to call when you stop for the night. Oh, and when you get to Sarasota, I'll want to know that you've arrived safely."

"Yes, Mother," Jan teased, leaning his head against the back of the sofa. "I'll keep you posted every step of the way, but it's sure not gonna be the same without you on this road trip. You're my favorite cycling partner."

CHAPTER 14

*B*ong! *Bong! Bong! Bong! Bong!*

Emma's eyes snapped open, and she cast a quick glance at the clock on the far wall. After doing some mending this afternoon, she'd relaxed in her recliner for a while. Then, unable to keep her eyes open, she'd fallen asleep. Now it was five o'clock.

"That noisy clock you bought the other day has just let me know that it's time to start supper," Emma said to Lamar, who sat on the sofa nearby, reading the newspaper. She yawned and stretched her arms over her head.

"Sorry about that," Lamar apologized. "When I found the clock in the secondhand store, I didn't realize it would be so loud. I can turn the ringer off if you'd like."

"*Danki.* It might be better if you did." Emma expelled another noisy yawn.

"Did you have a nice nap?" Lamar stifled a yawn, then laughed.

"Hearing you yawn makes me feel the need to yawn, too."

"Jah, hearing someone yawn can be quite contagious." Emma grinned. "When I was a young girl, I and a bunch of my classmates were supposed to be quietly reading, while our teacher Sara Beiler graded papers. Some of us got mischievous and took turns yawning, and in no time we had the teacher yawning, too. Sara never caught on to what we were doing, and it was all we *kinner* could do to keep from laughing out loud. We were lucky that day that we didn't get in trouble."

Lamar clucked his tongue. "My, my, you were a little dickens when you were young," he teased.

"Oh, you know, it was just kid stuff." Emma yawned once more and covered her mouth with the palm of her hand. "I don't know why, but I've been tired ever since our quilt class ended today."

"Tired physically or emotionally?" Lamar asked.

"I think it's more emotional than anything," she said. "It's difficult to see others struggling and not be able to do anything about it."

"Is there anyone in particular you're thinking of?"

She nodded. "Jennifer, for one. She's on the brink of becoming a new mother and shouldn't have to worry about how she and her husband are going to provide for their baby when it comes."

"We can give them some more food," Lamar suggested. "Or maybe buy them a gift card they can use at one of the grocery stores in their neighborhood."

"That's a good idea. I think we should do that. Unfortunately, just seeing that they have food in the cupboards won't pay their bills."

"We could give them some money, I suppose."

Emma removed her glasses and cleaned a spot that was smudged. "I'm not opposed to that idea, Lamar, but I think from what Jennifer's said, her husband might take offense if we gave them money. Maybe if we knew them better. . ."

"I wish I knew of some restaurant that needed a cook," Lamar said. "I'd surely put in a good word for Jennifer's husband." He rose to his feet. "Speaking of restaurants, why don't we go to that nice one up the street, where Anna and Kim work? It'll save you from having to cook this evening."

"Oh, I don't mind cooking; I'll just keep it simple. I appreciate your offer, Lamar, but I really don't feel like going out this evening."

"Okay. I'll turn the clock's ringer off, and then we can go to the kitchen and I'll help you fix whatever you want."

"We have some cold meat loaf and potato salad in the refrigerator, so maybe I'll make a fruit salad to go with those and use some of our juicy oranges. I also have some strawberries and pineapple that I purchased at the produce market the other day, so that can be our dessert."

"Sounds good. We haven't had fruit salad in a while," Lamar said. "I can help by slicing up whatever fruit you want to use."

Emma smiled. Once more, she was reminded of how fortunate she was to be married to such a kind, thoughtful man.

As dinnertime approached, Mike started feeling kind of shaky again. After returning from the quilt class, he'd spent the afternoon working in the yard and hadn't taken time to eat lunch. A few times he'd had to stop when fatigue overtook him.

"Big mistake for not eating sooner," Mike muttered, reaching for a jar of peanut butter from the refrigerator. Since he didn't have the energy to cook anything tonight, a peanut butter and jelly sandwich would have to suffice. It was something he could make quickly and get into his stomach, which was growling loudly.

Mike got out the bread and slathered peanut butter on one piece and jelly on the other. Then he poured himself a glass of milk and took a seat at the table. He'd just taken his first bite, when the telephone rang.

"Oh great," he mumbled. "It's probably some irritating advertising call. Those always seem to come in around dinnertime." Mike was tempted to ignore it, but on the chance that it might be his wife, he left the table and went to check the caller ID. Sure enough, it was Phyllis.

"Hi, hon," he said, mouth still full of sandwich.

"Did I catch you in the middle of supper?" Phyllis asked.

"Not so much." He moved back to the table and took a drink of milk. "Just having a peanut butter and jelly sandwich."

"That's all you're eating for supper?"

"Yeah, but it fills the hole." Mike took another drink and gulped it down, looking out the window toward the bay.

"Are you okay? You don't sound like your usual self tonight."

"Naw, I'm fine. Just tired is all. Guess I overdid it doing yard work today." Mike reached for the sandwich and took a bite. His shakiness had subsided some, but he still felt kind of weak. No way was he going to tell Phyllis that, though. She'd be torn between coming home to look after him and taking care of her sister.

"How'd the quilt class go today?" she asked.

"Fine. How's Penny doing?"

"Okay, but she's not ready to be on her own yet. She really appreciates me being here, especially with the snowstorm we're having right now. I think it's a blizzard, actually." Phyllis paused briefly. "I'm glad Penny has a generator. So many people here are without power, but Penny's prepared for something like this." She laughed lightly. "My big sis always did have a good head on her shoulders."

"I hope you two stay put and don't go anywhere. You're not used to driving in the snow—especially with someone else's vehicle," Mike said with concern. "Sure wish I was there with you right now."

"We're managing okay. The weather station's been warning people about this blizzard for a few days, so I went out and got some extra groceries the other day," Phyllis said. "Penny doesn't live far from the store, and I truly think everyone goes there just for the bread and milk. There was hardly any left in the store when I got there. Anyhow, Mike, I'm glad I thought to bring along some warmer clothes for this trip." She laughed. "I'd feel like a Popsicle if I'd only brought shorts and sandals."

"Guess people prepare for a snowstorm a little differently than when we get ready for a hurricane. At least up north, they don't have to board up the house or move inland," Mike said.

"You're right about that. It's sort of exciting to see all this snow, but at the same time, I really miss you and can't wait to get home. I'm starting to forget what that warm sunshine feels like, and I sure miss smelling the ocean breeze."

"I'll take our warm winters over those frigid ones any day." Mike grabbed a napkin and swiped at the sweat on his forehead. Even though he'd eaten half the sandwich, he still didn't feel right. His skin felt clammy. Now, along with everything else, the area around his mouth tingled a bit. *What in the world is going on with me?* Mike wondered. What he really wanted to do was head to the living room and lie down on the couch.

"Mike, are you listening to me?"

"Uh, what was that?"

"I was wondering if you've heard anything about your boat yet."

"Nope, nothing recently, but the last time I checked I was told it would be a few more weeks." He took a seat at the table.

"I'll let you go so you can finish your sandwich. I'll call again in a few days."

Mike said good-bye to Phyllis and grabbed the other half of his sandwich. *Maybe come Monday morning I will call the doctor,* he decided. *It doesn't make sense the way I've been feeling today, and I really would like to know if there's something seriously wrong.*

———

"How'd your day go, sweetie?" Kyle asked as he and Erika sat at the kitchen table, eating the pepperoni pizza he'd brought home for supper. It wasn't the healthiest meal, but it was quick and easy. Besides, it was Erika's favorite kind of pizza.

"My day was the same as usual," she mumbled around a piece. "How was yours?"

"Exhausting." He reached for his glass of water. "Never had so many emergencies all in one day."

"Accidents or kids who are sick?" she asked.

"Both."

Erika grunted. "Life stinks, and folks just need to get used to it. I'd hate to be a doctor and see people hurting all the time."

I watch you hurting, he thought. *Sometimes that's worse than anything I see at the hospital, Erika. I'd give anything if I could give you back the ability to walk.*

"How'd the quilt class go today?" Kyle asked, feeling the need to change the subject before he gave in to the blame game again.

"Well, it wasn't quite as boring as the week before."

"Oh? What happened?"

"A gecko got into the Millers' house and gave a couple of people a merry chase." Erika reached for her glass of lemonade. "Oh, and one of the women had to drop out of the class to take care of her sister who has a broken leg, so her husband took her place."

"That was nice of him."

Erika wrinkled her nose. "I don't think he really wanted to be there, and he especially wasn't having fun when he almost passed out."

Kyle's eyebrows lifted. "What brought that about?"

Erika shrugged. "I'm not sure, but he seemed to feel better after he ate some of Emma's coffee cake. I told him I thought he should see a doctor, 'cause he could have low blood sugar."

"That's possible, but of course, it could have been something else causing his symptoms. I'm glad you suggested he see a doctor, though. That was good thinking on your part."

"I'm not stupid, Dad."

His face heated. "Never said you were. Why do you always have to get so defensive, Erika?"

"I'm not. And why do you always treat me like a baby?"

Because you act like one sometimes. Of course, Kyle didn't voice his thoughts. Erika would have really gotten defensive.

"Let's not argue," Kyle said, reaching for another slice of pizza. "I don't have the energy to spar with you tonight."

Her lips compressed, but she made no comment. Kyle was beginning to think he would never get through to his daughter. He could only hope and pray that someone else could.

———

As B.J. sat on the porch of the bungalow he'd rented, watching the waves lap against the shore, he reflected on the debilitating fatigue he often felt, and wondered if his cancer had worsened. He remembered his doctor back home telling him that if he wasn't going to continue his treatments, then he needed to get his affairs in order and try to enjoy whatever time he had left.

And that's just what I'm doing, B.J. thought. Since he'd come to Sarasota, he'd developed a more positive outlook than when he'd been diagnosed with cancer. Maybe it was because the warm sunshine felt so good. Or it could be a renewed interest in his artwork since he'd begun taking the quilting classes. Either way, B.J. was living life the way he wanted, and by learning how to quilt, he hoped to hand down something special to his granddaughter when he left this old earth.

B.J.'s thoughts turned to his friend Sam Murphy, whom he'd met at the oncologist's office during one of his appointments. He'd talked to Sam on the phone last night and learned that Sam's cancer was getting worse. Sam sounded as though he'd given up when he told B.J. that his doctor had said he probably had about three or four months to live.

"Why do well-meaning doctors think they have to tell their patients how long it will be till they kick off?" B.J. muttered after taking a sip of his iced tea. He just wanted to live each day to the fullest, and not think about what lay ahead. After all, everyone had to die sometime—some sooner than others.

B.J. pulled out his hanky and blotted a splotch of tea that had dribbled out of his glass and landed on the front of his shirt. *If God wanted us to know the exact day of our death, He would have had it written on our birth certificate or something.*

A seagull screeched overhead—*reep, reep, reep*—and B.J. lifted his gaze upward, watching as the noisy bird flittered around, chasing another gull. When the gulls flew out above the water, B.J.'s thoughts turned to his friend again.

Sam had mentioned how supportive his family had been since hearing of his diagnosis. He said he didn't think he could make it without their encouragement. Sam's daughter had even told him that being there to help him was the least she could do for all the sacrifices he'd made during her childhood. She counted it a privilege to be there for him.

It might be a privilege for Sam's daughter, B.J, thought, *but maybe she's not as busy as my daughters are. They both have their own lives to live, and there is no way I'm going to get in the way of that. I don't want anyone feeling obligated to take care of me.*

He reached for his glass and took one final drink. *Maybe I'll get lucky and die in my sleep; then I won't have to worry about this any longer. That would solve the nasty little problem for everyone.*

CHAPTER 15

Noreen yawned and pulled the pillow over her head, hoping to drown out the sound of the neighbor's yappy dog. But the terrier kept barking, and the pillow did little to diffuse the irritating sound. Ever since her neighbor had purchased the puppy last week, Noreen had begun to lose sleep. That dog's yipping had probably scared every bird away, too.

Despite Noreen's irritation, she felt sorry for the mutt. It was a cute little pup, not much bigger than a rabbit. Didn't those neighbors know they shouldn't leave an animal that young alone in the yard? What if it found a way under the fence and ventured off their property? If the dog got out, it could get hit by a car or someone might steal it. Worse yet, what if an alligator got it? Noreen shivered, remembering the Millers' incident with the gator.

I may have to approach those people if their dog continues to bark and whine all the time, Noreen told herself. She didn't know the middle-aged couple on that side of her house very well, but she hoped they were reasonable people and would see the importance of keeping their puppy safe, even if they weren't concerned about the dog's barking.

With an exasperated sigh, she threw the covers aside and crawled out of bed. Stopping in front of her dresser to look at herself in the mirror, she frowned. Today was Tuesday, and it had been three days since she'd colored her hair. In spite of several washings, it was still just as dark as it had been on Saturday.

Self-conscious about the way she looked Noreen had skipped church Sunday morning and remained in her house all day yesterday, too. She certainly couldn't keep hiding from the world, however. Noreen liked to keep busy and enjoyed her freedom to go someplace whenever she felt like it.

Unless I plan to stay here indefinitely, guess I'd better find an appropriate hat or scarf to cover my head.

Noreen thought about Emma Miller and the stiff white head covering she wore. *If I had a hat like that to wear, I would sprinkle a little cornstarch in the front of my hair, to resemble the gray that used to be there, and no one would be any the wiser.*

She chuckled, her dour mood briefly dispelled as she pictured what she would look like wearing an Amish woman's hat. *I'd have to find an Amish dress to wear, too, or I'd really look ridiculous.*

Dismissing that thought, Noreen opened one of her dresser drawers and rifled through some colorful scarves. She tried on a few, but none covered her hair adequately. Next, she opened her closet door and took down all the hats on the shelf. After trying each of them on, she determined that nothing looked good enough to wear. Her only option was to go shopping for a new hat or scarf. If she found something that covered her hair sufficiently, she would wear it to the quilting class this Saturday. Since the school reunion was still a few weeks away, her hair would hopefully look better by then. If not, she may forget about going. Noreen stuck her tongue out at her reflection in the mirror. *Too bad it's not a Halloween party instead of a quilting class, because I'd certainly fit in.*

———

Knowing she had to be at work at noon, Kim had decided to get up early and take Maddie for a romp on the beach. The dog had spent the last hour running up and down, kicking up the sand and chasing seagulls, while Kim looked for shells. On one of her days off, she hoped to drive down to Venice to look for sharks' teeth. She'd heard they were there in abundance and thought it would be fun.

Too bad I don't have anyone to go with me, she thought. *It would be more fun that way. Guess I'll put the idea on hold for now.*

Kim kicked off her sandals and squatted beside a clump of broken shells. The shimmery white sand felt cool as her toes wiggled below the surface. While looking up every once in a while to watch Maddie play, Kim sifted through the sand, hoping to find some good shells that weren't broken. She was happy to have found a few, and then, digging deeper, her fingers touched something smooth and round.

"What's this?" she murmured, pulling the item up through the sand.

Turning it over in her hand, she soon realized it was a man's ring. Continuing to look it over, she saw the initials *B. W.* engraved on the inside of the gold band. A black onyx stone was mounted in the middle of the setting, and it had some sort of an emblem on one of the sides, with what looked like the inscription of a year on the other.

I'll bet this is someone's high school class ring, Kim thought as she examined it closer. The ring was a bit worn, so it was hard to tell what the lettering was around the insignia. Kim couldn't make out the year, either, but she was fairly sure it was a school ring.

I wonder how long this has been buried in the sand.

Hearing a shrill whistle, Kim looked up and saw a tall, bearded man with shaggy brown hair, wearing jeans and a biker's vest, and with a leather band around his head. He appeared to be heading her way. *Oh great. I wonder what he wants,* she thought, standing as she slipped the ring into the pocket of her shorts.

"Do you know who that dog over there belongs to?" he asked, pointing at Maddie, who'd just darted into the surf.

"She's mine. Why do you ask?"

"Well, she's got something in her mouth, and I don't think she oughta be running free on the beach. Don't you have a leash for her?"

Irritation welled in Kim's chest. Just who did this guy think he was talking to her like that? He didn't even know her and had no right to say anything about her dog.

"Maddie is fine; she's just having fun. Probably found a piece of driftwood to play with," she countered.

The biker took off his sunglasses and placed them on top of his head. "I think it's a bird—probably a gull."

Kim gasped. "Is—is it dead?"

He shrugged his broad shoulders. "Beats me. But if I were you, I'd go find out."

Kim hesitated a minute, then tromped to the edge of the water. "Maddie, come here, right now! And let that bird go!"

To Kim's relief, Maddie plodded out of the water and did as she was told, dropping the gull at her feet. The bird, although shaken, appeared to be unharmed and eventually flew off toward the sea.

"So your dog's name is Maddie, huh?"

Kim glanced over her shoulder and saw the burly man moving closer to her. *Oh great. Now what? I wish he'd go away.*

"Did you hear what I said? I asked if the dog's name is—"

"I heard, and yes, her name is Maddie."

When the guy squatted down and reached out to stroke Maddie's head, Kim noticed he had the word *Bunny* tattooed on his arm. She was tempted to ask him about it but didn't want to prolong this conversation.

"I've got a German shepherd, too," he said. "Fact is, my dog, Brutus, could probably pass for your dog's twin brother."

"Where is your dog?" Kim asked, clipping Maddie's leash to her collar.

"He's in Shipshe. My friend Terry's takin' care of Brutus while I'm gone, which suits me fine 'cause they really get along."

Kim tipped her head as she pushed a pile of sand back and forth with her big toe. "Shipshe?"

"Yeah, Shipshewana, Indiana. That's where I live. Took some time off work to come down here so I could visit some friends and spend a little time on the beach." He thrust out his hand. "The name's Jan. Jan Sweet."

Kim fought the urge to laugh out loud but kept her frown in place. She'd never heard Jan for a guy's name before. It sure didn't fit this big brawny fellow. He'd probably had a hard time living with a name like that and most likely been teased about it.

———

Jan could tell by her pinched expression that the cute little blond was miffed at him. Maybe she wasn't used to some stranger barging in and asking about her dog. Maybe she thought he was coming on to her and using the dog as an excuse to make conversation. *Or she could be thinking I'm just a nosey fellow who oughta mind his own business. Guess these days one can't be too careful, though.*

When the pretty lady didn't accept Jan's friendly gesture or offer her name, he lowered his hand and began petting the dog again. "How old is she, and how long have you had her?" he asked.

"She's six years old. I got her at the pound a month ago. Now if you'll excuse me, I need to get going 'cause I'm scheduled to work at noon, and I don't wanna be late." Clutching the dog's leash, she marched off in the opposite direction, leaving Jan by himself.

He watched her walk away and grinned when she glanced back at him briefly before heading off the beach. Seeing the German shepherd made Jan feel a bit homesick. He'd only been gone two days and had arrived in Sarasota early this morning. Already, he missed Brutus. Even more so, he missed Star and wished she could have come along with him. Traveling on the open road, just him and his Harley, was usually pure pleasure. Not this time, though. During the two days he'd spent traveling, all he'd thought about was his daughter and how he missed riding with her. At one point, Jan had been tempted to turn around and head back home but decided against it because he really wanted to see Emma and Lamar and find out how they were doing. Besides, for the last several months, he'd put in long hours with roofing jobs and really needed a break not only from the work, but from the cold weather they'd had recently in northeastern Indiana.

Putting his sunglasses back on, Jan stared out at the sparkling blue water, enjoying the warmth of the sun on his face and arms. It was a far cry from the frigid temperatures back home. The sounds were different here, too.

Closing his eyes, Jan listened as the waves splashed against the shore, while seagulls cried in unison as they flew overhead. Some of their calls sounded like high-pitched laughing. In the distance, Jan could have sworn he heard a ship's horn.

He opened his eyes, and looking across the water, he saw no sign of any ships. Maybe he'd just imagined it.

Jan breathed deeply, enjoying the smell of the salty air and hearing some kids' laughter as they played along the shore. It seemed like everyone he saw here wore smiles. It made Jan feel carefree, like he was a kid again. He'd have to put on his shorts or swimsuit and come back soon so he could swim or just lie around on the beach. Right now, though, he was anxious to head over to the Millers' and see how they were doing.

CHAPTER 16

Emma had just started making ham and cheese sandwiches for lunch, when a knock sounded on the front door. Since Lamar was in the backyard picking some lemons, she set the bread aside and went to answer the door.

Fully expecting to see one of her neighbors, Emma was shocked when she discovered Jan Sweet on their porch.

"Surprise!" Jan said with a twinkle in his blue eyes. "Bet you never expected to see me here in Pinecraft, did you?"

Emma reached out and gave Jan a hug. "No, I surely didn't. When did you get here, and how long can you stay?" She motioned to Jan's motorcycle, parked in the driveway. "Now don't tell me you rode that all the way from Shipshewana."

He chuckled. "One question at a time please, Emma."

Holding the door open for him, she smiled, feeling her cheeks warm. "Come inside, and I'll start over with the questions. Have you had lunch yet? I was just getting ready to fix ham and cheese sandwiches for Lamar and me, and we'd love to have you join us," she said, leading the way to the kitchen. "Lamar's out back right now, picking lemons, but oh my, is he ever going to be surprised to see you, Jan. In fact, I can't get over it myself."

"I don't want you to go to any trouble on my account," Jan said, leaning against the counter near the sink, "but a sandwich does sound pretty good about now."

"It's no bother at all; there's plenty of ham and cheese." She motioned to the table. "Take a seat, and we can visit while I finish making the sandwiches."

Jan did as Emma suggested, and a few seconds later, Lamar came in through the back door. He took a few steps, halted, and his face broke into a wide smile. "Well, look who's here! This is sure a surprise. What brings you to Sarasota, Jan?"

Jan stood and shook Lamar's hand. "Came to see you and Emma, of course. Thought it'd be nice to get a little sunshine, too," he added with a grin.

"Sure can't blame you for that," Lamar said, handing two fat lemons to Emma. "Can you stay and join us for lunch, Jan? We've got some catching up to do."

"I already invited him," Emma said.

"She didn't have to twist my arm too hard, either." Jan seated himself at the table again.

"How long are you here for?" Lamar questioned.

"A couple of weeks. Star will be joining me then, and we'll stay for a week or so after that. She would have ridden down with me on her bike, but she had to fill in for someone at work and couldn't get the time off."

"Oh, my, I hope she's not planning to ride down here on her

motorcycle all by herself," Emma said, feeling concern. She knew that some English folks thought it was dangerous for the Amish to use horses and buggies for their main mode of transportation, but she thought it would be a lot more dangerous to ride a motorcycle.

Jan shook his head. "Star will be catching a plane when she comes down to Florida, so you don't have to worry about that."

Emma blew out her breath, while slathering some mayonnaise on the bread. "That's a relief. It's just not safe for a young woman to be traveling alone these days—especially on the open road."

"Do you have a place to stay while you're in Sarasota?" Lamar asked, looking at Jan.

"Not yet, but I thought I'd look for a cheap hotel. Since I'm gonna be here awhile, I don't want anything too expensive."

"Why don't you stay here with us?" Emma and Lamar said in unison.

Emma chortled. "It seems that my husband and I are thinking alike. You know, Jan, we have an extra bedroom, and we'd love to have you as our guest."

"I appreciate the offer, but that's too much to ask."

"No, it's not," Emma said, vigorously shaking her head. "We'd enjoy having you stay with us, and we'd be disappointed if you didn't."

"Emma's right." Lamar agreed. "It'll give us a chance to get caught up with each other's lives and find out how things are going back home."

Emma put the finishing touch on the sandwiches. "It's all settled then. As soon as we're done eating, you can bring your things into the house."

"Now, how can I refuse an offer like that?" Jan gave them a wide smile. "Once Star gets here, I'll find us a hotel."

"That won't be necessary," Emma was quick to say. "Our living-room couch pulls out into a bed, so one of you can sleep right there."

"We're gonna bow for silent prayer now," Lamar said when Emma set the platter of sandwiches on the table and took a seat. "But if you'd rather pray out loud, Jan, that's fine with us, too."

Jan shook his head. "Naw, that's okay. I'm a believer, and I go to church whenever I can, but I ain't really comfortable prayin' out loud. So I'll just bow my head and say a silent prayer with you and Emma."

"That'll be just fine," Lamar said, casting Emma a smile.

All heads bowed, and when they'd finished praying, Emma jumped up and said, "Oh dear, I forgot the iced tea." She hurried across the room and returned a few minutes later with a tray that held a pitcher of iced tea, three glasses, and several lemon slices. She also placed a bag of potato chips on the table.

"I don't really need those." Lamar thumped his stomach. "Just a sandwich and the tea will be enough for me."

Emma sat down and scooted the bag of chips close to Jan's plate. "I'll bet you'd like some, though, right?"

With an eager expression, he grabbed a handful of chips. "It sure is great to see you folks again. How have you been anyways? Are you happy being here for the winter?"

"We sure are," Lamar said. "I love spending time on the beach, and the warm weather has been good for my aches and pains."

"That's great news." Jan grabbed a sandwich and took a bite. "So what do you enjoy about Sarasota, Emma? Do you also like to spend time on the beach?"

"It is nice," she admitted, "but I think Lamar enjoys it more than I do."

"Don't forget to tell Jan about the excitement we had here not long ago," Lamar said, stirring a slice of lemon around in his tea.

"Oh Jan, wait till you hear this." Emma leaned forward, eager to share with Jan. "You won't believe it, but we had an alligator in our backyard. Lamar should probably be the one to tell you about it, though, since he was out back when the gator was discovered."

Jan's eyes widened. "Wow, really? What happened?"

Emma watched Jan's expression as Lamar described the incident, including that he'd been thinking it was a robbery in progress. Hearing about that morning all over again made her feel as though it had happened to someone else instead of right in their own yard. Emma smiled as Lamar ended his story by telling how Jake and Rusty captured and relocated animals for a living.

"I'll give it to those two men," Lamar said, shaking his head, "because they sure knew what they were doing and handled the situation with ease. I could never have done that."

"Wow!" Jan exclaimed. "You were lucky those guys showed up when they did, and doubly fortunate it wasn't a robbery."

"I couldn't agree with you more," Emma said. "Everything turned out fine for all of us. Even for the alligator, since it was removed safely and relocated."

"You'll have to show me where the alligator was," Jan said. "I'd like to go out and look at your fruit trees, too. Never saw a lemon tree before."

"Neither had we till we came to Florida, and we have an orange tree, too." Emma took a handful of chips and placed them on her plate. "Oh, and that's not all the excitement, either. The other day one of our neighbors told us that the robbers had been caught, so that was a big relief."

"I'm glad you're both safe," Jan said, gulping down the rest of his tea.

"So are we," Emma agreed.

"We'll take a walk outside after lunch," Lamar said. "So, what's new in Shipshe, Jan?"

"Not a whole lot, really. Terry and Cheryl are still going out, and. . . Well, I probably shouldn't say anything since nothing's official, but Terry's planning to ask Cheryl to marry him."

Emma clapped her hands. "Oh, that is good news! I hope they don't get married this winter, though. We'd love to be there for the wedding."

"Since he hasn't even asked her yet, it's not likely they'd tie the knot before spring, or it could even be summer or fall." Jan grabbed a few more chips.

"What about some of our other quilting students?" Emma questioned as she poured Jan more tea. "Do you have news on any of them?"

"Yep. Paul and Carmen got married a few weeks ago."

"We knew about that, because we got an invitation to their wedding," Emma said. "I just hope they understood why we couldn't be there."

"I'm sure they did." Jan swiped his napkin over his mouth where some mayonnaise had stuck to his lip. "Oh, and another bit of news. Blaine got engaged to Sue, and he'll soon be opening his own fishing tackle store."

Emma looked over at Lamar and smiled. "It's good hearing such happy news about people who have come to our classes, isn't it?"

"Jah, it sure is," Lamar agreed. He pointed to the potato chips. "If you don't mind passing me the bag, Jan, think I'll have a few, after all."

"Have you heard anything from Stuart and Pam Johnston?" Emma asked.

Jan shook his head. "But I did see Ruby Lee a week ago, Sunday, when Star and I went to church."

"How's she doing?" Emma asked.

"Great. Things are going well at her husband's church, and they've been getting even more new people."

"I'm glad to hear that." Emma got up from the table and returned with a plate of raisin molasses cookies. "Are you ready for dessert?" she asked, placing the cookies in front of Jan.

"Sure thing!" he took three and plopped them on his plate.

"Did Emma tell you that we're teaching another quilting class?" Lamar asked.

Jan's mouth formed an O. "Really? Here in this house?"

"That's right," Emma said. "This place is much smaller than our home in Indiana, but we've been hosting our classes in the dining room, and it's working out just fine. We'll be having our third class this Saturday."

"Well, I'll be sure to make myself scarce," Jan said after he'd eaten the cookies. "Sure don't wanna be in the way while you're teachin'."

"Don't worry about that," Emma said. "You're welcome to join us if you want. You could share your own quilting experience with our new class."

Jan shook his head. "Think I'll pass on that, but I will have another cookie. These are sure good."

Emma smiled. "Thanks. They're one of Lamar's favorites."

Jan thumped his stomach. "I can already see that I'll have to go on a diet after this trip. You're too good of a cook, Emma."

She felt the heat of a blush on her cheeks. "You're just being nice."

"No, it's the truth."

Emma looked forward to having Jan stay with them over the next couple of weeks. It would be like old times, even if he didn't sit in on any of their quilting classes.

Randy had spent the morning job hunting again, this time in Bradenton, with no prospects at all. The longer he went without a job, the more discouraged he felt. *Maybe I should call my brother and see if he can help us out,* he thought as he thrust his hands into his pants pocket and ambled down the sidewalk. *But if I did that, it'd be like admitting defeat. I'll find something soon; I just have to.*

As Randy turned the corner, heading back to his pickup, he spotted a baby crib in one of the store windows. Pink and blue balloons waved in the breeze, as if welcoming customers inside. A big banner hung above the store's entrance, advertising a sale, including some merchandise at 50 percent off.

Think I'll go in and take a look around, he decided. *Maybe I'll find something nice that's been marked down.*

Entering the store, Randy meandered around, checking out all the baby things—several styles of cribs, playpens, car seats, strollers, and even some musical mobiles. Their baby girl would need all of those things.

He walked over to study the cribs. He'd never realized there were so many types. There were convertible cribs in all different wood grain selections. Some even had changing tables attached. There were also portable cribs, mini-cribs, and the usual standard crib.

Randy stood there smiling. He really liked the convertible crib, crafted in a deep cherry, like it was made for a princess. But that one was way overpriced. Another crib caught his eye, with a big "half price" sign attached. It was all white, and he realized it would work just as well as the more expensive one. He could just picture his beautiful baby girl lying in that crib, sleeping soundly and sucking her thumb.

While contemplating the different cribs, Randy came to the conclusion that a convertible crib would be more cost effective. When needed, the crib could be switched into a toddler bed. That way they wouldn't have to buy another piece of furniture when the baby was old enough to go from a crib to a bed. It was like buying two beds in one and would save them money in the long run.

Once he'd decided on the white crib, he spotted a matching dresser that could also be used as a changing table. A pink teddy bear sat in the crib, just beckoning him to buy it. After Randy put the bear in his cart, he wrote the item numbers down for the crib and dresser so he could tell the sales clerk after he'd finished shopping.

As he made his way around the store, Randy saw many other neat things. He picked out two sets of sheets for the crib—one with teddy bears and the other a plain pink. He spotted a mobile with different animals dangling from the center, and that also went into his shopping cart. Then he found a car seat, stroller, and a wind-up swing to put the baby in.

What kid wouldn't love that? Randy thought before he noticed a clerk and told her the item numbers of the furniture he wanted to purchase. He was going to love being a daddy, and no matter how hard he had to work, he'd make sure his daughter wanted for nothing. Of course, that would all depend on him finding a job.

Randy's hand slipped into his pocket, and after pulling out his wallet, he removed a credit card and approached the checkout line. *I may not have a job or any extra cash right now, but I can charge all the things our daughter will need. Maybe by the time the bill comes, I'll have found a job.*

CHAPTER 17

For the past hour, Jennifer had been sitting at the kitchen table, going over their bills and trying to balance their checkbook. Even with the small amount they had left in their savings plus Randy's unemployment check, their money wouldn't last long. It was a good thing they hadn't charged anything lately, because their credit card was close to being maxed out. *If Randy could just find a job,* she thought. *This is not a good time for us to be bringing a baby into the world. If I'd only known eight-and-a-half months ago that we'd be going through financial struggles like this. . .*

"Come see what I bought today, honey!" Randy shouted from the living room.

Jennifer jumped. She'd been so busy fretting about their finances that she hadn't even heard him come in. If he'd bought something, maybe that meant he'd found a job.

When Jennifer stepped into the living room, she halted, barely able to believe her eyes. There was baby stuff everywhere!

"What did you do, win the lottery?" she asked, with her mouth gaping open.

He grinned widely. "'Course not, sweetie. I'm not that lucky. I never win anything."

"Then how. . ."

"I used my credit card to buy these things for the baby."

"What?" Jennifer shouted as her hands started to shake. "How could you do something so foolish? Don't you care that we're already in debt up to our necks?"

Randy dropped his gaze to the floor. "I want our child to have new things, and I just thought. . . ."

"Well, you thought wrong. I've spent the last hour trying to juggle our bills and pay the ones that are overdue, and we certainly can't afford to add anything more to our credit card. As nice as all this looks, you'll have to take everything back."

"But Jennifer, the baby will be here in a few weeks, and we need to be ready. Don't you want to see what all I bought?"

"No, I don't, and we can't afford any of it. As I said the other day, we can look for some used furniture and other baby things and only get what we absolutely need." Jennifer's tone softened when she saw the look of disappointment on her husband's face. "Even if you found a job tomorrow, we wouldn't have enough money for all this. We have too many bills that need to be paid." She moved closer to Randy and touched his arm. "I'm sorry, but these things really do need to go back."

Randy shuffled his feet a few times, and he finally nodded. "You're right. I made a hasty decision and got carried away. I'll load the stuff into my truck and head back to the store right now."

Mike stared blankly at the magazine he'd picked up, feeling more nervous as each minute ticked by. He'd called his doctor's office yesterday, and since someone had cancelled their appointment, he'd been able to get in this afternoon. Now, as he sat in the waiting room, he'd begun to worry. What if something was seriously wrong? What if he couldn't run his charter boat business any longer due to ill health? How would he provide for Phyllis? But he had to know what was causing him to feel so lousy, and if it was bad news, he'd figure out how to deal with it, just like he always had when he'd been dealt a bad hand. Life was full of ups and downs, disappointments, and unexpected disruptions to one's plans, but that didn't mean a person should give up.

As Mike had learned at an early age from his dad's example, it was how a man handled situations that proved his worth. A guy could whine about the injustices of life, or he could buck up and make the best of the situation.

That's what I'll have to do if the doctor tells me there's something seriously wrong, Mike told himself. *I will not wimp out on my wife, and I won't give in to self-pity because that won't solve a thing.* Still, Mike hoped he didn't have diabetes. How could he possibly give himself a shot if he had to be on insulin? He hated needles, and he liked sweet foods. The last thing he wanted was to be mindful of everything he ate.

"Mr. Barstow, we are ready to see you now."

Mike rose from his seat and followed the nurse into one of the examining rooms. She got his weight, took his vitals, and asked several questions about the symptoms he'd been having. Then she left Mike alone in the room to wait for the doctor.

Several minutes went by, and Mike grew more fidgety. He'd always hated waiting for things. He figured the doctor was busy, but if that was the case, why did the nurse call him in when she did? *If I was missing work on the count of sitting here, I'd be really upset,* he fumed.

Finally, Dr. Ackerman stepped into the room. "It's nice to see you, Mr. Barstow. I hear you're having some problems."

"Yeah." Mike quickly explained about the shakiness, sweating, and dizziness he'd experienced, and ended by saying that with each episode, he'd felt better after eating.

"The first thing I'm going to do is order some blood tests, and I'll also do a physical today." The doctor filled out a lab form and handed it to Mike. "Get this done in the morning, and go in fasting. Don't eat or drink anything but water after midnight tonight. I want to check your blood sugar level, among other things. Oh, and please stop at the front desk on your way out and make an appointment to see me the middle of next week. Your lab work should be back by then." He motioned to the examining table. "Have a seat up there, and I'll check you out."

Mike did as he asked. No matter how things turned out, he was not saying anything to Phyllis about this until he had to. There was no point in worrying her about something she could do nothing about.

<hr />

Sure wish I didn't have to return all this stuff, Randy fumed as he entered the store. *But I know Jennifer's right; we really can't afford to get any further in debt. She's probably still mad at me for doing something so stupid.*

"I need to return everything I bought earlier today," Randy told the salesclerk who had waited on him earlier.

"You're kidding, right?" She squinted, looking at Randy as if he'd said something horrible. "What's the problem, sir?"

Randy couldn't seem to swallow his pride and admit that he couldn't afford these things. There was no way he'd own up to that. "Uh. . .well, a funny thing happened," he stammered, trying to come up with a good excuse. "See, when I got back home, my wife was all excited and said she'd just gotten a phone call from her parents." Since the clerk didn't know

Randy or Jennifer, or any of their families for that matter, he continued to add to the story. "My in-laws are coming to see us soon, and they said they'd be bringing all sorts of things for the baby, including furniture." Randy coughed, and then feeling his face heat up, he added, "So, until I see what they're bringing us, there's no point in me keeping any of these items. Sorry about that."

"Come with me then," the clerk said in a tone of irritation. "I'll start the refund process." Suddenly, the clerk stopped and swung around, causing Randy to almost bump into her. "I hope you remembered to bring your receipt, because we can't do a refund without it."

"I did; it's right here." Randy held up the yellow slip. "Oh, and I'm gonna need some help bringing in the bigger items that are out in my truck."

"I'll call someone to help you with that." The clerk's furrowed brows let Randy know she was anything but pleased about this.

For cryin' out loud, Randy fumed. *I'm sure I'm not the first customer who's ever brought anything back.*

As Randy headed out the door, he caught sight of a sign telling about a contest to win some free baby things, including furniture. He was surprised he hadn't seen it before. Could he have walked right past it? Or maybe the contest hadn't been posted until after he'd left the store earlier today.

Guess it wouldn't hurt for me to fill out the form and enter the contest, he decided. *Although I don't know why; I've never won anything before.*

Randy stopped, filled out the form, and dropped it into the box. *Maybe I should have chewed some gum and stuck it on my entry form,* he thought. *That way, whoever draws the winning name would be more apt to pull mine out 'cause it'd probably stick to his finger.*

Randy shook his head. *Now that was a crazy thought, and it'd be cheating, besides. What's come over me, anyway? First I made up a lie to the salesclerk about why I returned all the baby stuff, and now I'm thinking of how to cheat my way into winning a drawing. I need to get a grip.*

CHAPTER 18

"How about I take you two out for supper tonight?" Jan suggested as he, Lamar, and Emma sat on the front porch, enjoying the sunshine late Thursday afternoon.

"Oh, you don't have to do that," said Emma. "I'm more than happy to fix supper for us here."

"You've already provided several meals since I got here, not to mention letting me stay in your spare room," Jan reminded them.

"We're happy to do it." Lamar turned to Emma. "Aren't we?"

She bobbed her head. "Most definitely."

"Even so, I'd like to treat you folks to a meal out once in a while, and unless you've already got something started for supper, we can start by going out tonight."

Emma reached over and patted Jan's hand. "Alright then, if you insist. So, where would you like to go?"

"That's up to you," Jan replied. "I haven't been here long enough to know of any good places to eat. Do you guys have a favorite restaurant?" He patted his stomach and chuckled. "As you might guess, I enjoy most any kind of food."

"We could go to the restaurant up the street, where Kim and Anna work," Lamar suggested.

"Who are Kim and Anna?" Jan wanted to know.

"Anna is Amish, and she's from one of our earlier quilting classes— the one your friend Terry was in."

"Oh yeah. If I remember right, Anna moved down here with a friend."

"That's correct. She's working as a waitress at a restaurant nearby. Kim is one of my current quilting students." Emma smiled. "Oh, and she's single and drives a motorcycle. She's also quite pretty, so you might be interested in meeting her."

Jan shook his head. "Naw, I don't think so, Emma. I'm gettin' along just fine without a woman to complicate my life."

"*Wie geht's*, Lamar and Emma?" an elderly Amish man asked, interrupting their conversation as he approached, leading a small dog on a leash.

Lamar waved. "Hello, Abe. We're doing fine. How are you?"

"Doin' as well as any eighty-year-old can." Abe grinned. "I've been meaning to stop by. Thought maybe we could head over to Pinecraft Park for a game of shuffleboard some time."

"Sounds good to me," Lamar responded with a nod.

"Heard you had a gator in your yard."

"Jah. It was quite an experience. When we get together for shuffleboard, I'll tell you all about it." Lamar motioned to Jan. "Abe, this is our good friend, Jan Sweet. He's from our hometown in Shipshewana, and he'll be staying with us for a while."

"Pleased to meet you, Jan." Abe nodded as his little beagle hound yanked on the leash.

Jan gave a saluting wave. "Same here."

"Don't blame you for coming down south to get away from the cold weather. My wife, Linda, and I come from Ohio, and we just couldn't take the cold winters anymore. So five years ago, we sold everything and moved to sunny Florida." Abe grinned and gave his full gray beard a quick tug. "We've never regretted it, neither."

"I'll bet, too," Lamar said with a nod. "Emma and I probably won't sell our home in Shipshe, but it's nice to know we have a place here where we can spend our winters."

"If I get to likin' this weather too much, I might be tempted to stay in Florida," Jan commented. "I could ride my bike all winter and never have to worry about dealin' with snow. 'Course, I ain't likely to move, since my business and my daughter are in Indiana."

"I see you have a new walking partner, Abe," Emma commented.

He gave a nod. "Jah, that's right."

"That's a cute little dog. What's its name?" Emma questioned.

"This is Button. We just got her yesterday." Abe squatted down and pet the dog's head. "Never thought we'd get another dog, but we used to have a beagle when we lived in Ohio. Shortly before we moved here, old Gus got real sick, and we had to have him put to sleep. It was one of the hardest things Linda and I ever did, and because of it, we vowed never to get another pet. We didn't think we could go through that again, but the longer we've been down here, the more we've missed the fun we had with Gus all those years, so we finally talked ourselves into getting another dog."

"She certainly is cute." Emma giggled, watching Button chew on Abe's shoelaces. "She's so tiny. How old is she, Abe?"

"She's actually ten weeks old, but she's a miniature beagle and won't get as big as most standard beagles." Abe bent down to pick up the pup and stood. Button started licking his face right away. "Linda and I have to get used to a puppy all over again. We kinda forgot, with Gus being so laid back, how rambunctious a little one like this can be."

Everyone laughed as Button tried to grab the brim of Abe's straw hat. "Guess I'd better get going," he said. "As you can see, Button is getting impatient and looking for something to eat. In one day's time the little stinker ruined two pairs of my socks." Abe's chest moved rhythmically as he chuckled. "I suppose it could be a good thing, though. Linda won't have to get after me to pick up my things. Anyway, it's good seeing you, Emma and Lamar, and we'll get together soon." He looked over at Jan and smiled. "Nice meeting you."

"Likewise," Jan responded.

"Tell your wife I said hello," Emma called as Abe, carrying the puppy, headed down the road.

"Looks to me like that pup's got his master eating out of the palm of his hand." Lamar laughed. "I think Button has won my friend Abe's heart."

"He seems like a nice neighbor," Jan commented. "Are all the folks here in Pinecraft as friendly as Abe?"

"Pretty much," Emma said. "This is a good neighborhood, and it's a comfort to know there are dependable people who'll keep an eye on our place here when we're back home in Indiana."

"Too bad you couldn't train an alligator to be a watchdog," Jan teased. "You'd never have to worry about being robbed, that's for sure."

"You've got that right." Emma snickered. "Well, how about we head to the restaurant now? It's close enough that we can walk, and I don't know about you men, but my stomach's starting to growl."

"My appetite is growing, too," Lamar said, getting up and folding his chair.

"I was hoping you'd say that," Jan agreed. "Let's go have us a nice evening, and as you Amish like to say, 'Let's eat ourselves full!'"

Goshen

Star paced the living-room floor, fretting because she hadn't heard from her dad, other than one brief call after he'd arrived in Sarasota. She'd left him a couple of messages, but he hadn't returned any of her calls. Wasn't he checking his voice mail? And what all was he doing down there? Surely he would have caught up on visiting with Emma and Lamar by now.

She slapped the side of her head. *What was I thinking? I should have gotten the Millers' phone number from Dad before he left home. Think I'm gonna try calling his cell number again, 'cause I'm getting tired of waiting around and worrying that something might have happened to him.*

Star grabbed her cell phone and punched in her dad's number, frowning when she got his voice mail again.

"Dad, this is Star. I've been trying to call you, and I don't know why you haven't responded. Please call me back as soon as you can."

Star clicked off and sank into a chair. *This wouldn't be happening if I'd gone to Florida with Dad. Sure hope everything's okay. If I don't hear something from him soon, I'm gonna ditch my job and hop on the next plane to Sarasota.*

Sarasota

"How are things going with you?" Anna Lambright asked as she passed Kim on the way to the kitchen to pick up an order.

"Well, I've only dropped one plate and spilled a glass of milk so far, but other than that, things are going great," Kim replied with a grin. "I'm surprised no one's complained to the boss about me being such a klutz."

Anna touched Kim's arm. "I'm sure the customers know you don't do it on purpose. Besides, you're so polite and friendly to everyone, and that goes a long ways."

"I hope you're right, because I can't afford to lose this job."

"Me neither." Anna inhaled deeply. "The last thing I want is to feel forced to go home and listen to my folks say, 'I told you so.'"

"Are they still giving you a hard time about being down here?"

"They've let up for now, but I think it's because Emma called and had a talk with my mom," Anna said. "It's sad to say, but Mom and Dad will listen to Emma before they will me. They've never given me much credit for doing the right thing or being able to take care of myself."

"I think a lot of parents are like that when it comes to their young people getting out on their own."

"Don't they want us to have our own lives? I mean, shouldn't I have the right to make decisions and choose where I want to live?"

Kim nodded. "I think everyone deserves that privilege."

They reached the kitchen, and their conversation ended as they both picked up their orders.

Kim had just served a middle-aged couple their meal, when she turned to her right and saw Emma and Lamar Miller seated at a booth.

She blinked rapidly, unable to believe her eyes. Sitting across from them was the biker she'd met on the beach! *What in the world are they doing with him?* Well, she would know soon enough, because that was one of her tables.

———○———

Jan studied the menu they'd been given when they'd first sat down. There were so many choices, but his gaze kept going back to the buffet island to his left. He'd scoped it out on the way in and decided that if he didn't find something he liked better on the menu he'd go for the buffet. In addition to several kinds of meat, it offered mashed potatoes, scalloped potatoes, stuffing, a pasta dish, three vegetable choices, and everything one needed to build a hearty salad. Jan had eyeballed a couple of dessert items on the buffet, too, so he knew there was no chance of him leaving here hungry. Unless he used some restraint, he figured he'd be miserable when he walked out the door.

"Emma. Lamar. It's good to see you."

Jan jerked his head at the sound of a woman's voice. He looked away from the menu, and when he recognized the cute little blond he'd met on the beach, his mouth dropped open.

"We were hoping you might be working tonight," Emma said, smiling at their waitress. She turned to Jan and said, "This is Kim Morris, one of our quilting students. Kim, I'd like you to meet our good friend, Jan Sweet."

Kim stood several seconds, staring at Jan like he had two heads. "You—you're that guy I met on the beach."

He nodded. "Sure never expected to see you again. How's your dog?"

Kim's lips compressed. "Maddie is fine. And for your information, I take good care of her."

Jan shrugged. "Never said you didn't. I was just pointing out that—"

"Do you two know each other?" Lamar interrupted.

"Sort of," Jan mumbled. "We met on the beach the first day I got here. I had no idea you and Emma knew her, though."

"How do you know the Millers?" Kim asked, looking at Jan with a curious expression.

"I took Emma's quilting classes before she and Lamar were married."

Kim blinked. "Really? I'm surprised that—"

"That someone like me would want to learn how to quilt?"

Kim's face reddened. "Well, you don't exactly seem like the type."

Jan snickered. "There's a lot about me that I'm sure would surprise you."

"Jan is staying at our place while he's here on vacation," Emma said. "So I'm sure you two will have a chance to get better acquainted."

Jan jiggled his eyebrows, feeling kind of playful all of a sudden. Remembering back to last fall when Terry had taken Emma's quilting class so he could get to know Cheryl and ask her for a date, Jan was beginning to understand his friend's reasoning. But he could see from Kim's disgruntled expression that the last thing she wanted was to get to know him better. Well, like it or not, she'd better get used to the idea, because come Saturday, Jan planned to stick around and be part of the quilting class.

CHAPTER 19

Jan knew the quilt class would be starting soon, so he decided to check his voice mail before the students arrived. "Stupid phone! How did all these messages get on here without me knowing it?" Jan muttered to himself. He was surprised to find that most of them were from Star. Feeling guilty when he heard how upset she was, he gave her a call. When he got her voice mail, he figured she was probably at work, so he left a message. "Hi, Star, it's me. Sorry I missed all your calls. I just discovered that my phone was muted, so I never heard it ring. Haven't checked my messages for a few days, either. I've been staying with Emma and Lamar. They have a spare room and said they were glad to have me here with them. We've been having a great time catching up on things."

Jan was tempted to mention that he'd met Kim, but decided against it. He didn't even know Kim that well, and if he told Star that he planned to hang around during the quilting class in order to get to know Kim, she'd probably tease him. *If my buddy Terry knew, he'd give me a hard time about it, that's for sure.* There'd be no end to Terry's ribbing.

Slipping his cell phone into his jeans pocket, Jan stepped out of the guest room and joined Emma and Lamar in the dining room. "All ready for the quilting class?" he asked, looking at the colorful quilt Lamar had draped over a wooden rack.

"Yes, we sure are," Emma replied. "So what are your plans for the day?"

Jan pulled his fingers through the ends of his beard. "If you don't mind, think I'd like to stick around during the class."

Emma's fingers touched her parted lips. "Really, Jan? I thought you didn't want to sit in on the class."

Yeah, but that was before I knew the pretty blond I met on the beach was one of your quilting students, Jan mused. Of course, he didn't voice his thoughts.

"Well, I thought it over and changed my mind. Decided it might be kind of fun to meet your new quilting students." Jan wasn't about to admit that the only reason he'd decided to hang around for the class was so he could get to know Kim better. He could barely admit that to himself.

———

One by one, the students arrived, and Emma watched with curiosity at Jan's eager expression when Kim showed up. Was it possible that he had more than a passing interest in the young woman?

Now, wouldn't that be something? Emma thought. *Jan's friend Terry has a special woman in his life now, and it would be nice if Jan found someone, too. Well, I'd best not meddle. If it's the Lord's will for Jan and Kim to be together, He will put it all in place.*

After everyone had gathered around the table, Emma introduced Jan and explained that he had been one of her first quilting students.

She didn't mention, however, that the reason he had come to her class was because his probation officer had suggested it as a creative outlet. If Jan wanted to share that information, it was up to him.

"How do you like it here in sunny Florida?" Mike asked, looking at Jan.

"It's great! I'm likin' the warmth, not to mention the company." Jan winked at Emma and grinned at Lamar. Then he cast a quick look in Kim's direction and smiled at her, too. "So far, I've met some real nice people."

"How long are you planning to stay?" Noreen questioned.

"My daughter, Star, is planning to join me when her vacation starts in two weeks, and we'll probably hang around another week or two after that."

"What about your wife? Will she be coming to Sarasota, too?" Kim questioned.

Jan shook his head. "Don't have a wife. Star's mom and me split up over twenty years ago, when Star was less than a year old."

"Oh, I see." Kim turned to Emma. "What are we going to do on our quilting projects today?"

"You'll continue to sew your pieces of fabric together, and then I'll show you how to cut out the batting," Emma replied. "While you're waiting your turn to use a sewing machine, you can either talk with Lamar about some of the other quilt patterns he's designed or visit among yourselves."

"I've come up with several new ideas for patterns recently," Lamar said, rubbing his hands together. "I think my trips to the beach are giving me inspiration to create some new designs."

"I feel that way, too," B.J. interjected. "Only my designs are on canvas."

"So you're an artist?" Jan questioned.

B.J. nodded. "When I was a boy, my dad used to brag about my artistic abilities, and my mother said I was born with a paintbrush in my hand."

Jan chuckled. "My folks always said I was born to ride a motorcycle 'cause I liked my first bike with training wheels so much."

Kim perked right up. "Is that your Harley I saw parked in the driveway?"

"You bet it is."

"Kim has a motorcycle, too," Emma said, even though she'd already mentioned that fact to Jan.

Jan blinked his eyes rapidly, then a slow smile spread across his face. "That's cool! Do you mind if I go out and take a look at it right now?"

Kim hesitated at first, but then she said, "Guess that'd be okay. Since Noreen, B.J., and Erika are using the sewing machines right now, I'll go check out your bike, too." Kim looked at Emma. "Is that okay with you?"

"I have no objections at all," Emma said.

Jan jumped up, and Kim did the same, then they both rushed out the door.

Emma couldn't help feeling pleased. Maybe there was some hope for Jan and Kim to become a couple. They had their bikes in common, at least.

———

"That's sure a nice bike," Jan said, after he'd checked out Kim's black Harley with pink stripes. "I see you even have a helmet to match. That's pretty cool!"

"Your bike is nice, too," she said, motioning to Jan's black-and-silver motorcycle. "It's bigger than mine and looks like it'd be good for long road trips."

"Yeah, and since there's room enough for two, sometimes Star rides with me. She has her own bike, but I decided to add a sissy bar to mine.

That way when she or someone else rides with me, it's more comfortable for their back."

They talked motorcycle stuff for a while, and then Jan gathered up his nerve and asked if Kim would like to get a bite to eat with him after class. "We could either ride our own bikes, or double up on mine. Maybe we could grab a burger and fries at a fast-food place and then head to the beach."

Kim looked up at him, tucking a stray piece of blond hair behind her ear. "I—I don't know about that...."

"Do you have other plans for this afternoon?"

"No, not really, but if I went I'd have to take my own bike. So when we got ready to leave the beach I could just head straight home rather than coming all the way back here to get my bike. I'd have to keep my eye on the time because of Maddie, too. It's bad enough that she's home by herself when I'm at work, and I hate leaving her in the outside pen too long, because she barks, which irritates the neighbors."

Jan grunted. "I can relate to that. But it's better to have the dog penned up than running around the neighborhood causing trouble. I went through that with my dog already and almost lost him because he took off from the yard. So I finally had to pen him up while I was at work, and it's been much better that way."

"That's true for Maddie, too." Kim glanced at her watch. "I can't believe we've been out here almost thirty minutes. I didn't realize we'd been talking that long."

"Sorry," Jan apologized. He resisted the temptation to reach out and twirl Kim's fallen curl around his index finger. Tucking his hands in his jeans pocket, he said, "It's probably my fault, for flappin' my gums. Sure hope I didn't cause you to miss anything important in there."

"I'm sure it's fine," Kim said. "It's most likely my turn to use one of the sewing machines, though."

"Uh, before we go inside, you never really did say if you'll go to the beach and have lunch with me today."

"Sure, why not?" she said with a nod.

As they turned and headed for the house, Jan couldn't keep from smiling all the way. He was anxious for the class to be over so he and Kim could be on their way. He'd never imagined coming to Florida and meeting someone like her. Things like this just didn't happen to him. Of course, he figured nothing would come of it—not with them living several states apart. Besides, Kim would probably turn out to be like all the other women Jan had dated—a passing fancy.

Chapter 20

How are you feeling today?" Lamar asked Mike as he sat at the table, waiting his turn to use one of the sewing machines.

Mike shrugged. "I'm okay, I guess. Better than last week. But then I've been eating regular meals, which I think has helped."

"That's good to hear," Lamar said. "You gave us all a pretty good scare when you got dizzy and shaky last Saturday."

"Yeah, I had another spell at home, so I made an appointment and got in to see my doctor within a few days."

"How did that go?"

"The doc said he wasn't able to give me a diagnosis yet, but he did a thorough exam and sent me to get some blood tests. I should know something when I go in next week."

"It's good that you went," Lamar said. "Emma and I will be anxious to hear the results of your tests, and I certainly hope it's nothing serious. Of course, we'll be praying for you, Mike."

"Thanks." Mike couldn't believe Lamar's concern. Most people who didn't know a person that well probably wouldn't have even thought to ask how he was doing, much less offered to pray for him. Mike was beginning to realize that Emma and Lamar were caring people who lived their religion and showed it to others by what they said and did.

Maybe when Phyllis gets home, the two of us ought to start going to church, he decided. *She's mentioned it a few times, but I've always been too tired or too busy to go. Between now and then, it probably wouldn't hurt if I said a few prayers of my own, 'cause I'm nervous about the outcome of my blood tests.*

———

"Sorry for taking so long," Kim apologized to Emma after she and Jan had returned to the house. "We got a little carried away talking about our bikes."

"That's okay," Emma said. "The machines are free now, and you're just in time to start sewing,"

Kim smiled. "Oh good. I'll get right at it then."

While Kim went to one of the sewing machines, Jan meandered over to the table where B.J. sat with Noreen and Erika. He seemed genuinely interested in what they were doing. Though she resisted the idea, Kim had to admit, there was something about Jan that intrigued her.

I can't believe I agreed to go out with him after class, Kim thought as she took her seat at the sewing machine. *I barely know Jan, and since he's not from around here, there's no chance of us ever getting to really know each other or develop a relationship. Maybe that's for the best,* she decided. *Less chance of any romantic involvement that could lead to another dead end for me. Well, I've already said yes to his invitation, so I may as well go and try to enjoy the afternoon.*

Kim started working on her quilt squares, and at the same time, she thought about the day she'd met Jan on the beach and how irritated she had been when he said she ought to keep an eye on her dog. But after visiting with him outside by their bikes, she'd seen him in a different light and actually found herself yearning to know him better, even though he would be leaving in a few weeks.

I can't worry about this right now, Kim told herself. *I need to concentrate on making my wall hanging.*

———

At eleven o'clock, Emma suggested that everyone take a break for refreshments.

"What'd you fix for us today?" Mike asked. "I hope it's not oranges again."

Emma shook her head. "I made a couple of strawberry pies, and there's also a fruit platter with strawberries, bananas, and grapes."

"Guess to be safe, I'd better stick to the fruit and leave the pies alone," Mike said.

"That's good thinking." Lamar gave Mike's shoulder a squeeze.

"While I'm getting the refreshments, the rest of you can visit or keep working on your squares," Emma said, starting for the kitchen door.

"I'll help you with that." Jennifer left her seat and followed Emma to the kitchen.

"How did your week go?" Emma asked as she took the pies from the refrigerator. "Did your husband find a job yet?"

Jennifer's shoulder drooped as she slowly shook her head. "Randy's getting really discouraged, and he proved that when he did something totally out of character the other day."

"What happened?"

"He charged up a bunch of furniture and other things for the baby that we really can't afford."

"Oh dear." Emma placed the pies on the table. "How will you pay for everything if he doesn't find a job soon?"

"Even if Randy found a job today, we'd have a long ways to go in catching up with our bills. But we don't have to worry about paying for the baby things, because I insisted that he return them." Jennifer sank into a chair and lowered her head. "I felt bad for him. He seemed so proud and happy when he showed me what he'd gotten for the baby. This whole situation with him being out of work is taking a toll on our marriage."

Emma remained silent as she let Jennifer continue.

"I couldn't let even more money problems get in the way of us trying to keep it all together. If I wasn't due to have a baby in a few weeks, I'd go back to the styling salon where I used to work, but even if I could, I wouldn't make enough to support us and the baby."

Emma placed her hands on Jennifer's trembling shoulders. "I know it isn't much, but I have a box of food I want to send home with you today."

"I appreciate it," Jennifer said tearfully, "but I'm not sure how Randy will respond to that. He'll probably see it as a handout, because he's too proud to admit that we need help."

"Would you like me to ask Lamar to speak to your husband?"

Jennifer sniffed. "That might help—if Randy's willing to listen." She paused and wiped her nose on a tissue she'd pulled from her pocket. "You know, Emma, when I got home from your class last week and showed Randy the fruit and cookies you'd sent home with me, he said he'd like to have you and Lamar for supper sometime to say thanks for your kindness."

Emma flapped her hand. "What we did was nothing big, and no thanks is needed."

"But if you came for supper, it would give Lamar a chance to talk to Randy," Jennifer said.

Emma nodded slowly. "You might be right about that. If you'll let us know what night would work best for you, we'll plan to be there."

"Any night this week should be fine. Why don't we make it Friday?"

"Friday would be good for us," Emma responded.

Jennifer tapped her fingers along the edge of the table. "I hate to even ask this, but do you think your friend Jan would feel bad if he wasn't included? It's not that I would mind having him," she quickly added. "I just don't think Randy would open up to Lamar if someone else was there."

"I understand," Emma said. "And I'm sure Jan won't mind fending for himself that evening. Maybe he'll even have a date by then."

"This pie is sure good, Emma," Jan said as everyone sat around the table, enjoying the refreshments Emma had provided.

"Thanks, I'm glad you like it." Emma looked over at Noreen, and her gaze came to rest on the green scarf she'd worn around her head in turban fashion today. Emma had been tempted to ask about it but didn't want to be rude.

Perhaps Noreen couldn't get her hair to look the way she wanted this morning, Emma thought. *Maybe she had what I've heard some Englishers call a bad hair day. Well, it's Noreen's right to wear whatever she wants. After all, I wear my head covering, and no one here has questioned me about it.*

"Tell us more about your artwork, B.J.," Lamar said. "Are you self-taught, or have you had professional lessons?"

"I painted and drew pictures on my own throughout my childhood and teen years," B.J. said, "but after high school I went to college and majored in art."

"What school did you go to?" Erika asked. It was the first time today that she'd joined in the conversation.

"The college was in New York," B.J. replied.

"So is that where you're originally from?" Erika questioned.

B.J. shook his head. "I grew up in Columbus, Ohio."

"Did you say 'Columbus'?" Noreen asked with a curious expression.

"That's right, but after I graduated from college, I didn't move back home. Took a job as an art teacher in Chicago, which is where I still live."

"What a coincidence," Noreen said. "My sister and I grew up in Columbus."

"Really?" B.J. reached for a cluster of grapes.

"That's right. We lived on the north side of town."

B.J.'s eyebrows lifted. "That's interesting. So did I."

"I'm curious," Noreen said, leaning slightly forward. "What does B.J. stand for?"

"Bruce Jensen," he replied. "But I've gone by B.J. since I was in college, when some of my friends started calling me that."

"Did you say Bruce Jensen?" Noreen's mouth twisted at the corners, and she stared at him as though in disbelief.

He gave a quick nod.

"Did you by any chance have a girlfriend in high school whose name was Judy Hanson?"

B.J.'s face blanched. "Why, yes, I did. What made you ask that question?"

Noreen lips quivered. "Judy was my sister, and you're obviously the man who broke her heart." She pushed back her chair with such force that it nearly toppled to the floor. "I'm sorry, Emma, but I have to go!" Noreen quickly gathered up her things and rushed out the door.

CHAPTER 21

H
ow many times are you going to clean things in here?" Lamar asked as he watched Emma scrub the kitchen counters. "I think they're clean enough, don't you?"

"You're right, Lamar, but staying busy helps when something's on my mind."

"And what would that be?"

Emma dropped the sponge into the sink and turned to face him. "I'm upset with how things turned out today, and I'm beginning to think we'll never be able to help any of our students."

"Now don't you go thinkin' negative thoughts like that," Lamar said with a shake of his head. "Things aren't really that bad."

"Are you serious?" Emma leaned against the counter and folded her arms. "Not only is Erika still being very negative, but Jennifer shared with me how depressed her husband has become because he's still unemployed. All I could do was offer her some food."

"I'm sure she appreciated it, Emma."

"I know, but it just didn't seem like enough. I don't have any answers for her, and I wish we could do more."

"Well, you said Jennifer invited us to their house for supper on Friday night, so maybe we can take them another box of food."

"That's a good idea, and I'm sure it will help some." Emma sighed deeply. "I'm also worried about Mike. I could see how anxious he was about his health, yet he wouldn't really open up and share his fears."

"He talked some to me," Lamar informed her. "I think he'll feel better once he gets the results of his blood test next week."

"I hope it's nothing serious," Emma said. "And with his wife away, I'm sure Mike feels even worse."

"You're probably right," Lamar agreed. "I told Mike we'd be praying for him."

"That's good, Lamar. We also need to pray for B.J. and Noreen. He looked devastated when Noreen yelled at him, and she seemed terribly upset when she ran out of our home."

Lamar tugged on his ear. "I wonder what was up with that."

"Apparently B.J. did something to hurt Noreen's sister, and Noreen's angry about it." Emma slowly shook her head. "We've never had a class like this, Lamar. Everyone has a problem, but no one seems willing to say much about it, or ask for our help."

"They don't need to ask," Lamar reminded. "We just need to be there and offer our support. Remember all the other classes? Even though we had our doubts at first, in the end, things turned out for the best."

"That's true, and I have to remember that God seldom swoops down and fixes everything. Some things take time, and people need to be willing to allow Him to help them cope and manage their problems."

"Well said. And you know, Emma, one good thing did happen today," Lamar commented.

"What was that?"

"I do believe that Jan may have found himself a lady friend."

Emma smiled. "I think you could be right about that."

———

"What a beautiful day it is to be on the beach," Kim remarked as she and Jan sat on a bench facing the water, eating burgers and fries. "For me, this is the best part of living in Florida, having the gulf and its beaches so close at hand."

"Think I could get used to this kind of life." Jan tossed a fry to a squawking seagull and laughed when three more gulls moved in and tried to grab it.

"If you like it here, why don't you relocate?" Kim asked.

He shook his head. "I can't. I'm a roofer, and my business is in northeast Indiana."

"You could start over. That's what I did when I left my home in Raleigh, North Carolina. Of course, I didn't have my own business to worry about."

Jan threw several more of his fries on the sand and watched as the hungry birds attacked. "It'd be hard to start over with a new business here. I'd probably have some stiff competition in an area as big as Sarasota and the surrounding towns, and it would take some time to get my name out there."

"I suppose you're right." Kim finished her burger and leaned back with eyes closed and head tilted toward the sun. "My advice is to enjoy every moment of your vacation. By the time you leave, you'll be nice and relaxed and probably go home with a really nice tan."

Jan gave no reply. He didn't give a rip about getting tan or being relaxed.

When he'd first met Kim on the beach with her dog, he'd been intrigued. Now, he just wanted to spend the time he had left in Sarasota getting to know the perky little blond sitting next to him. He couldn't take his eyes off her, and almost choked on a french fry, seeing Kim's face lifted toward the sun. Her smooth tan skin and those long, thick eyelashes lying against her cheeks were almost his undoing. Her silky hair coming loose from behind her ears and gently bobbing with the warm breezes made him wish once again that he could wrap a strand of it around his finger.

"Are you all right?" Kim asked when she opened her eyes. "You're looking at me strangely."

Jan coughed and swallowed to regain his composure. "Yep, I'm just fine. Those dumb seagulls made me laugh and I almost choked." *Boy, did that sound stupid,* he thought. *But I couldn't come right out and tell her the truth.*

"Yes, they are crazy birds." Kim pointed toward the water. "Would you look at that?"

"What is it?" he asked.

"There's a dog out there, standing on a paddle board, and a woman is pushing it along." She giggled. "Don't think I've ever seen anything like that before."

Jan smiled. "Guess it takes all kinds."

"You're right. That's what makes the world such an interesting place." Kim closed her eyes again. "It feels so good to just sit here and soak up the sun. I feel totally relaxed."

"Same here." Jan thought about how he and Kim had ridden their own bikes to Lido Beach, which meant they couldn't visit on the way. It didn't matter, though. Ever since they'd first stepped onto the sand, they'd been talking pretty much nonstop. They'd shared things about their families, jobs, and what kinds of things they enjoyed doing just for fun. Jan couldn't remember when he'd felt this comfortable with a woman—not even with Star's mother, Nancy, whom he'd nicknamed Bunny. He'd only spent part of a day with Kim, and already he felt as if he'd known her for years. He'd been attracted to Nancy physically, but their personalities were as different as fire and ice. Even better, he and Kim had a lot in common. They both owned motorcycles, liked to bowl, enjoyed eating pizza, and ironically, they each owned German shepherds.

What a shame they lived so many miles apart. Why couldn't he have found a gal like Kim back home? Even if they established a friendship while he was here, it would probably end when he returned to Indiana. It would be too hard to have a long-distance relationship. Phone calls weren't the same as spending actual time together.

Appealing as it sounds, I sure can't pull up stakes and move down here, Jan reminded himself as he took a drink of root beer.

"You're awfully quiet," Kim said, opening her eyes. "Are you bored with my company now?"

Jan jerked his head. "What? No! Just the opposite, in fact."

She smiled. "Does that mean you've enjoyed being with me as much as I have you?"

He gave a nod, pleased that she'd said what he'd been thinking.

"Can I ask you something?"

"Sure thing. What do you want to know?"

Kim pointed to his arm—the one with "Bunny" tattooed on it. "I'm curious about that name."

"It's a nickname for someone I used to date—my daughter's mother, in fact." Jan slapped the side of his head. "I didn't have much in the way of brains when I had that tattoo done. Guess I figured I'd spend the rest of my life with Bunny."

"Things don't always turn out the way we think they will," she said.

"Nope, they sure don't."

They sat quietly for a while, watching kids squealing with excitement as they ran out to meet the water, and couples walking hand-in-hand along the sandy beach. Turning to Kim, Jan touched her arm briefly and said, "Would you be willing to go out with me again? Maybe we could go bowling, catch a movie, have another picnic on the beach, or take a ride on our bikes."

"That sounds like fun."

"Which one?" he asked, tipping his head.

"Everything you suggested."

He snapped his fingers. "Great! Let's do all four."

"All in one day?" Her eyebrows lifted.

"Sure, why not? We could start by taking another ride on our bikes and come back here to the beach. We can lie in the sun, splash around in the water, and eat some lunch. Then we can take in an afternoon show and end the day at the bowling alley."

"Whoa now! That all sounds nice, but maybe we should space those things out a bit. I have a job, you know, and don't forget about Maddie. I don't like leaving her alone for long hours."

"Maybe we can do something together on your next day off, and either take Maddie along or just not be gone all day."

"My next day off is tomorrow. Since it's Sunday, the restaurant will be closed, but I did plan on going to church in the morning. Guess I could go to the early service, though."

"Would you mind if I tag along?" Jan asked.

"No, not at all. I'd enjoy the company."

"I hope you don't think I'm bein' too pushy," he said, "but since I'll only be here a few weeks before my daughter joins me. . ."

"Oh, that's right. You did say something earlier about her coming here."

"Is that a problem?"

"No, of course not. I'd like to meet her."

He grinned. "And you shall, 'cause I'm sure Star will enjoy meeting you, too."

"Guess what, Randy?" Jennifer asked when she arrived home from class and found him sitting slumped on the front porch.

"I have no idea," he mumbled. "And I don't feel like guessin' neither. Just tell me, okay? I'm not in the mood for guessing games."

"There was a new guy in our class this morning—a friend of Lamar and Emma's. He's a big, rugged-looking biker, and he drove all the way down here from Shipshewana, Indiana."

Randy lifted his head and shrugged. "So, what's that to me?"

"Nothing personal, but I thought you might be interested in hearing about—"

"Sorry, but I'm not."

Jennifer winced. She hated seeing her husband in such a sullen mood. And she didn't have to ask the reason for it. He'd obviously spent the day job hunting and had come up empty-handed again.

"There's a box in the trunk of my car," Jennifer said. "It's a gift from the Millers."

"What'd they give you this time?" he asked, glancing at her car parked in their driveway.

"It's full of food, but I didn't look inside to see what all is in it."

"Humph! You know how much I hate handouts."

"I don't like to accept charity from others, either, but in our situation, we need all the help we can get."

"Yeah, you're right about that. Guess we'd better have them over for supper to show our appreciation. Why don't you give 'em a call and see if they're free to come over one evening this week?"

"Actually, I already invited them. I suggested Friday night, and Emma said that would be fine." Jennifer placed her hands on Randy's shoulders. "We can just keep it simple, okay?"

"Sure, whatever." He rose to his feet. "I'll go get the box out of the car, and then we can figure out what I should fix for our guests."

"I cannot believe the man I thought was so nice is actually my sister's old boyfriend!" Noreen fumed as she drove through town. She had gone shopping after she'd left Emma and Lamar's, like she always did whenever she was upset, but it had only fueled her anger. Seeing herself in the store mirrors, wearing a turban on her head, had only added to her anxiety. She was glad no one had asked her about it at the quilting class. She would have been mortified to admit what she'd done to her hair, let alone allowing them to see the dark color.

The color of my hair is nothing compared to the agony Bruce put my poor sister through when he broke up with her, Noreen told herself. *Didn't he even care that she was carrying his child? Judy was just a teenager, in the prime of her life. She hadn't even finished high school yet.*

Noreen gripped the steering wheel so hard her fingers ached, as the memories from the past flooded her mind. *Apparently all he cared about was running off to college and forgetting his responsibilities to the innocent young woman he'd taken advantage of. And to think, my sister thought she loved that man! If Judy were still alive, I'd make Bruce meet her face-to-face and beg for her forgiveness. But it's too late for that. Thanks to that man, Judy is gone, and I'll never let him meet the child he abandoned before the innocent baby came into this world.*

CHAPTER 22

Erika sat in her wheelchair near the front door, dressed in her church clothes but not wanting to go. She dreaded having people stare at her with pity or worse yet say something they thought would cheer her up. According to Dad, those well-meaning folks had her best interests at heart, but she didn't want their words of encouragement. Even though she was sure they might mean well and want to cheer her up, what they said had the opposite effect.

Last Sunday, while sitting in the greeting area of church waiting for Dad, Erika overhead some of her friends talking about the fun they were having at their high school games. It was basketball season, and being junior varsity cheerleaders, her friends accompanied the team to all of the games.

Erika's first intention was to go over and join them, but after hearing their conversation, she decided against it. Not wishing the girls to see her, she'd repositioned her wheelchair to the corner where a large artificial plant sat. That way she could eavesdrop, while peeking through the plant's dusty leaves, without her friends noticing. It ended up being a mistake, because hearing the excitement in their voices as they chatted about the latest game became painful. But stuck behind the plant, she had no choice but to remain where she was and listen.

So far, their basketball team had an unbeaten season, and the next game was against their biggest rival. They'd never won a game against that school, but maybe this year things would be different. At one time that would have meant something to Erika, but now, she couldn't care less. She dreaded the pep rally the school would have on the afternoon of the approaching game. Because she was in a wheelchair, she'd have to sit conspicuously alongside the bleachers in the gymnasium. The thought of being forced to watch her friends go through their cheering routines made Erika even more miserable. Knowing she should be out there helping to rouse school spirit caused her to feel worthless and apart from everyone else.

Erika closed her eyes, remembering how she and her friends had tried out for the cheering squad. They'd all looked forward to high school with anticipation of what it would it bring, but what happened to her that summer changed everything.

I would have made the squad if not for my diving accident, she thought, opening her eyes.

Erika dreaded going to high school and church. *Sure wish I could get out of going today. I'm so tired of it all.*

When Dad came out of his bedroom, he smiled at Erika and said, "Ready to go?"

She shook her head. "Can't we do something else today? I get tired of going to church every Sunday and seeing the same people with fake smiles on their faces."

Dad's face tightened. "They're not fake smiles, Erika."

"Well, the things they say to me seem phony."

He shook his head. "You're just too sensitive."

She folded her arms. "You would say that. You never agree with me about anything."

"That's not true, and you know it."

She gave no reply. *It wouldn't matter what I said. Dad always thinks he's right.*

"We're not staying home from church," Dad said, "but we can do something fun afterward."

"Like what?"

"How about we go to the beach? It's a beautiful sunny day, and—"

"No thanks. There's nothing for me to do on the beach anymore." Erika frowned. "I can't swim or even play in the sand, and it's no picnic to sit there and watch others have all the fun."

Dad knelt on the floor in front of her chair and took hold of Erika's hands. "I understand how you feel, but—"

"No, you don't." Tears gathered in Erika's eyes, and she blinked, in an attempt to keep them from dripping onto her cheeks. "Everyone says they understand just to try and make me feel better, but nobody with two good legs could possibly know how I feel."

"I'm trying, Erika." Dad patted her arm and stood. "I just wish you could find something that would give you pleasure and bring meaning to your life. I'd hoped the quilting class might do that for you."

She wrinkled her nose in disgust. "Those people are weird, Dad."

He scowled at her. "I know Emma and Lamar dress different than we do, but I don't think they're weird."

"I wasn't talking about them. I meant the other quilting students." Shaking her head, Erika muttered, "Yesterday there was a biker in the class, with a scruffy beard and several tattoos. He's from Indiana, and

I guess he'll be staying with Emma and Lamar for a while."

"Don't be so judgmental, Erika. He might be a nice man."

"Whatever." She turned her wheelchair toward the front door. "If we have to go to church this morning then let's get it over with. There's a new computer game I wanna try out this afternoon."

Dad smiled. "That's good. I'm glad you have something to look forward to."

Erika shrugged.

———

"Are you sure you don't mind me bringing Maddie along?" Kim asked Jan as they headed to the beach in her little red car, which they had also taken to church.

"Nope. Don't mind a'tall. That way, she won't have to be locked up all day." Maddie lay on the seat between them, and Jan reached over and stroked the dog's head. "My dog, Brutus, likes to go places with me, too, whenever I take my truck. If I had him with me now, I'll bet when we got to the beach he'd have a ball traipsing through the water and be chasin' after every seagull he saw."

"How'd you end up with Brutus?" Kim asked.

"Got him from a friend of mine when he was just a pup. I remember you said you got Maddie at the pound."

"Yeah. I'd read an article in the paper that the Humane Society was asking for help. After breaking up with my boyfriend, I was feeling kind of down and thought doing something helpful might get me out of my mood." Kim paused, noticing that Jan was watching her intently. "I bought a few sacks of dog food to donate, and after arriving at the animal shelter, I ended up looking at all the animals," she continued. "I was shocked to see so many that needed a good home. And well, to make a long story short, Maddie and I seemed to connect, and I felt like

I was saving her life." Kim smiled. "Little did that dog know that she actually saved mine."

"I know exactly what you mean," Jan agreed. "Brutus is almost like family to me."

"Maybe sometime you can come to Florida in your truck and bring your dog along," Kim said, feeling Jan out to see if he had any interest in returning to Sarasota and hoping he did.

"Maybe so, only driving the truck wouldn't be near as much fun as ridin' my bike."

"Tell me more about your daughter," Kim said. "What's she like, and what interests does she have?"

A huge smile spread across Jan's face. "Star's amazing. She sings and plays the guitar. Oh, and she writes most of her own music."

"That's impressive. Has she ever had any of her songs published?"

"Yeah, a couple, but I'm hopin' she'll get a few more breaks, 'cause she's got a talent that deserves to be recognized."

"Sounds like Star is a special young woman. I'm sure you're proud of her."

Jan bobbed his head. "You got that right. Every chance we get, we spend time together."

Kim smiled. Jan might look a bit rough around the edges, but even after knowing him for such a short time, she could tell he had a heart of gold. She'd been surprised yesterday when he'd shared several things about his past, including how Star's mother had run off with her when she was a baby. It was sad to think that Jan had been cheated out of the opportunity to be a father to his only daughter until they'd met by chance during one of Emma's quilting classes.

Kim didn't understand how any mother could have taken her child and run from the child's father, unless they were being abused. Even though she didn't know Jan all that well, she felt sure that wasn't the case. From what Jan had said yesterday, Star's mother was kind of a flake who'd gone from one relationship to another, while Jan had wanted to settle down and raise a family.

I can relate to that, Kim thought with regret. *But none of the men I've dated have had marriage on their mind.* She glanced at Jan out of the corner of her eye as he continued to pet Maddie. *I'd better not get my hopes up about Jan, either, because with the miles between our homes, it's not likely that our relationship will go very far.*

As B.J. sat on a wooden bench at the beach, painting a picture, he thought about Noreen being his ex-girlfriend's older sister. He'd met Noreen a couple of times before she got married and moved away, but Judy had called her sister "Norrie," so he didn't realize her name was actually Noreen. Not that he would have recognized Noreen when they'd met that first day of the quilting class, even if she had used the same first name. B.J. and Noreen had both changed quite a bit over the years.

A sense of regret welled in his soul. He'd almost forgotten about his high school sweetheart until her name was mentioned. B.J. and Judy had been serious about each other back then, and he'd thought he might even marry her someday, but his folks had put an end to the relationship, telling Bruce that he was too young to get serious and that he had his whole life and a career ahead of him. They insisted that he break things off with Judy and sent him away to college. When he came home at the end of his first year, he was surprised to learn that Judy and her family had moved, and no one seemed to know where they'd gone. His folks said it was for the best, that he could do better than a girl like Judy. Well, he'd found a good woman when he met Brenda, who'd later become his wife, but he'd never compared her to Judy. Not until now, at least.

Judy was a lot like B.J.—kind of shy and reserved—and she had a creative side. She wrote poems and short stories, which she'd often shared with him when they were alone. Brenda had been B.J.'s opposite, yet he'd been attracted to her from the moment they'd met at a party thrown by one of their mutual college friends. Brenda had been outgoing and talkative. He remembered how his mother, after meeting Brenda, had called her a social butterfly. His mom and dad had encouraged the relationship from the beginning, and B.J. hadn't objected because he was attracted to Brenda's magnetic personality and good looks. Her jet-black hair and sparkling blue eyes could have turned any man's head.

Judy, on the other hand, was rather plain, although not unattractive. She had light brown hair, which she wore in a ponytail much of the time, and didn't care about the latest fashion trends. She was down-to-earth and always looked on the bright side of things.

I wonder where Judy is now. B.J. pondered. *Noreen left Emma and Lamar's in such a hurry yesterday, I didn't get the chance to ask. I'll question Noreen about Judy when I see her at the next class, though. I'd like to reconnect with Judy—for old time's sake.*

Well, enough with the reminiscing, B.J. told himself. *I came here to paint, not dwell on the past.*

———

"Hey, isn't that B.J. from the quilting class over there on that bench?" Jan asked as he and Kim, leading Maddie on her leash, made their way across the white sandy beach.

She shielded her eyes and looked in the direction Jan was pointing. "You're right. That is B.J. It looks like he's painting something. See that easel in front of him?"

Jan nodded. "Should we go say hi?"

"I don't know. Do you think he'd mind if we interrupted him?"

"Guess we might disrupt his concentration," Jan said. "But what if he sees us over here and thinks we're snubbing him?"

"You're right. We don't want to be unsociable," Kim responded. "Besides, I'd kinda like to see what he's painting."

"Same here. Let's go on over then."

As they approached B.J., Maddie started pulling on her leash.

"All right, girl, but don't run off too far." Kim bent down and unhooked the leash from the dog's collar.

Jan snickered as Maddie let out an excited bark and dashed into the water. Kim would be lucky if she ever got the dog back on her leash.

"I see we're not the only ones from our class who enjoys this beach," Kim said, stepping up to B.J. "It's nice to see you today."

He smiled up at her and then nodded at Jan. "I heard you two talking yesterday about going to the beach, but I thought you planned to do that after class," he said.

"Oh, we did." Kim smiled at Jan. "We enjoyed it so much, we decided to come back again today after church."

"It's a good day to be here," B.J. said with a nod. "Nice and warm, with just a slight breeze. It's a perfect opportunity to get some painting done."

Jan studied the painting, already in progress. The ocean scene featured seagulls swooping close to the waves, and a couple of boats on the horizon. "You do nice work," he said, gesturing to the easel.

B.J. smiled. "I did an ocean scene from my studio in Chicago, but it's much better to paint here by the water. I think it helps to put more feeling into my work."

"It's beautiful." Kim looked closely at the painting. "I can almost feel the spray from the waves you've painted. You captured everything perfectly."

"Thanks. I do my best."

Jan was tempted to bring up the topic of Noreen, and what had gone down at the quilting class yesterday but thought better of it. It was none of his business, and if B.J. wanted to talk about it, he would.

From the choice words coming from Noreen before she'd stormed out of the Millers' house, Jan figured B.J. must have done something pretty bad. *Guess everyone has said or done something in the past that they're not proud of,* he thought. *I know I've done my fair share of flubbing things. I have to wonder, though—if what B.J. did was so bad, why didn't Noreen stick around to discuss it with him? It'll be interesting to see if she shows up for class this Saturday. Well, I'm gonna be there, that's for sure. Not to see what goes down between B.J. and Noreen, but so I can spend more time with Kim.*

CHAPTER 23

"How are things in North Dakota?" Mike asked as he sat in the living room Friday evening, talking to his wife on the phone. Mike was all settled in his easy chair and breathed deeply the aroma of the coffee he'd just brewed. With the TV on mute, he used the remote to flip through the channels, not really paying attention to what was on the screen, trying to focus on what Phyllis was saying.

"A little better than the last time we talked. It's not snowing right now, and it's good to have the power on again. Even though Penny has that backup generator, it's nice to have everything running off the main grid again." After a pause, Phyllis said, "How are things with you?"

"Okay." Mike gnawed on his lower lip, contemplating whether to tell his wife that he'd seen the doctor and gotten the results of his blood test. Would it be best to tell her now or wait until she got home? If he told her now she would worry about him. If he waited to tell her the news, she'd be upset. It was a no-win situation. He'd rather face a group of disappointed fisherman than explain his issues to Phyllis.

"Mike, are you still there?"

"Uh, yeah. Just thinking is all."

"About what?"

"Umm. . .there's something I need to tell you." He pointed the remote, turning off the TV, then reached for his coffee cup, blowing on the steam still rising from it.

"What is it, Mike?"

"I've been having a little problem lately, so I went to see the doctor last week, and—"

"What? And you're just now getting around to telling me that?" Phyllis's voice rose. "What's wrong, Mike? Have you been sick?"

"No, not really. Well, kind of, I guess."

"What's that supposed to mean?"

"I've felt kind of weird and shaky lately. So I finally went to see the doctor, and he had me go in for some blood tests. I got the results yesterday."

"You got the results a day ago, and you're just now telling me about it?" Mike winced when he heard the frustration in Phyllis's voice.

"Calm down, honey," he said, trying to keep his own voice composed. "I knew if I told you that, I'd get this reaction."

"So you figured it'd be best not to tell me at all?"

"That's not it. I just didn't want to worry you, Phyllis, especially while you're helping your sister."

"Well, it's too late for that, because I am worried. What was the outcome of your tests?"

"I have pre-diabetes, but—"

"Diabetes? Oh, Mike, no!"

He grimaced. "I wish you'd stop interrupting and let me tell you everything the doctor said."

"Sorry. I'm listening."

"I don't have full-blown diabetes yet. According to the blood tests, I'm in the early stages, and the doctor seems to think that if I exercise regularly and watch my diet I may never get to the place where I have to take pills or insulin shots."

She blew out her breath. "That's a relief. You really had me worried. Of course, you'll have to follow through and do as the doctor said."

"Yeah, I know. It's gonna be hard for me to give up sweets, though."

"There are many delicious desserts made with sugar-free ingredients," she said. "When I get home, I'll try a few recipes and see what you like. In the meantime, promise me that you'll be good and eat right."

"Yes, Mama."

"I'm serious, Mike."

"I know, hon, and I promise to toe the mark."

"So how's the quilt class going?" she asked, her tone relaxing some.

"Fine. Some big biker fella who's a friend of the Millers joined us last week. Guess he took one of their classes up in Shipshewana, Indiana."

Phyllis snickered. "I can't picture Emma and Lamar becoming friends with a biker."

"It was a surprise to me as well, but those two are the nicest people. I think they could be friends with anyone—except maybe some hardened criminal who nobody could reach."

"Just from my first meeting with Emma and Lamar, it wouldn't surprise me if, were they ever to meet such a person, they'd try to reach out to him in kindness."

Mike laughed. "You could be right about that."

"Thanks for the ride," Lamar told their driver when he dropped them off at Jennifer and Randy's place that evening. "We'll give you a call when we're ready to come home."

"Oh, let's not forget the box of food we have in the trunk," Emma said as she stepped out of the car. They'd filled the box with flour, sugar, cereal, bread, eggs, pasta, milk, and several packages of meat. She hoped Randy and Jennifer would graciously accept their gift.

Lamar lifted the box, and they headed up the porch stairs. Emma reached out to knock, but the door swung open before her knuckles connected with the wood.

"It's good to see you. Please, come in." Jennifer greeted them with a cheery smile.

"Since you wouldn't let us bring anything to contribute to the meal, we brought you this," Lamar said as they followed Jennifer into the house.

"What is it?" she questioned.

"Just a few more items of food we thought you could use." Emma smiled. "And please don't say no, because we have plenty of food in our pantry, and we surely don't want to take this box home."

"We appreciate your thoughtfulness; isn't that right, Randy?" Jennifer asked, gesturing to the box after her husband stepped into the room.

He shook hands with Emma and Lamar, then looked into the box. "You're giving us more food?"

Lamar nodded. "It's just a little something to help out."

Randy hesitated but finally nodded. "Thanks, we appreciate it."

"While Randy takes the box to the kitchen, why don't the rest of us go into the living room so we can visit before supper's ready?" Jennifer suggested, holding the small of her back as she led the way to the other room.

Emma and Lamar took a seat on the couch, and Jennifer sat in the rocking chair across from them, rubbing her stomach.

"You look tired, Jennifer. How has your week been going?" Emma asked, feeling concern.

Jennifer patted her ever-growing stomach. "This little girl has been pretty active lately, and I'm not sleeping as well as I should."

"I'm sorry to hear that," Emma said. "How much longer until the baby comes?"

"Just four more weeks, unless I'm late." Jennifer gave her stomach a couple more pats. "I think our baby is anxious to be born, because she seems to be kicking all the time."

"Some babies can be pretty active," Emma said. "I remember when I was expecting my daughter, Mary, she often got the hiccups, and it would wake me during the night."

"I just checked the oven, and supper's ready," Randy said, joining them in the living room. "I hope you folks like enchiladas."

"Can't say that I've ever had them," Lamar spoke up. "But I'm willing to try anything."

Emma and Lamar rose from their seats and followed Jennifer and Randy into the small but cozy dining room. Emma could see that Jennifer had set the table with her best china, and a pretty floral centerpiece sat in the middle of the table.

After they all took seats, Lamar said, "At home, Emma and I usually offer a silent prayer, but here in your house we'd be pleased if you prayed out loud."

Jennifer glanced at Randy, and his ears turned red. "Uh, yeah, well. . . Jennifer, why don't you pray for the meal?"

Jennifer fingered her napkin. Emma wasn't sure whether this young couple felt uncomfortable praying in front of others, or if they normally didn't pray before a meal, but she sensed the awkwardness of the moment. To ease the tension, she quickly said, "Or maybe you'd prefer that we all pray silently instead."

"No, it's fine; I'll pray for the meal," Jennifer said. After everyone bowed their heads, she prayed in a soft-spoken voice, "Dear Lord, I thank You for this food, and for the hands that prepared it. I also want to thank Emma and Lamar, who have been patiently teaching me to quilt and generously gave us some food. In Jesus' name, amen."

When everyone opened their eyes, Jennifer passed the tossed green salad around the table, followed by the dish of enchiladas.

"This certainly smells good," Emma said, spooning some of the Mexican dish onto her plate.

"You're right about that," Lamar agreed. "And if it tastes as good as it smells, I think we're in for a treat."

While Emma poured some dressing over her salad, Lamar took a bite of enchilada. As he chewed, his face, neck, and ears turned red. Coughing, he quickly reached for his glass of water.

"What's wrong?" Jennifer asked, looking at Lamar with concern. "Did you swallow incorrectly, or is it too spicy for you?"

Gasping for breath, Lamar croaked, "It—it's hotter than anything I've ever tasted."

Jennifer took a taste, then quickly spit it back onto the plate. Her forehead wrinkled as she looked sternly at Randy. "What did you do to the enchiladas? They're hotter than a blazing furnace!"

Randy's brows furrowed. "I–I don't know what happened. Thought I'd poured just the right amount of picante sauce over the top of them. And it was the mild kind, not hot."

"I've never tasted anything this hot that's supposed to be mild." Jennifer grabbed her glass of water and took a drink.

Emma stared at her plate. She was glad she hadn't tasted her enchilada yet. If it was hot enough to affect Lamar and Jennifer as it did, she'd probably have choked to death.

"I'm going to get the jar of sauce." Randy rose from the table and left the room. When he returned with the jar, he placed it on the table and pointed to the label. "See, it says right here that it's mild."

"Maybe you should taste it," Jennifer suggested.

Randy opened the lid, stuck his spoon inside, and put the whole spoonful in his mouth. "Yow! That's anything but mild!" He coughed, sputtered, and gulped down his glass of water.

"That jar of sauce must have been mislabeled," Jennifer said. "You should take it back to the store."

"I'll do that tomorrow," Randy said, "but right now we need something else to eat, so I'll grill some burgers with the package of ground beef that was in the box the Millers gave us." He looked across the table at Emma and Lamar. "I'm really sorry about this. It wasn't a good way to repay your kindness."

Lamar waved a hand. "Don't worry about it, Randy. Barbecued burgers will be just fine." He pushed his chair aside and stood. "In fact, I'd enjoy helping you grill them, and while we're doing that, it'll give us a chance to chat."

Randy gave a nod. "Sounds good to me. Let's get that grill started."

Emma smiled. She was glad to see Randy relax a bit and be willing to accept, not only the food they'd brought, but Lamar's help.

———

"I'm glad you suggested we go bowling tonight," Kim said when Jan picked up his ball and got ready to take his turn.

He smiled and nodded. "Back home, bowling is one of my favorite things to do on a Friday night."

"Do you have a bowling partner?"

"Star usually goes along, and sometimes we bowl against my friend Terry and his girlfriend, Cheryl." Jan wiggled his eyebrows playfully. "It's kinda fun to compete and see who can rack up the most pins."

"Well, you won't have to worry about that tonight, 'cause even though I enjoy bowling, I'm not very good at it," Kim said. "I'll probably have more gutter balls than strikes."

"Let's not worry about competing." Jan grinned. "I just wanna have fun and get to know you better."

Kim gave a nod. "Same here."

As they took turns bowling and keeping score, Jan appreciated what a good sport Kim was. She never got upset when she messed up, and even when he made a strike or a spare, she cheered him on. He found himself liking her more all the time, and that scared him. Could he trust Kim not to break his heart the way Star's mom had?

I've gotta quit thinking like this, Jan told himself. *In the short time I've known her, I can already tell that Kim is nothing like Nancy.*

Jan glanced to his right and saw a middle-aged man dressed all in black sitting on a bench at one of the alleys up from them. The guy had thick dark hair and sideburns, and of all things, he was wearing sunglasses.

Jan nudged Kim and snickered. "Look over there. I think an Elvis-wanna-be is in the building."

Kim looked that way and laughed. "You're so funny, Jan. No wonder I'm having such a good time tonight."

He wiggled his eyebrows again, stifling a belly laugh. "Thank you. Thank you very much."

———

As the evening progressed, Kim found herself enjoying her time with Jan more than she'd ever expected. Not only had he offered her some bowling tips, but even when she rolled a few gutter balls, he never made fun of her.

When they finished bowling, they headed out to an Asian restaurant Kim had been meaning to try. Each table had its own chef, who cooked the meal on an open hibachi grill right in front of them. After he'd cut the tails off the shrimp, he flipped them into his white chef's hat, adding a bit of humor to the whole experience.

Kim glanced over at Jan and could see by his broad smile that he was having a good time and enjoying the meal. She liked his easygoing, positive attitude, and wished once more that Jan didn't have to return to Indiana when his vacation was over. *When I've worked at the restaurant long enough for some vacation time, maybe I'll take a trip to Shipshewana and see where Jan lives,* she thought. *Who knows—I might even like it there and decide to stay.*

CHAPTER 24

"How'd your date with Kim go last night?" Lamar asked as he, Emma, and Jan sat at the kitchen table Saturday morning, eating breakfast.

Jan grinned widely. "Good. Really good." He reached for his glass of freshly squeezed orange juice. "I like her a lot."

Emma looked at Lamar and smiled when he winked at her. It was good to see Jan in such good spirits. He'd been through a lot over the years and deserved to be happy. Emma couldn't help but wonder, though, how Jan and Kim could keep their relationship going once Jan returned home. Also, things seemed to be moving rather quickly between the two, and that concerned her a bit. She hoped no one would end up getting hurt.

"Say, Jan, I've been wanting to make a trip to Venice to look for sharks' teeth," Lamar said. "Would that be something you'd be interested in doing?"

Jan nodded enthusiastically. "You bet! When did you wanna go?"

"Anytime you'd like. 'Course, it can't be on a Saturday, because of the quilt classes, and then, Sunday is our day for church."

"No problem. We can make the trip whenever you want. I'll have to see about renting a car, though, since I only have my motorcycle with me." Jan smacked his forehead. "Hey, here's an idea. I could get a sidecar and have it attached to my bike. Wouldn't it be fun to tool around together that way? Emma, you could ride in the sidecar, and Lamar can sit behind me on the bike. How far is it from here to the Venice beaches?"

"I'd say about twenty miles or so," Lamar replied. "I'm not sure we'd want to travel the way you suggested, though. Emma and I are a little old for that sort of thing. Right, Emma?"

She gave a decisive nod.

"Not a problem," Jan said. "I'll see about renting a car for the day. That way there'll be plenty of room for all three of us to go."

"You two don't need to worry about me. Just go ahead and have fun," Emma said. "I'll be perfectly fine here at home while you're gone. Oh, and maybe you could see if one of our drivers will take you to Venice. That would probably be cheaper than Jan renting a car."

"Aw, come on, Emma, you've gotta go along. I thought I'd invite Kim to join us, and it'll be more fun if you're there, too." Jan reached for his cup and took a drink. "Hey, I've got it!" he said, nearly choking on his coffee. "Kim has a motorcycle, but she also owns a car. I'll bet anything she'd be willing to drive us there."

Emma didn't really care about looking for sharks' teeth, but it would be nice to visit with Kim, walk the beach, and search for pretty shells. "Okay, if Kim goes, then I will, too." Emma blew out a puff of air. "I feel better knowing we'll be taking a car. I just can't see myself riding in one of those sidecar things."

"I understand, but I haven't ditched the idea of getting a sidecar. I'd actually like to see how my bike maneuvers with one of those on. While I'm here in Florida, I may get one installed before I head home. That is, if I can find a dealer around here that sells 'em." Jan rubbed the bridge of his nose. "If I got a sidecar, Star could ride in that on the way home instead of sitting on the back of my bike, like we'd planned for her to do. Might be more comfortable on the long trip. And since I hate leaving Brutus at home so much, or having to ask someone to watch him when I go on some motorcycle trips, he could ride along." He chuckled. "Can't you just see my dog sittin' next to me in a sidecar? I wonder how he'd look wearing goggles."

They all laughed. "That would surely be something, alright," Emma agreed.

Jan rubbed his hands together. "Now back to goin' to the beach in Venice. Here's another thought. Maybe we should wait till Star gets here. I think lookin' for sharks' teeth would be something she'd enjoy doing, and it'd be a chance for her to get acquainted with Kim."

"That's a good idea, Jan." Emma smiled, looking at Lamar, who was nodding his head in agreement. "It will be so nice to see Star again, but Jan, don't you think you should ask Kim first, if she would mind driving us all to Venice?"

"'Course I'll ask, but I'm almost sure she won't mind." Jan gave his left earlobe a tug. "In the short time I've known Kim, I've found her to be real easygoing. In fact, if she was here right now, I can almost bet she'd have already suggested taking her car."

Emma reached for her cup of tea and took a sip. *If Jan wants Star to get to know Kim, then he must be getting serious about her already, Now, wouldn't that be something if Kim decided to move to Indiana and she and Jan got married? It would be a pleasure to have another one of my quilting students living nearby so we could visit once in a while.*

Emma enjoyed staying in touch with her previous students. It was nice to see some of the quilting projects they had done on their own—not to mention keeping up with what was going on in their lives. Just the other day she'd received a letter from Pam Johnston, who'd attended Emma's first class. Pam mentioned that she and Stuart were planning to take their children to Disney World during their spring break and said if Emma and Lamar were still in Florida, they might come down to see them, since Orlando was only a few hours' drive from Sarasota.

We'll be going home in the spring, Emma thought. *I need to be close to my family there and could never be happy staying here on a permanent basis. Oh, I hope Lamar doesn't get any ideas about living here year-round.*

"Emma, did you hear what I said?" Lamar asked, nudging her arm.

"Uh, sorry, I didn't. Guess I was deep in thought. Would you please repeat it, Lamar?"

"I asked if there's anything you need me to do before our students get here this morning?"

"Thank you, but I think everything we need has been set out." Emma turned to Jan and said, "Will you be joining us again today?"

He gave a quick nod. "Wouldn't miss it!"

Goshen

Star picked up her guitar and took a seat on the end of her bed. It had been awhile since she'd composed a new song, and since she didn't have to work this morning, it was a good time to come up with some words that would express the way she felt about her dad. Star wished she and Jan could gain back the twenty years they'd lost when her mom had taken her and run off, but that wasn't possible. What mattered was the time they had to be together now and in the future.

Star was glad her dad didn't have a serious girlfriend. It was probably selfish, but she wanted him all to herself. It was bad enough she had to share him with Brutus. The mutt always seemed to be vying for his master's attention—especially when Jan had been away from home for a while. She could only imagine how the dog would carry on when Jan returned from Florida. He'd probably become Jan's shadow for several days.

"Though we can't turn back the hands of time, we have the future to look forward to," Star sang as she strummed her guitar. "Like grains of sand slipping through our fingers..."

Star's cell phone whistled, letting her know she had a call. She placed the guitar on the bed and picked up the phone. Looking at the caller ID, she smiled, pleased to see it was her dad.

"Hey, stranger, what's up? I haven't heard from you for a few days."

"Sorry about that," he said. "I've been occupied."

"Doing what?" she asked.

"Helping out at Emma and Lamar's and spending time with Kim. She's the cute little gal I told you about—the one who's taking the quilt class and has a German shepherd named Maddie."

"Oh, I see." Star hoped her dad wasn't getting serious about Kim, because a long-distance relationship wouldn't work. Besides, he didn't need a woman to complicate his life and come between them.

"I was gonna wait to tell you this when you got here, Star, but I think I've found the perfect woman."

Star lifted her gaze toward the ceiling. "Yeah, Dad, right. You barely know this Kim person."

"I realize that, but we have a lot in common, and it's like... Well, it feels as if we're soul mates."

Star's fingers clenched the phone. "No way, Dad! You can't know that in such a short time."

He grunted. "You're not being very supportive, but I'm sure you'll feel differently once you've met Kim."

"I doubt it," she mumbled.

"What was that?"

"Nothing. I've gotta go now, Dad. I'm busy." Star hated to hang up so soon, but this conversation was not what she'd expected. Her dad's announcement had really thrown her for a loop.

"That's okay. I need to hang up anyway. The quilt class will be starting soon, and I don't wanna miss it."

"Okay, whatever."

"I'll pick you up at the airport next Thursday," he said. "Oh, and Star. . ."

"Yeah, Dad?"

"I'm looking forward to seeing you."

"Same here. Bye, Dad."

When Star clicked off her cell phone she flopped back on the bed with a moan. Dad thought he was in love with a woman he hardly knew. *Well, when I get to Sarasota, things will change. I'll talk some sense into Dad and make him see what a mistake he's making. And if trying to reason with him doesn't work, then I'll have to take more drastic measures, because I can't let that woman come between me and my dad!*

Sarasota

"Is Jennifer here yet?" Kim asked Emma, after she'd entered the Millers' house. "There's something I want to tell her."

"Not yet, but I'm sure she'll be here soon," Emma replied.

"Hey, Kim, I'm glad you're here," Jan said with an eager expression as he sauntered into the room. "There's something I'd like to ask you."

"Oh, what's that?"

"Lamar mentioned this morning that he'd like to go down to Venice to look for sharks' teeth, and I thought if you'd like to go along that you might be willing to drive us all there, since you have a car."

Kim smiled. "That sounds like fun, and it's actually something I've been wanting to do. So yeah, I'd be happy to drive you there."

"We'll help with the gas," Lamar spoke up.

"Oh, don't worry about that," Kim responded with a wave of her hand. "It'll be my pleasure."

Emma shook her head. "If we're going along, then we insist on helping out with the gas."

"We can talk about that when the time comes. When did you want to go to Venice?" Kim asked, directing her question to Jan.

"Any day you have off," Jan replied. "But I'd like to wait till Star gets here, 'cause I think she'd enjoy looking for sharks' teeth, too."

"When did you say your daughter will get here?" Kim asked.

"She's flying in on Thursday."

"That's perfect. I have next Friday off," Kim said. "Would that be a good day for all of you?"

Lamar nodded, and so did Emma.

"That's great!" Jan bumped shoulders with Kim. "I can hardly wait."

"Same here," she agreed. "I'm anxious to meet your daughter. Oh, and Emma, we'll have to put our heads together and take a few things along for a picnic lunch. Maybe we can eat right there on the beach. I think it'll be a terrific day."

"I hope I'm not late," Jennifer said when she entered the Millers' house a short time later. "I don't know why, but the traffic was terrible this morning."

"You're not late at all. Only Kim and Jan are here, but Jan's in the spare room right now, and Kim's in the dining room at the table," Emma said. "You can go right in if you want to."

Jennifer hesitated a minute. "Before I do, I was wondering if Lamar suffered any ill effects from Randy's spicy enchiladas."

Emma shook her head. "No, he's fine. I don't think he ate enough of it to cause any real distress."

"That's good to hear. Randy was so embarrassed by what he did."

Emma patted Jennifer's arm. "Well, he needn't have been, because it wasn't his fault."

"I know, but Randy's a cook, and he always tries to do his best." Jennifer held her hands tightly at her sides as her eyebrows pulled together. "I think the longer he's unemployed, and the closer it comes for me to have the baby, the more worried he becomes. If he doesn't find a job soon, we may have to leave Sarasota and move in with one of our parents."

"Would that be such a bad thing?" Emma questioned.

Jennifer nodded. "It would be admitting defeat, and since our parents aren't well off, us moving in with them would cause a hardship."

"Hopefully, it won't come to that. I know it's hard, but try to keep a positive attitude and trust God," Emma said. "One of my favorite verses of scripture is Proverbs 30:5: 'Every word of God is pure: he is a shield unto them that put their trust in him.'"

Jennifer smiled. "That's the same verse Lamar quoted to Randy when they were outside grilling the burgers. Randy shared that with me after you folks left. He said Lamar gave him a pep talk about how important it is to trust God, even when things look hopeless." Jennifer gave Emma a hug.

"We're pleased that you have both shared your feelings with us. That helps us know how to pray." Emma paused. "Oh, and before I forget,

Kim wants to talk to you. Why don't we go in to see her now?"

When they entered the dining room, Jennifer took a seat in an empty chair next to Kim.

Kim turned and clasped Jennifer's arm. "I'm glad you're here. I wanted you to know that the restaurant where I work is looking for a cook."

A sense of hope welled in Jennifer's chest. "Really? Have they interviewed anyone yet?"

"I don't know. I stopped over at the restaurant before coming here to pick up my paycheck, since I forgot to get it after work yesterday." Kim's cheeks turned pink. "Guess I was too excited about my bowling date with Jan. Anyway, I think you should call your husband now and let him know about the job. He should go over there as soon as possible to apply."

"You can use our phone in the kitchen," Emma spoke up.

"Thanks." Jennifer hurried from the room. Maybe this would be the day that her prayers were answered.

CHAPTER 25

I can't believe I'm wearing this stupid turban again," Noreen fumed as she drove down Bahia Vista toward Pinecraft. She'd washed her hair several times during the week, but the color hadn't faded much at all.

Well, at least the neighbor's dog had quit yapping so much, and she was grateful for that.

Noreen grimaced as another thought popped into her head. *I dread having to face Bruce Jensen again today.*

When Noreen first met the man, she'd thought he was nice and perhaps even her type. *I could have made the same mistake my sister did if I'd become involved with him,* she thought. *I'll bet he never loved Judy, or he wouldn't have run out on her when he found out she was carrying his child. Instead, he ran off to college in another state, never giving a second thought to my sister or their baby.*

The closer Noreen got to Pinecraft, the more upset she became. Well, she wasn't going to let Bruce keep her from finishing the wall hanging she'd started. She just wouldn't talk to him about Judy. Better yet, maybe she would bring it up at the Millers' today and embarrass B.J. in front of the whole class!

———

When B.J. pulled in front of the Millers' house, he spotted Noreen getting out of her car. "Oh, great," he mumbled. "The last thing I need is a confrontation with her out here in the yard." He did want to talk to her, though, because he had some questions to ask about Judy. But he figured it would be better to wait until after class. Maybe he would invite Noreen to lunch, where they could talk privately without the rest of the quilting students listening in on their conversation.

B.J. slunk down in his seat, hoping she wouldn't notice him. If he waited until Noreen went inside the house before making his appearance he might be better off. He glanced at the driveway and saw Kim's motorcycle and a few other vehicles and knew everyone else had probably arrived.

Looking back at the house, B.J. relaxed a bit when he saw Noreen go inside. He waited a few more minutes before getting out of the car. As he walked slowly up the walk to the porch, a van pulled in.

B.J. watched as Erika's father lifted her wheelchair from the van and placed her in it. He felt sorry for the girl. Her life had been altered by an accident that could have been avoided, and now her activities were restricted and she was bound to that chair.

Life isn't fair, B.J. thought. A person never knew what was around the next bend. They could be in an accident, become terminally ill, or lose all their possessions due to some horrible disaster. There were times when he wondered if it would have been better if he'd never been born.

Enough with the negative thoughts. It's time to go inside.

———

B.J. glanced across the table and noticed Noreen's scowl. He wished she'd quit looking at him with that sourpuss expression. Did she hate him that much for breaking up with her sister? Why couldn't she let go of the past? *It's just so petty,* he thought.

In an effort to avoid Noreen's piercing gaze, B.J. turned to face Mike, who sat on his right. "How'd your week go?"

Mike shrugged. "Okay, I guess."

"Did you get the results of your blood tests?" Lamar questioned from where he sat at the head of the table.

Mike nodded. "Found out I have pre-diabetes, but the doc said if I watch what I eat and exercise regularly, my blood sugar numbers should improve."

"That's good to hear," Lamar said, smiling.

B.J. nodded. He wished what was wrong with him could be controlled by diet and exercise. *Try not to think about it,* he reminded himself. *Just live each day as it comes and enjoy every moment you have left on earth.*

"I got in touch with Randy, and he's going over to the restaurant right now to see about that job," Jennifer said as she returned to the room and took a seat beside Kim.

Kim patted Jennifer's arm in a motherly fashion. "I hope it all works out."

"Yeah, me too. It gives me a ray of hope, at least."

"Please let us know how it all turns out," Emma said.

"Yes, I will."

"Well, now that we're all here, we'd better get started. Today we'll be cutting out the batting for your wall hangings, and then we'll begin the quilting process."

"Oh great. More sewing on that dumb sewing machine." Erika wrinkled her nose, like some foul order had permeated the room. "I had

189

a hard time holding the material straight last week when I sewed the pieces of material together." It was the first thing the girl had said since she'd gotten here, and as usual, it was something negative.

"Actually, the quilting will be done by hand, with a needle and thread," Emma explained. "But before we begin the actual process, you'll each need to cut a piece of cotton batting about two inches larger on all sides than your quilt top."

"The excess batting will be trimmed even with the quilt top after the quilting stitches have been done," Lamar interjected.

B.J. and the rest of the class watched as Lamar and Emma demonstrated how it should be done.

"I'll explain the details of the quilting process once you've all cut out your batting," Emma went on to say. "So let's begin that now."

Everyone did as she asked, and as they cut, Noreen looked over at B.J. and said, "You're doing it wrong. The piece you cut is too small." She clicked her tongue. "I suppose some people can't do anything right."

"What's that supposed to mean?" B.J. asked.

"Nothing," she mumbled.

They worked awhile longer, then Noreen turned to B.J. and said, "You sure messed up where my sister was concerned."

"I was going to wait until we could talk in private," B.J. said, "but since you brought the subject up, I'd like to know what I did to Judy that was so terrible. I mean, a guy ought to have the right to break up with a girl without her sister carrying a grudge all these years and treating him like he's got the plague."

Noreen set her work aside and glared at B.J. "Since you obviously don't mind the whole class knowing about your sordid past, I'll tell you exactly what you did to Judy."

The room became quiet as B.J. leaned closer to Noreen and said,

"Please do."

"First of all, you took advantage of my sister's innocence and talked her into sleeping with you."

Seeing the look of shock on everyone's face, B.J. wished there was a hole in the floor so he could crawl into it and hide. This was so embarrassing!

B.J. was about to offer an explanation, but Noreen spoke again. "When you found out that Judy was carrying your child, why did you run off to college to fulfill your dream of becoming an artist? Couldn't you have stayed in Columbus and taken responsibility for your actions?"

The shock of hearing this sent B.J.'s mind whirling. He couldn't deny that he and Judy had been intimate, but she'd never told him she was pregnant. He'd broken up with her because his parents said if he didn't they wouldn't pay for his schooling, and he'd really wanted a degree in art. What a shock to learn that Judy had been carrying his child.

Noreen's finger trembled as she shook it at B.J. "Choosing your career over my sister was pretty selfish, don't you think?"

"If I had known Judy was pregnant, I would have married her."

"I'll bet you would."

"You have to believe me," he said. "I'm not the kind of man who would shirk his responsibilities." Sweat beaded on B.J.'s forehead as a sense of panic welled in his chest. "Give me the chance to apologize to Judy and meet our child. Please tell me where she lives, or at least give me her phone number."

Noreen shook her head. "It's too late for that. Judy is gone, and so is your son."

CHAPTER 26

B.J.'s eyes widened as his mouth dropped open. "I—I have a son?"

Heat flooded Noreen's face, and she covered her mouth with the palm of her hand. She hadn't planned to let Bruce know that he had a son, but she couldn't take back what she'd said. She would have to be careful not to tell Bruce any more, for her sister's ex-boyfriend had no right to know anything about his son. Worse yet, if the truth came out, Judy's son would be crushed, and Noreen feared it might ruin her relationship with him.

"Where is Judy, and where is our boy?" B.J. asked in an emotion-filled voice.

Noreen drew in a calming voice. All eyes and ears seemed to be upon her, and she wished she could crawl under the table. "My sister is dead. She died from complications during childbirth." She choked back the sob rising in her throat. Even after all these years, it was difficult to talk about. Now, with the father of Judy's son staring at her from across

THE HEALING QUILT

the table, it was more painful than she ever thought possible.

B.J. winced as though he'd been slapped. "I—I'm so sorry about Judy. I had no idea. Why didn't someone tell me this?"

"Would you have cared?" Noreen asked, searching through her tote bag for a tissue.

"Of course I would, and I still do." He paused and clutched his chest, as though in pain. "What about the baby? Did he die, too?"

Noreen was tempted to say that Bruce's son had also died, but she had a feeling he'd be able to see through her lie. "Judy's baby was adopted by a good family," she said, blowing her nose and dropping her gaze to the table.

"Do you know who they are? Do you have any information about the boy's whereabouts?"

"No, I do not, and I don't want to talk about this anymore." Dabbing at the moisture beneath her eyes, Noreen picked up her scissors to finish cutting the batting.

B.J.'s eyes narrowed. "I think you do know where he is. I have a feeling you're keeping it from me."

She shook her head vigorously. "I've told you all that I know. If you had wanted to be a part of your son's life, then you shouldn't have run off like you did."

His jaw clenched. "I told you I did not know Judy was pregnant."

Mike cleared his throat real loud, and everyone turned to look at him. "It's obvious that you two have some issues, but this isn't the place to be airing them out. The rest of us came here to learn how to quilt, and you're taking up our time with your personal problems. You oughta deal with all of this after class. I can't speak for everyone else, but you two going back and forth at each other is making me uncomfortable."

"Mike is right," Erika spoke up. "This isn't the place to be airing out your differences."

"Actually, it might be exactly the place," Jan interjected. "During the quilt classes I took at Emma's home up in Shipshe, everyone in the class had some sort of problem. We were all like a bunch of broken shells on the beach, and it seemed like there was no way to put the pieces together. But once we started talkin' about things, we felt better." Jan looked at Emma and smiled. "Our special teacher here not only taught us how to quilt, but gave us spiritual guidance as well."

"I take no credit for that," Emma was quick to say. "It was the Lord, guiding and directing my words. And because my students were open to change, He was able to heal hearts and give those who'd been hurting a new perspective." She paused a moment. "In Ezekiel 34:16 it says, 'I will seek that which was lost, and bring again that which was driven away, and will bind up that which was broken, and will strengthen that which was sick, saith the Lord God.'"

"That's a great verse, Emma," Jan said. "I think many of your students, includin' yours truly, were broken people in need of healing."

Noreen's shoulders stiffened, wishing she could flee the room. Well, she'd run out last week, but she wouldn't do it again. It would be a sign of weakness. "I don't need any guidance, or a new perspective," she muttered. "I signed up for these classes to learn how to quilt, and for no other reason. So let's get on with our lesson."

Emma looked at Lamar, hoping he might say something, but all he gave was a quick nod. Assuming that meant she should proceed with the lesson, Emma waited while everyone worked on their batting, and she sent up a silent prayer that this class would end on a good note. She never dreamed her quilt classes would hold so many surprises, but it seemed that each one of them had so far. Well, at least these quilting students were finally beginning to open up. She just hoped it would end with healing. For now, though, she needed to concentrate on teaching today's lesson.

Once Emma saw that everyone had finished cutting their batting, she held up one of the small wooden frames Lamar had made. "In order to create a smooth, even quilting surface, all three layers of your quilt will need to be put in a frame like this," she said. "If you were making a larger quilt, you would need a quilting frame that could stretch the entire quilt at one time." Emma paused to be sure everyone was listening; then she continued. "Since your wall hangings are much smaller than a full-size quilt, you can use a smaller frame such as this."

"That looks sort of like the embroidery hoop I've seen my grandma use," Jennifer said.

Emma nodded. "That's correct, and it's important when using this type of hoop to baste your entire quilt together through all three layers. This will keep the layers stretched tightly while you are quilting."

"Just be sure you don't quilt over the basting," Lamar added. "Because it will be hard to remove later on." He snickered. "Oh, and be careful not to stitch your blouse or shirt to the quilt, like one of our previous students did."

Jan rolled his eyes. "I'll bet it was my buddy Terry. That sounds like something he'd end up doing."

"You're right. That did happen to Terry," Emma agreed.

Jan slapped his knee. "Figured as much."

Emma then told the class about needle sizes, pointing out that it was best to try several and see which one seemed the most comfortable to use. "It's also a good idea to use a thimble on your middle finger for pushing the quilting needle, because the needle has to go through three layers of fabric to create the quilting pattern." Following that, she passed around a tray full of various thimbles. "Now, if everyone will choose a needle and thimble, you can begin the quilting process."

Emma waited until everyone had done as she asked, the whole time watching the body language between Noreen and B.J. They obviously both carried a lot of pain, and perhaps some serious regrets. She hoped they would be able to work it out and prayed that God would show Lamar and her if there was anything they could do. The Lord seemed to be using this quilt class already, by bringing B.J. and Noreen together after all these years. It had happened before, when Star and Jan learned they were father and daughter during Emma's first set of quilting classes. Then last year, Emma had been reunited with her sister, Betty, whom she hadn't even known about. Surely it was no coincidence in how that had all happened. If Noreen and B.J. could just set their hostilities aside and talk things through, perhaps their reunion might turn into something good.

Setting aside her thoughts, Emma explained that the next step would be to mark the design they wanted on their quilt top. "However," she added, "if you just want to outline the patches you've sewn with quilting stitches, no marking is necessary."

"You'll need to quilt close to the seam so the patch will be emphasized," Lamar interjected. "Oh, and don't forget, your stitches should be small and even. They also need to be snug but not so tight that they'll cause any puckering."

"I'll demonstrate on my own quilt patch," Emma said, picking it up and showing everyone the correct way to pull the needle and thread through the material to create the quilting pattern.

Mike's forehead wrinkled. "That looks too hard for me. My hands are big and the only thing I've ever sewn is a button on my shirt—and Phyllis had to help me with that."

"Speaking of Phyllis, how is her sister doing these days?" Emma asked.

"Better, but her leg's not healed well enough so she can be on her own yet," Mike replied. "They've been having some nasty weather in North Dakota lately, so Phyllis won't come home until she's sure Penny can manage okay without her."

"That's understandable," Kim spoke up. "It would be bad enough to be laid up with a broken leg, but trying to get around on crutches while wearing a cast could be dangerous, not to mention difficult."

"You've got that right," Mike agreed.

"Can we get back to our lesson now?" Noreen looked at Emma. "Will we be expected to finish the quilting process today?"

Emma shook her head. "Whatever you don't get done can be finished next week. During our final lesson, you will finish your wall hanging by putting the binding on." Emma glanced at B.J., who now seemed almost subdued as he continued to work on his project. "Now if any of you needs help today, just let either Lamar or me know." Emma motioned to Jan, sitting close to Kim. "I'm sure Jan would be willing to help out, too, since he's taken the class and is familiar with the procedure."

"I'd be more than willing to help." Jan smiled at Kim. "So don't hesitate to ask if you need anything."

She smiled in return. "Thanks, Jan. If I keep sticking myself with this needle, I may turn the whole project over to you."

He shook his head. "Naw, you're doin' just fine."

Emma moved over to stand beside Erika. "How are things going with you? Are you getting the feel for quilting?"

Erika shrugged. "I guess so. It seems easy enough."

"Not for me," Mike said. "I'm all thumbs. Some people think baiting a hook is hard, but that's nothin' compared to quilting."

"It just takes practice," Emma said. She gave Erika's shoulders a tender squeeze. "What you've done so far looks very nice. I think you have a knack for quilting."

Erika looked over her shoulder at Emma, and the faintest smile crossed her lips. "Thanks."

At least that's a step in the right direction, Emma thought as she moved back to the head of the table. *Now if we could just help Noreen and B.J. resolve their differences, I'd feel a lot better about things today.*

CHAPTER 27

At eleven o'clock, Emma suggested that everyone stop quilting and she served a snack of orange slices, fresh strawberries, and banana bread. That was fine with Jennifer. Her back was beginning to ache from sitting so long, and it made her uncomfortable to witness the undercurrent going on between B.J. and Noreen. Every time B.J. asked Emma a question or needed help with his stitching, Noreen said something derogatory.

That poor man, Jennifer thought as she bit into a juicy strawberry. *I wonder if he and Noreen can work out their differences. Everyone makes mistakes. Besides, it doesn't sound like B.J. knew anything about the consequences of his actions years ago.*

Walking around for a bit to get the kinks out of her legs and back, Jennifer looked around the tidy room that Emma kept. A battery-operated clock on one wall, a quilted wall hanging on another—and then there were the sewing machines, lined up in a row along the windowed wall, with the table they'd all been sitting around in the center of the room. There was no clutter, for everything in the room seemed to have a purpose.

Jennifer pressed on the small of her back, and it relieved the pain somewhat. She was definitely ready for this baby to be born.

Her thoughts shifted as she looked at the clock on the far wall. She could hardly wait to get home today to talk to Randy and find out how things went at the restaurant. She was almost afraid to ask, but oh, how she hoped he'd gotten that job.

———

"If everyone is finished with their refreshments you can continue working on your quilting projects," Emma instructed her students.

"I'm finished and ready to get back to work." Noreen pushed away from the table. "But let me help you carry the empty plates to the kitchen."

Emma's first thought was to tell Noreen that she could manage the dishes on her own, but thinking this would be a good opportunity to speak with her about B.J., she changed her mind. "Thank you, Noreen. I appreciate that."

"I can carry some dishes, too," Kim spoke up.

"That's alright," Emma said with a shake of her head. "I appreciate your offer to help, but there aren't many dishes, so I think Noreen and I can manage just fine."

"Oh, okay." Kim sat back down, and Emma and Noreen gathered up the dishes and left the room.

When they entered the kitchen, Emma told Noreen that she could put the dishes in the sink. "I'll wash them later this afternoon."

"How do you deal with not having a dishwasher?" Noreen asked, looking around the room.

Emma laughed. "I can't miss what I've never had. Why, I've been washing dishes by hand since I was a young girl. When my sister, Rachel, and I were too short to reach the sink, we had stools to stand on."

Noreen grimaced. "Before I got married, I used to wash dishes by hand, too, but it was definitely not my favorite thing to do."

"I guess we all have chores we'd rather not do."

Noreen gave a nod. "I suppose I should go back and get busy on my wall hanging. I don't want to get behind."

When Noreen started for the door, Emma quickly said, "Before you go, there's something I'd like to say."

"What's that, Emma?" Noreen asked, turning to face her.

Emma moistened her lips with the tip of her tongue, hoping her words would be well-received. "I don't mean to interfere, and I'm not trying to stick my nose in where it doesn't belong, but I wanted you to know that should you need to talk about your situation with B.J., I'm here to listen."

Lowering her gaze to the floor, Noreen quietly said, "I'll keep that in mind." Then she hurried into the next room.

Emma stayed in the kitchen a few moments longer, offering a prayer on Noreen's behalf. She obviously didn't want to discuss the situation, so Emma would just keep praying.

———————

"You're doin' a great job with that," Jan said, leaning over Kim's shoulder.

She smiled up at him. "Thanks. The stitching is a little tedious, but it's fun to be creative like this."

"I know what you mean," he agreed. "When I took Emma's quilting class, on the advice of my probation officer, I think some of the other students thought it was kinda weird to see a big guy like me with a needle and thread in his hands."

"You were on probation?" Erika jumped into the conversation.

Jan gave a nod.

"What'd you do?"

"Got busted for a DUI. Do you know what that means, Erika?"

She rolled her eyes. "Of course I do. I may be disabled, but I'm not stupid."

"Never said you were." Jan grunted. "You're too sensitive about bein' in that wheelchair, if you ask me."

"Well, I didn't ask," she shot back.

Emma quickly stepped forward and said, "We only have a few minutes left today, so if anyone has a question, now is a good time to ask."

Erika lifted her hand.

"What's your question?" Emma asked.

"What are we supposed to do with our wall hangings after they're done?"

"Whatever you like." Emma smiled. "I'm sure most of you will want to keep yours, but of course, if you want to give the finished project to someone as a gift, that's perfectly fine, too."

"I might give mine to the hospital where my dad works," Erika said. "I think it would look nice hanging in the waiting room inside the children's wing. That's why I'm including a smiley face in the center of my wall hanging."

"That's an excellent idea," Lamar spoke up. "Don't you think so, Emma?"

Emma nodded. It was good to see Erika coming out of her shell. And the fact that she wanted to give her wall hanging away was a good indication that she was thinking beyond her own struggles.

"Erika, now that you know how to sew, maybe you could make some other things the children at the hospital could enjoy," Emma said.

Erika tipped her head. "Like what?"

"What about some cloth dolls?" Jennifer suggested. "I'll bet any of the little girl patients would like to have a doll to play with and cuddle."

"That's a good idea. What do you think about that, Erika?" Emma questioned.

Erika shrugged. "I'll give it some thought."

Well, at least she didn't say no, Emma thought.

When Emma announced that class was over for the day, Noreen gathered up her things and skirted out the door. B.J. felt a sense of panic. He needed to talk to Noreen and try to find out more about his son. He felt sure she was hiding something.

Mumbling a quick good-bye to Emma and Lamar, B.J. rushed out the door. Seeing that Noreen was already at her car and about to get in, he hollered, "Please, wait, Noreen! I need to speak with you."

Ignoring him, she jerked the car door open, but she dropped her purse and half of the belongings fell out. She bent to pick it up, throwing the contents back in, giving B.J. time to step up to her car.

"Here, you forgot this," B.J. said, bending down to get the tube of lipstick that had rolled slightly under her car.

"I saw it." Noreen grabbed the tube when he handed it to her and threw it in her purse. B.J. noticed how she wouldn't even look at him, even though they were hunkered down, face-to-face.

"What are you afraid of, Noreen?" he asked. "Why won't you tell me more about Judy's death and the child you said was adopted?"

As Noreen rose to her feet, the turban on her head caught on the edge of the car door and ripped right off. "Oh no!" she gasped, as her midnight-black tresses tumbled out. "Now look what you made me do!"

B.J. bent to pick up the turban that had fallen on the ground. If he hadn't been so concerned about getting answers from her about Judy and their child, he might have laughed, seeing Noreen standing there like that. Laughing at her was the last thing he wanted to do, however. She was already mad enough at him. No wonder she'd worn the turban to the last two quilt classes. Apparently she'd dyed her hair black and didn't want any of the quilting students to see it. Well, he couldn't blame her for that. It looked terrible!

"Give me that!" Noreen snatched the turban out of B.J.'s hands, hopped into her car, and slammed the door. Then she started her engine and peeled out of the driveway in a spray of gravel. B.J.'s shoulders slumped. At this rate he would never get the answers he sought.

———

As Jennifer headed for home, she thought about everything that had happened during the quilt class. If it hadn't been for the tension between Noreen and B.J., she would have enjoyed herself, for she found quilting to be a stress reliever.

After I finish the wall hanging, I'll get started on a quilt for the baby, she decided. *And when Randy gets a job and there's more money coming in, maybe I can make a queen-sized quilt for our bed.*

Jennifer turned on the radio and hummed along to a couple of her favorite tunes. It made the drive less boring. Her ankles were a little swollen from sitting so long this morning, so she decided to get some things done at home and move around more this afternoon.

When she finally pulled into her driveway, she was relieved to see Randy's truck. Anxious to hear about his job interview, Jennifer climbed out of the car and stepped onto the front porch. "Now, what is this?" she murmured, picking up a small box lying near the door. It had a picture of a crib mobile inside on it. *I wonder where that came from.*

Stepping inside, Jennifer halted. In the middle of the living-room floor sat Randy, surrounded by baby furniture and unopened boxes. She couldn't believe it! "What is going on, Randy? All these things must have cost a fortune!"

"I know, I know. It's a lot to take in," Randy said, looking around the room. "But don't get upset, because I—"

"I was just going to ask where the little box by our door came from, and now I see all of this! Did you go back to the store and charge a bunch of baby things again?" Jennifer's jaw clenched as she awaited his answer.

Randy shook his head. "Calm down, Jen, and let me explain. I found them on the front porch when I got back from the restaurant this morning. I must have forgotten to bring in that smaller box you found. I have no idea where it all came from, and seeing all of this surprised me as much as it did you." Randy paused a moment and stood. "But before we talk about this more, just listen to this, honey." He reached for her hand. "I got the cook's position at the restaurant on Bahia Vista Street! Isn't that great news?"

She relaxed a bit and started to giggle. "Oh Randy, what an answer to prayer! After I called you about the job opening, I could hardly wait to get home to see how it went." Jennifer hugged him tightly, then rested her head against his chest, her whole body relaxing.

"Maybe things are starting to look up for us now," he said.

Leaning back to look at his face, Jennifer nodded tearfully. "I'm so glad about your new job, and I'm anxious to hear all the details, but first, what about all these baby things? How did they end up on our porch?"

"I don't know. There was no note or anything. But let's not worry about who gave us these gifts," he said, resting his chin on top of her head. "Someone obviously wanted us to have all this furniture, and we can sure use it. Wow, I can't believe that two good things happened today."

Jennifer smiled. "I'm grateful for the baby things and relieved that you didn't charge them. I just wish I knew who to thank."

"Me too, but let's just be thankful, okay?" Randy tilted her face up toward his and kissed her.

CHAPTER 28

I wonder if I could have won that drawing for baby furniture that I entered, Randy thought as he left the house Thursday morning to head to his new job. He hadn't given it much thought until now, but if he had won the drawing, then all the baby things that had been left on their porch would make sense.

I've still got plenty of time till I have to be at the restaurant, so think I'll stop by the store on my way to work and ask who won that drawing.

Monday had been Randy's first day on the job. He'd worked the breakfast and lunch shifts, and things had gone well. The owners of the restaurant were nice and had even stopped by the kitchen to tell him that several customers that morning had mentioned how good the food was. He hadn't been working a week yet, and already he was getting compliments. Boy, did that feel good, and to be working again felt even better.

Things seem to be looking up for us, Randy mused, turning onto the street where the store was located. *Since I have a job now, I don't have to worry about our bills, and the nursery is full of everything we'll need for the baby. Now all we need to do is try to be patient and wait for our little girl to be born.* He glanced at his reflection in the rearview mirror. *I wonder if she'll look like Jennifer or have more of my traits. Sure hope she doesn't end up with a nose that's a bit too long, like mine. Our little girl should have a cute turned-up nose, like her mother's.*

Randy parked his truck near the store and headed inside. He hoped he wouldn't encounter the salesclerk who'd been miffed when he'd returned the original baby furnishings. He couldn't really blame her for that. Most likely the sale personnel worked on commission, and she'd made a sale and lost it just as fast on the same day.

When Randy spotted a clerk in the baby section, he was relieved that it was a different woman. He stepped up to the counter and asked about the drawing that had recently been held. "I'm thinkin' I may have won, because last Saturday a bunch of baby items were left on our front porch."

"The winner would have been notified by phone first," the middle-aged clerk said. "Then once the address was verified, you would have been asked to come to the store to pick up your items."

Randy scratched his head. "Are you sure about that? I mean, if someone from the store tried to call and we weren't home, maybe the baby things were delivered and left on our porch."

"That wouldn't have happened."

"Can you at least tell me who the winner was?" Randy asked.

"Sorry, but I don't have access to that information, and even if I did, I would not be permitted to give it out. As I said before, if it had been you, there would have been a phone call."

"Okay, thanks for your time." Randy turned and hurried out of the store. This whole thing really had him puzzled. If he hadn't won the drawing, then who had left all that stuff at their home?

"Good morning," Anna Lambright said as she passed Kim near the breakfast buffet at the restaurant.

"Morning." Kim smiled. "I've missed seeing you. Guess that's what happens when we work different shifts."

Anna nodded. "I actually prefer the morning shift. It gives me a chance to get some afternoon sun on the beach. Have you been there lately?"

"Since tomorrow's my day off, I'll be going to Caspersen Beach in Venice with Emma, Lamar, Jan, and his daughter, Star." Kim smiled. "We're going to look for sharks' teeth, and I'm really looking forward to that."

"I didn't realize Jan's daughter was in Sarasota."

"She's supposed to arrive today. Jan should be picking her up soon."

"So you'll get to meet her for the first time?"

"Yes, and I'll admit, I'm a little nervous about it. But if she's anything like Jan, I'm sure she'll be nice."

Anna poked Kim's arm playfully. "You like him a lot, don't you? I can see it by the gleam in your eyes."

Kim laughed self-consciously. "Does it really show?"

"Yeah, but that's okay. If being with Jan makes you happy, that's a good thing."

"Thanks. Well, guess we both need to get to work. We don't want any of our customers complaining because they had to wait too long for their orders this morning."

"We sure don't. If I don't talk to you before, have a nice time at the beach tomorrow. I'll be thinking about you when I'm here working."

"I'm sure you'll get your chance to go to the beach again soon."

"You're right. My friend Mandy and I hope to go to Siesta Keys Beach." Anna gave Kim's arm a light tap. "See you later."

As Kim went to the kitchen to turn in her order, she thought about Jan and how much she'd come to care for him in such a short time. She was almost sure he felt the same way, because of the expression in his eyes when he looked at her.

I wonder if he's holding back because he knows he'll be going home in a few weeks. Maybe that's why Jan hasn't tried to kiss me, she thought. *He might not want to give me hope that there could be anything more than just a passing friendship between us. It's gonna be hard, but I need to accept that fact and be prepared for when he leaves.*

Jan parked his motorcycle in the parking lot and sprinted for the airport terminal. Star's plane should be arriving any minute, and he wanted to be waiting for her. He was anxious to see Star and glad they would get an opportunity to spend some time together here in the warmer climate.

Jan didn't have long to wait, for a few minutes later, he spotted Star heading his way. Her dark brown hair bounced in rhythm with each step as she came closer, and her face broke into a wide smile when she saw him. Was it Jan's imagination, or did his daughter look a bit older today? It hadn't been that long since he'd last seen Star, so he couldn't quite tell what the change really was.

"Hey, Dad, it's good to see you," she said, giving him a hug.

"It's great to see you, too, kiddo. I've missed you a lot."

"Ditto."

"If you don't have any checked luggage to pick up, we can head out to the parking lot." Jan gestured to the door leading outside.

"Nope. I knew I'd be riding home on the back of your bike, so everything I need is right here," she said, pointing to her backpack.

"That's great. Let's get going then."

As they walked across the parking lot, Jan looked over at his daughter. "I can't put my finger on it, but there's somethin' different about you."

"Do you like it?" Star fluffed up her hair. "Thought I'd go with a shorter style, and I got a body wave, too. It's a bit bouncy, but I really like the change."

"It's cute, Star. Yeah, real cute. Makes you look older, too."

"Well, it's time I start looking my age. I'm in my twenties now and can't look like a teenager forever."

Jan would have given anything to have been a part of Star's teenage years. He had missed out on so much of her life. It was hard not to look back and be full or regrets, but he knew he had to put the past to rest as best as he could. Star was back in his life now, and going forward was all that mattered. No more would he be missing out on anything pertaining to his daughter's life, and he looked forward to every bit of it.

When they reached the spot where Jan's motorcycle was parked, Star's eyebrows squeezed together. "What's this for?" she asked, pointing to the new sidecar Jan had purchased on Monday. "I hope you don't think I'm ridin' in that."

"Only if you want to. Thought you could put your backpack in the sidecar and then ride on the back of the bike with me. But when we head for home in two weeks, you might be more comfortable riding in the sidecar than on the back of the bike."

She shook her head vigorously. "No way, Dad! Sidecars are for old ladies and dogs."

He chuckled. "That's the main reason I got it, Star. Thought it'd be fun to give Brutus a ride."

Star rolled her eyes and whacked his arm. "You're gettin' strange ideas in your old age, Dad."

He grinned. "Not so strange, really. Think I'm just gettin' more settled."

Star shook her head, pulling her curls aside and clipping them at the back of her head. "Don't think you'll ever be settled. You're a free spirit, just like me."

"Can't I be a free spirit and settled at the same time?" he asked after they had put on their helmets. "Look at you. You're already making changes, like your hair."

"Yeah, right. So, are we going straight to Emma and Lamar's? It'll be nice to see them."

"Yep. We're goin' there right now. They're looking forward to seeing you, too. Oh, and Star, I've made plans for us to do something fun tomorrow with Emma and Lamar."

"What's that?"

"We'll be driving down to one of the beaches in Venice to look for sharks' teeth. Doesn't that sound like fun?"

"Sure, I guess so. But how are we gonna get there? There sure isn't room in your sidecar for both Emma and Lamar."

"Kim will be driving us in her car."

Star's body stiffened as she held her hands rigidly at her sides. "Kim's going, too?"

"Yeah. It'll be a good chance for the two of you to get acquainted."

"Who says I want to get to know her? I mean, she's really nothing to me."

"Well, she is to me, and I want you to know her."

"Let's get going," Star said, nudging Jan's arm. "I'm hot, tired, and hungry to boot."

"I'm sure Emma will have lunch waiting for us when we get there,"

Jan called over his shoulder as they took their seats on the bike. Turning on the engine, he headed out of the airport parking lot. He didn't care for Star's attitude toward Kim. It seemed as if she didn't want to meet his new girlfriend.

Kim is my girlfriend, isn't she? Jan asked himself as they sailed down the road. *Sure seems like it to me.*

CHAPTER 29

Sitting in the backseat of Kim's car between Emma and Lamar, Star clenched her teeth. The vehicle was small, and she felt cramped and couldn't see out either of the side windows. She had to settle for looking straight ahead, watching Kim's eyes in the rearview mirror as she drove them down Highway 41 toward Venice.

Star was usually uncomfortable when someone else was driving, and today was no exception. It didn't help that Kim kept glancing at Dad as they held a conversation. It was sickening to watch her dad smiling, nodding, and hanging on every word Kim said. Kim was no better. She kept laughing at the stupid little jokes and corny stories Dad told as they traveled along. Star would be glad when they got to Venice so she could get out of the car and be on the beach. *If Dad keeps acting like a teenager with a crush, I'll lose my appetite.*

"You're awfully quiet," Emma said, gently patting Star's arm. "Are you feeling okay today?"

"I'm fine. Just tired is all."

"That's understandable. We did get up pretty early this morn
not to mention the hours you traveled yesterday on the plane."

"I'll be fine." Star studied Emma. She was wearing a navy blue dr
black shoes, and black stockings, and her white head covering was ne
in place.

Lamar was dressed in a pale blue shirt and a pair of denim-looki
trousers held up with black suspenders. His straw hat rested in
hands and would no doubt offer him shade when the sun heated thin
up later today.

Star's dad, on the other hand, had on a pair of jeans, with his swi
trunks underneath. He also wore one of his biker vests, which covere
his back and chest, leaving his muscular arms showing. Star wondered
he'd worn it to show off for Kim.

She glanced down at the black shorts she'd worn, along with a ligh
beige tank top. At her dad's insistence, she'd brought her swimsuit alon;
but doubted that she'd wear it. She'd rather lie on the beach and soak up
the sun than go swimming. Star thought she might also try some song-
writing. She'd brought along a notebook and pen, in case she became
inspired by the sound of the waves or seagulls that would no doubt be
soaring overhead. If she kept busy with that, maybe she wouldn't be
expected to make conversation with Kim.

"I should have let you sit by the window," Emma said, breaking
into Star's musings. "You've never been to Florida before, and there's
so much to see on this route we are taking. Have you ever been along a
coastline like this?"

Star shook her head. "I saw it from the plane when I was flying
down here, but I've never been to the beach on the gulf before."

"Today should be fun for you then," Lamar interjected. "Before too

long, you'll be able to walk right out and put your feet in the water."

"I'm anxious to see it," Star admitted. "The closest thing to big water I've ever seen was Lake Superior when Mom and I lived in Minneapolis. It was only one time, though, when Mom was dating some guy from Duluth. He took us to a place called Two Harbors for the day."

"The lakes make up a large body of water, too," Lamar said. "It's a lot like the ocean when you're looking out toward the horizon and all you can see is water. Ocean waves are a lot bigger than what you'd see on a lake, though."

Star nodded. "I remember there were small waves on Lake Superior."

"Going to the lake sounds like a nice memory for you," Emma commented.

"It was a memory alright." Star remembered how she'd felt like a nuisance that day, so long ago. It had been pretty clear Mom's boyfriend Eddie wanted Mom all to himself. *Thank goodness Mom broke that relationship off quickly.*

Star wondered how things would go today between her dad and Kim. Would Kim resent her and act like she was in the way? Well, Star would make sure she wasn't in the way, because she had little to say to Kim. And if she said what was really on her mind, she would upset both Kim and Dad.

Feeling drowsier, Star leaned her head back against the seat and closed her eyes. "Wake me when we get there," she murmured.

Venice, Florida

"According to my GPS, this is the place," Kim said, pulling into the parking lot at Caspersen Beach. "And look, there are restrooms and a place to wash the sand off our feet, so that'll be handy."

Everyone climbed out of the car, and while Emma and Lamar

stretched their legs and Star headed for the restrooms, Jan went around to open the trunk, where they'd stowed all their beach supplies and picnic basket. He and Kim had purchased some beach chairs, in addition to two special scoops with long handles they could take turns using when they searched for sharks' teeth in the shallow part of the surf. Jan could hardly wait to try out one of those contraptions.

"I'm glad I brought plenty of sunscreen along," Kim said, joining him at the back of the car. "From the looks of the sky, and feeling how warm it is already this morning, I'm guessing we're in for a pretty hot day."

Jan patted his jeans. "Which is why I am wearing my swim trunks under here—so I can get cooled off in the water if I get too hot and sweaty."

"I'd thought about bringing my swimsuit," Kim said, "but I knew Emma wouldn't be wearing one, and knowing that the Amish dress modestly, I didn't want to offend her or Lamar." She glanced down at her turquoise shorts and rose-colored, sleeveless top. "Even this outfit, I wasn't too sure about."

"Aw, you look fine," Jan said. *More than fine,* he mentally added. "Star wore shorts today, too, so you're not alone, and I'm sure neither Emma nor Lamar will be offended."

Kim smiled. "Your daughter's a pretty young woman, Jan."

"Yeah. I think she got her mother's good looks, 'cause I still have mine." Jan chuckled and winked at Kim.

She swatted his arm playfully. "Seriously, I'm glad Star's here. I hope she and I will have a chance to really visit today. Since you and I were talking in the front seat on the way here, and she was sitting in the back, I didn't get the opportunity to ask her any questions." She paused while Jan reached into the trunk and took out the beach chairs. "I took US

41 so Star could see more of the scenery along the way. Maybe I should have suggested that she sit up front with me. Except for what I overhead her telling Emma and Lamar about the lake, I don't think she said much else."

Jan removed the rest of their things from the trunk. "Since we plan to spend a good portion of the day on the beach, you two will have lots of time to get acquainted. I'm sure you'll get to know her, so don't worry."

Between them, Jan and Kim managed to grab most of the things. Lamar carried the beach umbrellas, Star had the picnic basket, and Emma tucked an old quilt under her arm as they left the parking lot and headed down the path to the beach. "Good thing we thought to bring the umbrellas along," Jan added. "It'll be nice to have a shady place to get out of the sun for a while. And just listen. . . Think I can already hear the waves calling to me."

Sarasota

B.J. stared at the painting he'd started a few days ago. It was another beach scene, with the sun setting over the water in a rainbow of glorious colors. If he got it finished in time, it would make a nice thank-you gift for Emma and Lamar, which he hoped to give them at the last quilting class. So far, the seascape looked pretty good, and he was happy that he'd captured the colors just right, but something seemed to be missing. He just needed to figure out what and then add it in. Well, if he didn't get it done before the last class, he'd finish it when he returned home and mail it to them. He hadn't noticed many pictures on the walls in the Millers' house, but hoped Emma and Lamar would like this one. Trouble was, he had so little energy this week. *Probably the cancer taking its toll on me,* he decided. He'd felt better when he'd first arrived in Sarasota, and thought there might be some hope for him after all. But for the last few days, he'd felt his body weakening, and it made him wonder if it had been a mistake to leave Chicago and come here. Maybe he should have continued with his cancer treatments. The vitamins and herbs he'd tried so far hadn't done much to make him feel better. Perhaps he just needed to give them more time, or maybe he'd waited too long after his cancer diagnosis to try the more natural approach. Either way, B.J. knew he was in trouble, because he had coughed up blood the other day, and that wasn't a good sign. But he had to keep fighting and pressing on. In addition to the wall hanging he wanted to finish for his granddaughter and the painting for the Millers, B.J. had a son out there somewhere whom he wished to meet.

B.J. left his easel, turned on the CD player for some relaxing music, and reclined in his chair. *I just wish Noreen would talk to me without getting hot under the collar. I wonder what would happen if I looked up her phone number and gave her a call. But that might make her even angrier than she already is.*

Just then, B.J.'s cell phone rang. Glancing at the caller ID, he saw that it was his daughter, Robyn. B.J. hated to ignore Robyn's call, but the last thing he wanted to do was deal with her asking how he was doing. He dreaded the thought of telling his daughters the truth about his cancer, but sooner or later it would have to come out. He wasn't sure what would be worse: explaining that his cancer was spreading, or telling Jill and Robyn they had a stepbrother, who until recently, B.J. had known nothing about.

Finally, the phone quit ringing, and B.J. sat with his eyes closed, thinking things through. If he didn't get anywhere with Noreen this Saturday at the quilt class, then he would follow her home so they could talk.

The phone rang, startling Noreen as she sat in her recliner, half-asleep. She pulled herself out of the chair and went to answer it. "Hello."

"Hi, Mom. How's it going?"

Noreen yawned. "Uh, fine. How are you, Todd?"

"Doin' good. I didn't wake you, I hope."

"It's okay. I was just resting my eyes a bit. It's good to hear your voice, Son."

"Same here, Mom. Say, the reason I'm calling is Kara and I have some time off, and it's been awhile since we've seen you, so we thought we'd come to Sarasota for a visit."

Noreen's heartbeat quickened. As much as she wanted to see Todd and his wife, now wasn't a good time. Not with Bruce asking so many questions about Judy's son.

"Mom, did you hear what I said?"

"Umm. . .yes, I did."

"So, is it okay if we come down to see you?"

Think, Noreen, think. She swallowed hard. "Well, I'm kind of busy right now."

"Doing what?" he questioned.

"I'm taking a quilt class, and there are still two more lessons, so. . ."

"Are you tied up with the class every day of the week?"

"Well, no, but. . ."

"Kara and I can fend for ourselves while you're at the class. It'll give us some time to hang out on the beach or explore a few things in Sarasota that we haven't seen before."

"O–okay, if you're sure," Noreen finally conceded, unable to think of any other excuse. Her son and daughter-in-law meant the world to her, and she really did want to see them. It had been way too long since their last visit. Noreen just hoped Todd hadn't noticed her hesitancy.

She would just have to make sure Todd and Kara never met B.J. while they were visiting, because she certainly wasn't going to mention him.

CHAPTER 30

Venice

Your dad mentioned that you sing and play the guitar," Kim said, in an attempt to make conversation with Star. The women had been sitting on the old quilt Emma had brought along, while the men took a walk up the beach. So far, Star hadn't said more than a few words, not even to Emma.

Star merely shrugged, as she sifted grains of sand through her fingers.

Thank goodness Emma is here, Kim thought. *I feel invisible to Star.*

"Star not only plays and sings, but she's an accomplished songwriter," Emma put in. "In fact, she's had two of her songs published."

"That's awesome. I'll bet your dad's really proud of you."

"Yeah, I suppose," Star muttered, making no eye contact with Kim.

"I've always wanted to learn to play the guitar," Kim said, hoping Star would at least look at her. "Maybe you could teach me sometime."

Star pursed her lips. "That might be kinda hard since you live in

Florida, and we live up north."

"Maybe you could give Kim a few lessons before you go home," Emma suggested.

Star shook her head, looking back at Emma. "No can do. I didn't bring my guitar."

"Lamar has an old one you can borrow," Emma said.

Star's eyebrows shot up. "Lamar plays the guitar? I didn't think Amish people could own any musical instruments."

"Is that true?" Kim asked, turning to look at Emma.

"Some Amish do play the guitar or harmonica, but not in church. Sometimes when we get together with friends or family members we sing, and someone might play their guitar or harmonica," Emma explained. "Some of our young people have even been known to use a battery-operated keyboard."

Star whistled. "Now that's a surprise."

Emma laughed. "We're not entirely old-fashioned in our ways, and we do like to have fun when we gather with family and friends."

"You're right, Emma," Kim agreed. "I've witnessed that during our quilting classes whenever Lamar has teased you or told a joke."

Emma smiled. "My husband's a good man, and he's brought much joy into my life." She motioned to the men, who'd moved even farther down the beach. "Jan is a good man, too, and I think even in the short time you've known each other, he's come to care a good deal for you, Kim."

Kim glanced over at Star to gauge her reaction, but the young woman just sat, swirling her fingers in the sand.

A dragonfly darted between them, and flicking it away, Star rose to her feet. "Think I'm gonna take a walk down the beach a ways."

"Would you like some company?" Kim called as Star started to walk away. She thought this might be a good chance for them to talk privately and hopefully break the ice.

Star shook her head and kept walking in the opposite direction of the men.

"Oh great. My hopes of getting to know Star seem to be going nowhere." Kim leaned back on her elbows and sighed. "I'm afraid Jan's daughter doesn't like me very much. I think she might be upset that her dad's spending time with me."

Emma gave Kim's arm a tender pat. "She hasn't had the chance to get to know you yet. Just give her some time, and I'm sure she'll warm up to the idea of you and Jan seeing each other."

Kim drew in a deep breath and released it slowly. "I hope so, but then maybe it doesn't matter."

"What do you mean?"

"Jan and Star will be going back to Indiana in a few weeks, and then I'll probably never see them again." Kim slowly shook her head. "It's a shame, too, because even in the short time I've known Jan, I have really come to care for him."

Emma nodded. "I figured as much, but if things are meant to work out between you, then they will."

"I wish I had your confidence." Kim shaded her eyes as she watched Jan and Lamar turn and head back in their direction, and then remembering she'd put her sunglasses in her tote bag, she reached inside and put them on. "I sometimes have a hard time making decisions and don't always make right choices," she admitted. "I wish I had a guidebook that would show me what to do."

"Actually, there is," Emma said. "It's the Bible, and in Proverbs 3:6 it says, 'In all thy ways acknowledge him, and he shall direct thy paths.'" Emma crossed her ankles and clasped her fingers around one knee.

"When Lamar and I first met, I was confused about our relationship, but after praying about it, the Lord showed me what to do. If you trust God, and seek His will, He will show you what to do concerning Jan and his daughter."

Kim smiled. Emma was a wise woman with a heart for people. Sitting here, the old quilt beneath them, made Kim feel relaxed and hopeful. It almost felt like a healing quilt. She was glad she'd chosen to take Emma's quilting classes. But choice had nothing to do with her relationship with Jan. Things had just seemed to happen in the short time they'd known each other, and now she had strong feelings for him and wasn't sure what to do. *Will I be able to turn those feelings off once he goes back to Indiana?* she wondered. *I guess Emma's right; I need to pray about this.*

———

"Have you found any yet?" Jan called to Lamar, after they'd gathered up the long-handled scoops and waded into the water in search of sharks' teeth.

"Just a few. How's it going with you?"

"Not too bad. Found a couple of good ones, I think." Jan gestured to the plastic bag in his hand. "Got a few shells in there, too." He was glad he'd stripped down to his swim trunks. Otherwise, his jeans would be as wet as Lamar's trousers. Even though Lamar had rolled them up to his knees, his trousers were wet almost up to his waist from the waves washing in.

Jan watched with interest as a turtle came out of the water, walked up the beach, and meandered along the path that led to the road. A lot of interesting things could be found here on Caspersen Beach.

"Sure am glad that fella we ran into up the beach showed us what to do, or I probably wouldn't have found any sharks' teeth at all," Jan said, lifting his long-handled scoop to see what all he'd trapped.

Lamar straightened and rubbed the small of his back. "I don't know about you, but I'm about ready to take a little break. Why don't you see if either Kim or Star would like to take my place for a while?"

"I can't ask Star right now." Jan pointed down the beach. "Look, she's way down there, sittin' on a rock by the water. I'll see if Kim wants to try her hand at this, though. It's a lot of fun, and I'll bet she'd enjoy it as much as I do."

Jan followed Lamar to the place where Kim and Emma sat and knelt beside them on the sand so he wouldn't mess up Emma's quilt.

"Take a look at all the fossilized sharks' teeth we've found," Lamar said, holding his bag open for Emma to see.

Emma's eyes widened. "Oh my! Some of them are so small; I don't know how you even spotted them."

"They get trapped in the scooper," Lamar explained. "But I'll have to admit, it was hard to see some of those littler ones."

Jan showed Kim what was inside his plastic bag.

Her eyebrows lifted. "Wow, those are sure impressive! The only thing I've ever found on the beach that looked that interesting was a man's ring."

"Really? Where'd you find that?" Jan asked.

"On Lido Beach a few weeks ago. It had some initials carved in it. I think it may have been someone's class ring."

"What did you do with it?" Emma questioned.

"Took it home and put in my jewelry box." Kim pushed a wayward strand of hair off her forehead. "I'd return the ring to its rightful owner if I knew who it belonged to."

"Maybe you oughta take it to a jewelry shop and see if it's worth some money," Jan suggested.

Kim shook her head. "Think I'll hang on to it for now. Or maybe I'll run an ad in the paper about it."

"Why don't you bring it to class with you?" Emma said. "I'm curious to see what it looks like."

Kim gave a nod. "If I don't forget, I will."

"Right now, how'd you like to use one of the scoops and try to find some sharks' teeth with me?" Jan asked Kim.

"That sounds like fun, but if you and Lamar want to keep looking, I can wait."

"That's okay," Lamar was quick to say. "I'm ready to take a break. Bending over like that and then lifting the handle of the scoop made my back ache a bit." He smiled at Emma. "I know it's not lunchtime yet, but I could sure use a snack."

Emma smiled and motioned to their lunch basket. "I think that could be arranged."

Jan reached out his hand and helped Kim to her feet. Then Lamar handed her his scoop. "Now you need to show Jan how it's done," Lamar teased.

Kim laughed. "Emma and Lamar are sure great," she commented as she and Jan walked toward the water.

"You got that right." Jan glanced down the beach and saw that Star was still there. *She's not very sociable today,* he thought. *Maybe she just needs some time alone. She's probably enjoying the warm sun and salty air. Sure wouldn't be gettin' that if she was at home right now.*

———⋅———

As Star sat on a large rock with her legs outstretched, she couldn't help but enjoy the cool water as it splashed gently over her bare feet. Hearing a helicopter buzz overhead, she looked up. When it moved out of sight, she noticed several pelicans skimming the water as though searching for fish. It was funny to watch them fly straight up then dive right down to snatch their prey.

A slight breeze lifted the bangs from her forehead as she shielded her eyes from the glare of the sun. Glancing up the beach a ways, she saw her dad and Kim in the water, looking for sharks' teeth, no doubt.

Star pulled her hair back and secured it with a clippie. Her hair wasn't as long as it had been before, but there was still enough to clip back, letting the shorter ends fall free. She'd hated sitting there on Emma's old quilt as Kim plied her with questions and couldn't wait to get off by herself so she think and try to enjoy the day.

Glancing at the water again, she noticed farther out, where it appeared to be deeper, a group of teenagers laughing and shouting to each other as they frolicked in the waves.

I wonder what it would have been like to have had friends to hang out with when I was their age, Star mused. She thought about her own teen years and how she'd preferred to be a loner rather than making friends. She could almost hear her mom saying, "You've pushed people away most of your life. No wonder you have no friends."

Star hated to admit it, but Mom was right. She did push most people away. She'd seen too many complications where having friends was concerned. They could be friends one minute and turn on you the next. Star's dad was like having a best friend, but that was different. She knew him well enough to know he'd never turn on her. But he was doing a good job of ignoring her today.

Star drew her knees up to her chest, watching in disgust when her dad put his arm around Kim's waist. She nearly gagged when he kissed Kim on the mouth. Didn't he care that Lamar and Emma were sitting on the quilt, no doubt watching them?

After knowing the Millers as long as he has, Dad oughta realize that married Amish couples like them never display that kind of affection in public. And what in the world is he thinking, getting involved with Kim? If she's falling for him, the way I think he is her, then he's gonna break her heart when we go back home. Maybe Mom was right when she told me that Dad walked out on us when I was a baby. Maybe he lied when he said it was Mom who took me and ran off.

Looking away, Star knew her thoughts were running amok. Mom had already admitted that she'd been the one to leave. Still, it did seem odd that after all these years, her dad had never had a serious relationship with a woman.

Could there be a deep-seated reason for that? Star wondered. *Maybe he's never really gotten over his feelings for Mom.* She shook her head, trying to clear her jumbled thoughts. Even if that were the case, Star's mother was married now and living in Fort Wayne, Indiana, so it was too late for her and Jan to become a couple again.

Star glanced up the beach once more and saw Dad and Kim with their heads together, apparently looking at something in one of their scoops.

I don't know what I'm going to do about this, Star fumed, *but I've gotta think of something before Dad gets some dumb idea about moving to Florida.*

"This is hard work," Kim said as she dumped a scoopful of shells onto the sand. "And it's difficult to see if there are any sharks' teeth in all the debris." Truth was, she still felt a bit breathless after Jan's kiss. If the tender way he'd looked at her before the kiss was any indication of the way he felt, he had fallen for her as hard as she had for him.

"After you've scooped up some stuff, try lifting the wire basket in and out of the water to rinse the sand off, and then shake it back and forth. Most of the bits and pieces you don't want will sift right through the basket, hopefully leaving just the good things behind."

"For a guy who's never done this before, you sure know a lot about it," Kim said.

Jan smiled. "Guess I'm just a quick learner."

"Lamar seemed to be enjoying himself when he was out in the water with you," Kim mentioned. "It was fun to watch him plodding through the water with his pants rolled up to his knees."

"Yeah." Jan chuckled. "He said he's been wantin' to do this ever since he and Emma came down for the winter. I'm glad he invited us to come along."

"I wish I could have brought Maddie with us today," Kim said wistfully. "She would have had fun, too. But there wasn't room in the car for her, so I asked one of my neighbors to check on her for me today."

"We'll have to bring Maddie along the next time we go to the beach," Jan said. "I'll bet Star would enjoy seeing your dog, too. Especially since she looks so much like my Brutus."

Kim turned to look down the beach to where Star had been sitting and noticed that she wasn't there anymore. Then she spotted her seated on the quilt beside Emma and Lamar. They were chatting away like best friends.

I wish she would visit with me like that, Kim thought. *I'll never get to know Jan's daughter if she won't converse with me.*

Kim's thoughts were halted when someone started shouting. Looking out at the water, where some teenagers had been swimming, she noticed that they seemed to be out pretty far. At first, she thought they were just fooling around, but then one of them hollered, "Help! Help! My friend is drowning!"

With no hesitation, Jan dropped his scoop, jumped into an oncoming wave, and started swimming out to the kids.

Kim stood on the shore, hands sweating and heart racing as she grabbed Jan's scooper. She hoped Jan was a strong swimmer and that the kid he was trying to save wouldn't pull him down.

Chapter 31

"What's going on? What's my dad doing?" Star asked Emma and Lamar when she caught sight of Jan swimming out through the waves. "He sure can't be looking for sharks' teeth way out there."

"I—I don't know." Emma placed her hands parallel with her eyebrows, gazing out to where Star was pointing. "It looks like there are some young people out there, and Jan seems to be swimming in their direction. She turned to Lamar. "Can you tell what's going on?" The sun was at an angle that made the water glare back, and each ripple and wave glistened in the sun's reflection, making it hard to see.

Lamar shook his head, shading his eyes. "Not from this far, Emma. My vision isn't as good as it used to be."

"Mine either," she said. "And my glasses are only for close-up work."

"Well, my eyes are good, and I don't like what I see!" Star clambered to her feet.

Just then, Kim came running up from the water's edge, red-faced and panting. "Someone's in trouble out there, and Jan went to help, but we need to call for assistance right away." Dropping to her knees, she reached for her canvas tote, which she'd left on the quilt, and rummaged through it for her cell phone.

A sense of panic welled up in Star's soul, and with her heart pounding, she dashed to the shoreline. *Dear God, please don't let my dad drown. I need him so bad!*

"Maybe I should swim out and see if I can help Jan," Lamar said, starting to rise from the quilt.

Emma clasped his arm as he helped her get up. "Oh Lamar, I wish you wouldn't try to do that. I don't think you're up to something so strenuous."

Lamar frowned. "I can't just stand here and do nothing, and I'm not a *schwechlich mann,* you know."

"Of course you're not a weakly man," Emma was quick to say. "That's not what I meant."

Lamar folded his arms. "Sure sounded like it to me, but it doesn't matter. All that matters now is that they need help."

"Let's wait and see if Jan needs any assistance," Kim said after she'd made the 911 call. "If he does, then I'll swim out there myself. Ever since I was little I've been like a fish in the water."

"I guess that would be best," Lamar conceded. "Sounds like you're a stronger swimmer than me."

They stood watching while another small crowd of people gathered, pointing and observing as Jan swam toward the teens. A middle-aged man ran up to them and offered to call 911.

"Thank you, sir, but I already have," Kim answered and scurried back down to the water's edge to stand near Star.

"Oh dear." Emma sighed. She felt so helpless. She had heard the concern in Kim's usual bubbly voice. *And poor Star. She must be frantic with worry about her father right now.* All Emma could do was pray and hope for the best.

———

As Jan swam out to the drowning victim, he mentally recounted all that he'd learned during his training as a lifeguard shortly after graduating from high school. *Enter the water. Approach the victim from behind so he doesn't pull you down. Place your arms under the victim's armpits and bend your arms back so they're pointing at yourself, and hold on tight.*

Even though it had been more than twenty years, the instructions Jan learned back then had stuck with him. Thanks to his job as a roofer, he was in pretty fair shape physically. There was no doubt that swimming against this current was tiring.

Jan approached the teenage boy, who was now bobbing up and down, while gulping in water and gasping for air, and his training took over. He did everything just like he'd been taught. Jan pushed aside any fears about what could be swimming beneath the waters around them and concentrated fully on the boy.

The kid was in a panic, of course, and Jan had to remind him over and over to calm down. "Try to relax. You're gonna be okay. Trust me. I've got you."

Drawing in a deep breath, Jan swam toward shore, pulling the boy along. As he drew closer, he spotted Star and Kim standing near the edge of the water.

"I called 911, so help should be here soon," Kim said as Jan laid the nearly unconscious boy on the sand.

"Good," Jan panted. "But we can't wait for help to arrive. The kid could have water in his lungs, and he needs mouth-to-mouth resuscitation right now."

"I'll do it, Dad," Star volunteered, falling to her knees in order to help. "I've had CPR training. Besides, you look exhausted and oughta rest for a while."

"Star's right," Kim agreed, getting on the other side of the boy. "If necessary, she and I can take turns with the resuscitation."

Jan couldn't argue with their assessment, so he flopped down on the sand to catch his breath and watched as the women took over. Jan cast a quick glance toward the ocean and caught sight of a dolphin not far from where the teens had been. Looking back at the teenaged boy, he sent up a silent prayer, asking for the kid to be okay.

Emma and Lamar, as well as the other teenagers who had been in the water, gathered around with anxious expressions. Star turned the young man's head to one side, allowing the water he'd swallowed to drain from his mouth and nose. Then she turned his head back to the center and began mouth-to-mouth resuscitation, while Kim checked the boy's pulse. The small crowd of people that had quickly congregated stood far enough back to give them room.

Jan accepted a bottle of water that a middle-aged man offered him and said thanks when asked if he was alright. "Yeah, I'm okay." It was plain that everyone around was concerned.

When the boy started to breathe and cough, the crowd sighed with relief. Jan was hopeful that the kid would make it now.

A short time later, sirens wailed in the distance. Hopefully, the boy hadn't taken in too much water and wouldn't end up with complications.

Sarasota

Mike had just taken a seat on his front porch, to read the paper and enjoy the sun, when a sporty-looking black car pulled onto his driveway. A few minutes later, Mike's older brother, Keith, who lived in Orlando, got out of the car.

"Hey, Brother, it's good to see you!" Mike set his newspaper aside and stood. "What brought you to Sarasota today?"

Keith stepped onto the porch, and the brothers shook hands, then drew each other in for a hug and slap on the back. Afterward, Keith groaned as he sank into the wicker chair next to Mike's. "I was hoping you'd be here, because I need to talk."

Mike moved his chair closer to Keith's and sat down. He'd never seen his brother look so serious. "You seem upset. Is something wrong?" he asked, giving Keith his full attention.

Keith nodded, pulling his fingers through the ends of his thick blond hair. "I'm just gonna come right out and say it. Gina's left me."

Mike bolted upright, feeling as though an electrical current had been shot through him. "You're kidding, right?"

Keith slowly shook his head. "Wish I was."

"But why? What happened?" Mike could hardly believe his sister-in-law would have done such a thing. His brother had gotten married later in life, concentrating on getting settled into his career first. Gina was quite a bit younger than Keith, but from the beginning of their relationship she seemed to adore Keith. He'd given her everything she could have asked for—a big house, fancy car, and money to satisfy all of her whims. It made no sense that she would leave.

"Gina says I'm never around—that I'm not there for her and the kids anymore." Keith reached up and massaged the back of his neck. "She's seeing the clown who coaches Robbie's Little League team. Says he's more of a father to our son that I've ever been. Besides, the guy is a good-looking dude. At least, she thinks he is. Now tell me, how can I compete with that?" He moaned, leaning forward as though in great pain. "I just don't get it. I've worked hard all these years so my wife and kids could have nice things. They've wanted for nothing, and this is the thanks I get. I feel like I've been kicked in the teeth."

"I don't know what to say, Keith, except I'm sorry. Is there a chance you can win her back?"

"I don't think so. Gina made it pretty clear that she's done with me."

"Have you thought about going to see a marriage counselor?" Mike asked. "Would Gina be willing to try that?"

Keith shook his head. "I'm not about to let some shrink get inside my head. Besides, Gina's pretty involved with this baseball geek, and I doubt she'd agree to go for counseling. I think it's too late. I'm not sure how I could have been so dense, but I never even saw this coming."

"You ought to at least give counseling a try," Mike said, rising to his feet. "You can't walk away from fifteen years of marriage."

"You're right. It's tough. But if divorce is what she wants, then who am I to stand in her way?"

Irritation welled in Mike's soul as he glanced out at the bay. "It doesn't sound to me like you care that much if you're not willing to fight for your marriage."

"I do care," Keith snapped back. "It's just that Gina wants me to give up my career and hang around at home all the time."

"Maybe you should cut back on your hours at work," Mike suggested.

Keith looked at Mike like he'd taken leave of his senses. "No way. I'm not willing to do that. I've worked too hard to get where I am today. Not to mention having recently been offered a big promotion."

Mike knew that his brother's job as a sales rep for a big Orlando company put him on the road a lot. Last Christmas Mike had overhead Gina telling Phyllis that Keith was gone so much that she was beginning to feel like a widow. What had shocked him most that day was when Phyllis responded by saying that she could completely understood because she thought Mike cared more about his boat than he did her. At the time, Mike had brushed it off, thinking the women were overdramatizing. He'd rationalized his need to be on his boat so much. After all, didn't working long hours to give his wife nice things count for anything? Surely she should be able to figure out that his desire to make a good living proved how much he cared for her.

But hearing about his brother's situation caused Mike to stop and think about his own life and what was truly important to him. All these years Mike had thought his brother had the perfect life—a great career, good money, and a wife and kids who adored him. From as far back as Mike could remember he'd wanted to be successful like his older brother, but now he asked himself if success was really that important.

It was hard to figure people out or understand the logic behind their thinking, but Mike knew one thing for sure: he didn't want his own marriage to end up like Keith and Gina's. He'd been blinded by what he thought his brother had. When Phyllis got home, Mike planned to spend less time on the boat and more time with her.

CHAPTER 32

Hey, kiddo, how'd you sleep last night?" Jan asked when Star came out of the bathroom on Saturday morning, rubbing her eyes.

She frowned as she stretched her muscles and tilted her head from side to side. "I would've slept a whole lot better in a bed instead of on the couch."

"Why don't you take the spare room, and I'll sleep on the couch. I offered to do that when you first got here."

Star shook her head. "Naw, the couch only makes into a double bed, and the bed in the guest room is a queen. You need that bigger bed more than I do, Dad." She released a noisy sigh. "I don't see why we can't stay in a hotel instead of here with Emma and Lamar."

"They invited us to stay with them, Star, and I don't wanna hurt their feelings," Jan explained in a low voice so the Millers wouldn't hear. "You know as well as I do what good people they are, and sleeping on the couch a few more nights isn't going to hurt you. Besides, with the money we're saving, it'll give us more to spend on the way home."

"I guess you're right on both counts, but when are we leaving?" she asked with a hopeful expression.

"Thought we'd head out the Monday morning after the last quilting class. That'll give us plenty of time to make it home before you have to be back at work."

"What about your business, Dad? Don't you think you should go home sooner, in case a big roofing job comes in?"

Jan shook his head. "Terry's there. If something develops, he can handle it on his own. Besides, with the cold weather they're having up north, it's not likely that anyone's gonna want their roof replaced till spring."

"Guess you're right about that, too."

Jan paused before heading to the kitchen, where the aroma of fresh coffee beckoned him. "I know I told you this on the way home from the beach, but I'm real proud of the way you revived that boy who almost drowned."

"What I did was nothing, Dad. You were the hero, going out there to rescue him. When the boy's parents tracked you down afterward to say thanks, I could tell they thought you were a hero, too."

"I just followed my instincts. Sure couldn't stand there and let the kid drown." Jan smiled. "I was relieved when his parents said their son was going to be okay. That could have ended in disaster."

"Yeah, I know." Star took a few steps and halted. "Before we go into the kitchen, could I ask you a question, Dad?"

"Sure thing, kiddo, you can ask me anything."

She moistened her lips with the tip of her tongue. "It's about Kim."

"What about her?"

"I've been wondering how serious you two are about each other.

I saw you kiss her when we were at the beach in Venice, and. . ."

"I like her very much, Star," Jan was quick to say. "Kim and I have a lot in common, and I enjoy bein' with her more than any woman I've ever met." He bumped Star's arm playfully. "Present company excluded, of course."

Star dropped her gaze to the floor. "I see."

Jan put his thumb under her chin and lifted it until she was looking directly at him. "You're not jealous, I hope."

"No. Uh, yeah, maybe I am a little."

"Well, don't be. You're my daughter, and no one will ever come between us. You are still my number-one girl, and that'll never change. For the rest of the time we're here, I hope you'll give Kim a chance to get to know you better, because she's feeling some negative vibes coming from you." Jan pulled Star close and kissed her forehead. "Now let's get in there and see if Emma has breakfast ready, 'cause the Saturday quilters will be here soon."

"Don't see why we have to be here for that," Star complained. "Can't the two of us do something fun today? We could check out Siesta Key Beach or join one of those sightseeing tours at the marina."

"We'll do something fun after the class," he said. "I want to be here to see how things go, and maybe help out if I'm needed."

She grunted. "I thought the Millers were teaching the class."

He tweaked the end of her nose. "They are, smarty, but I want to be there in case Emma and Lamar get busy and someone has a question or needs extra help."

Star rolled her eyes. "Someone, like Kim?"

He shrugged. "Maybe."

Star opened her mouth as if to respond, but Emma called to them from the kitchen. "If you two are ready, breakfast is on the table."

Jan nudged Star's arm. "Guess we'd better get in there. We can talk later."

———

Noreen's hands felt clammy as she gripped the steering wheel. She dreaded going to the Millers' house for the fifth quilting class, because she hated the thought of seeing B.J. again. And knowing Todd and Kara would be here next week made her all the more apprehensive. If only they would wait to come for a visit until B.J. went back to Chicago. *I should be dancing on air knowing that my son and his wife are coming for a visit. Instead, I'm dreading it,* Noreen fumed. The more she thought about it, the more upset she became. *Bruce Jensen is messing everything up. I shouldn't be surprised, though; he's good at it.*

"I know one thing," Noreen barked, hitting the steering wheel to affirm her decision. "No matter how much prying B.J. does, he will never know about Todd!"

She looked in the rearview mirror, and grimaced at her reflection. Since B.J. had seen her hair last week when her turban fell off, she figured there was no point in wearing it again today, as he might say something about it in front of the others.

I don't know why I care what he thinks or doesn't think, Noreen scolded herself. Besides, she'd seen her hairdresser this week, gotten her hair cut, and had some highlights put in, which had toned down the black a bit. Her hair wasn't to her liking yet, but at least it looked better than when she'd first put that awful color in.

Glancing at her gas gauge, Noreen realized she'd let her tank get low, so she pulled into the nearest gas station. It wasn't like her to let it go below half. Her only excuse was that she'd been under so much stress and wasn't thinking clearly or paying attention to details, the way she normally did.

Noreen got out of her car, and as she pumped the gas, she thought about the class reunion she'd been invited to attend this evening. Ever since she'd dyed her hair, she'd struggled with whether to go or not. Through all Noreen's years of teaching, her hair had never been as dark as it was now. But was that a good reason to stay home? Most likely, the students wouldn't remember how her hair had looked back then, unless they got out their class yearbooks and checked out the teachers' photos.

If I don't go, I will miss seeing some of my old students, and any of my coworkers who might also be there, she told herself. *No, I'm going, even if I look like an old fool. Even if just for a few hours, maybe the enjoyment of seeing everyone again will take my mind off everything else that's been happening in my life lately.*

When B.J. arrived at the Millers', Noreen was just getting out of her car. He fully intended to ask her about Judy's son again, but by the time he'd gotten out of his car, she was already on the porch. He noticed everyone's vehicles were there, and most likely, the other quilters were waiting for them. Even so, while he had this opportunity, B.J. wanted to try once more to get some answers from Noreen.

Maybe Emma won't answer the door right away, and I'll get to Noreen before she goes into the house, B.J. thought as he made his way slowly across the yard. He was more tired than usual today and couldn't walk as fast as he normally did. There was no doubt that his illness was taking a toll on him, and he was powerless to stop it.

"Please don't start badgering me again," Noreen snapped when B.J. stepped onto the porch. "As I told you before, I don't know where Judy's son is, and I don't want to talk about this anymore. I just hope you can live with the fact that you took advantage of an innocent girl." Her mouth quivered. "If Judy hadn't gotten pregnant, she'd still be alive today."

"You don't know that," B.J. shot back, taking deep, deliberate breaths to slow his racing heart. "People die from many causes." *Like cancer,* he mentally added, gripping the porch railing, so he wouldn't lose his balance.

Now don't let me fall apart in front of Noreen. B.J. willed his weakened body to keep going, as he fought to overcome a dizzy spell.

Noreen turned her back on him and said nothing, just knocked on the door.

"I know you blame me for your sister's death, and if there was anything I could do to change the past, I surely would. Please try to understand," he implored. "Judy and I were both young, and I was still living under my parents' roof. I was just a teenaged boy, but if I'd known about everything, I wouldn't have left like I did. Please listen to me, Noreen." B.J. didn't like talking to someone's back, especially when they gave no response, but he continued anyway. "What teenage kid doesn't make mistakes? I'm not trying to make excuses for myself, but I had no idea about any of what happened. Not about Judy being pregnant, her having the baby, or about her death."

Noreen continued to ignore him and was practically pounding on the Millers' front door.

"Just try to put yourself in my place, Noreen," B.J. said, hoping she would finally realize what it was like for him to find out about his and Judy's child after all these years.

Noreen turned around suddenly, and looked as if she were about to say something, when Emma, with her usual cheery smile, opened the door. "Good morning. I'm glad you're both here."

When they entered the house, Emma looked at Noreen and her eyes widened. "Oh, you've done something different with your hair."

Noreen's cheeks turned pink. "Uh, yes. I changed the color and had it cut a bit shorter."

As worn out as he felt, B.J. stifled a laugh, and then hastily coughed to cover it up. Emma's shocked expression said it all. But she didn't laugh, either—just invited them to join the others at the table. Even in his own misery, B.J. could still find humor in this situation, and he couldn't wait to see the reaction of the other quilters when they saw Noreen's hair.

CHAPTER 33

I t's good to see you all here," Emma said as she looked at everyone seated around her table. "I hope each of you have had a good week."

A few heads bobbed, but Noreen, looking as if she had eaten a sour cherry, said nothing, and neither did B.J., who sat with his shoulders slumped and head down. It tugged at Emma's heartstrings, making her wish once again that there was something she could do to help these two. But she didn't want to be pushy. If they wanted her or Lamar's help, surely they would ask.

"We had an interesting Friday," Kim spoke up with enthusiasm. "Jan saved a boy from drowning."

"Really? Wow! Tell us about it," Jennifer said, leaning forward with a wide-eyed expression.

Jan shrugged his shoulders. "It was nothin' really. Just did what most anyone woulda done."

"You're being modest," Lamar interjected. "Out of everyone on the beach, you were the only one who swam out to rescue the boy. You gave it no thought, just jumped into action."

"That's right, and you could have drowned in the process," Kim said.

"Well, I'm perfectly fine, and so is the boy." Jan smiled at Kim. "And don't forget, you and Star took turns reviving the kid till the paramedics got there."

"Who's Star?" Erika asked.

"She's my daughter," Jan replied. "She flew down here from Indiana so we could spend some time together, see some sites in Florida, and visit our friends, Emma and Lamar."

"By the way, where is Star today?" Kim questioned. "I thought she might join our quilting class."

"She took my bike and headed out to see what Sarasota's all about."

"It's a shame she didn't stick around. Didn't you say she was in the quilting class you took, Jan?"

He nodded.

"I invited her to join us," Emma said, "but she said she'd rather do something else." Emma gestured to the wall hangings everyone had begun quilting the previous week. "I think we'd better get busy now and continue with the quilting process. Since next week is our final class, we'll do the binding that day, and then you can take home your finished projects."

Mike cleared his throat before speaking. "Phyllis called last night, and she'll be coming home on Monday, so she'll be able to attend the class next Saturday."

"That will be nice," Emma said, smiling. "Then you can show her everything you've learned about quilting."

"I'd thought about just letting her take my place but changed my mind," Mike said. "Something happened this past week that made me realize I don't spend enough time with my wife. I'm gonna change all that when Phyllis gets home. There's a lot of lost time to make up for."

———※———

While everyone quilted, Jan sat beside Kim, watching as she moved her needle in and out of the material like she'd been doing it all her life. *Wish I didn't have to go home a week from Monday*, he thought with regret. *I'd like to stay longer and spend more time with Kim. I could check with Terry, I guess. If we don't have any houses to roof in the next few weeks, maybe I could hang around Sarasota awhile longer.*

Jan stroked the ends of his beard as he contemplated the idea. *But then Star has to get back to her job, so unless she'd be willing to fly back to Indiana alone rather than riding home with me, I don't see any way I can stay here longer. Maybe I'll discuss it with her later today.*

Jan's thoughts took him back to the quilting classes he'd taken with Emma's first group of students. It had been during their fifth class that he'd learned Star was his daughter. And now, being here in this quilt class had brought another special person into his life. He fixed his gaze on Kim once more and smiled. She really was a special gal.

———※———

At eleven o'clock, Emma excused herself to get refreshments, and Lamar went with her. They returned several minutes later with some chocolate chip cookies and a tray with crackers and cheese.

"Delicious as usual," Jan said, biting into one of the cookies and smacking his lips.

Noreen rolled her eyes. *That man is so ill-mannered. I don't understand what pretty little Kim sees in him.* She accepted the cup of tea Emma handed her. *Each to his own, I suppose, but a man like that would never appeal to me.*

She glanced at B.J. *I can't believe I was actually attracted to that man when I met him at the first quilting class. But not anymore. My sister was sure taken with him, though, and I'm not sure why. Of course, he was much younger then, and from what Judy said, he was quite good-looking. It's strange, but B.J. looks much older today than he did on the first day of our class.*

Noreen studied B.J.'s face, noting the dark circles beneath his eyes, which appeared almost sunken today. *Maybe he hasn't been sleeping well lately,* she thought. *Or perhaps he isn't taking good care of himself.*

"Oh Emma," Kim spoke up, "I brought that old ring I told you about yesterday—the one I found on Lido Beach."

Emma moved closer to where Kim sat, on the left side of Noreen. "Oh yes, that's right. I'd like to see it."

Kim reached into her tote bag and withdrew a small box. Then she opened it and handed a ring to Emma.

"You're right," Emma said, turning it over in her hand. "I see some initials engraved in the band. It's hard to make them out, since they are pretty worn, but it looks like the letters B and W."

Noreen almost choked on her tea when she heard what Emma had said. "Why, those were my husband's initials. May I see the ring?"

Emma looked at Kim, and when she nodded, she handed Noreen the ring.

Noreen studied it a few seconds and gasped. "This was my husband's! He lost it in the sand a few weeks after we moved to Sarasota." Tears welled in her eyes. "I would know this ring anywhere, and I can't believe you found it."

"Wow! What are the odds of that happening? I can't fathom it myself." Kim left her seat and held out her hand to Noreen. "Here you go. Take the box, too." She paused a moment, then quickly added, "You don't know how close I came to advertising the ring in the Lost and

Found section of the newspaper."

"Thank you so much. I can't begin to tell you how much this means to me," Noreen said with feeling. "After we'd gone back to the beach the next day to see if we could find Ben's ring and then searched for hours, we finally gave up. We thought it was lost forever, or that someone might have found the ring and kept it." She sniffed and wiped the tears from her cheeks. "Oh, this has truly made my day."

"I think Kim finding it was meant to be," Emma said, patting Noreen's shoulder.

"That's right," Lamar agreed. "God works in mysterious ways."

"We've been blessed this week, too," Jennifer put in. "Someone left us a lot of baby things, but we don't know who to thank for it."

"Some people like to do things in secret, and they don't want any thanks," Jan said, reaching for another cookie.

"Would anyone care for some cheese and crackers?" Emma asked, motioning to the other tray.

"I'll take a few," Mike responded. "Now that I'm restricted from eating a lot of sugary things, other foods that are better for me taste pretty good."

Emma handed the tray to Mike, and after he'd taken a few crackers, she passed it to Erika. "I'd rather have a cookie," the young woman said.

"Here you go." Jan passed the cookie plate down to Erika.

"What about you, B.J.?" Emma asked. "Would you like crackers or cookies?"

B.J. shook his head. "No thanks, I'm not really. . ." His words were cut off when a coughing fit overtook him. He quickly pulled a hanky from his pocket and held it over his mouth.

"Are you okay? Would you like a glass of water?" Emma asked, wearing a look of concern, as did everyone else in the class. Even Noreen thought his cough sounded pretty bad.

He lowered his hand, and Noreen gasped when she saw a splotch of blood in his hanky.

"Oh my! B.J., you're bleeding!" Kim exclaimed.

B.J. nodded slowly and looked from person to person, stopping at Noreen and holding her gaze. "I have cancer." He paused and drew in a quick breath. "Short of a miracle, it won't be long till I'm dead."

CHAPTER 34

After B.J.'s surprise announcement, the whole room went silent, filled with strong emotions. He hadn't meant to blurt out that he was dying. *If I just hadn't coughed up blood,* he thought with regret, *no one would have been any the wiser.* Now he had to deal with their sympathetic expressions as they processed the idea that one of their fellow quilting students would soon be checking out of this world.

B.J. almost knew how they felt and experienced sorrow for them in the awkwardness of the moment. He was sure they probably felt the same way, only for a different reason. Realizing that the outcome of his cancer was coming sooner, rather than later, was still hard for him to grasp, even after all this time. It wasn't fair. Lately, there'd been some days that B.J. thought for certain would be his last. But on other days, everything seemed right with the world, and it felt like his cancer was just a bad dream.

Thinking back, he realized that he'd wasted a lot of time moaning and groaning about having a bad cold or the twenty-four-hour flu. If he'd only known then what he knew now. Unfortunately, he understood the meaning of misery, and not just the part about having cancer. Maybe though, in spite of everything, there was a little ray of sunshine. B.J. wasn't sure why this had happened, but for weeks now, his senses had become more heightened. Could it be because his spirit knew there was so little time left? Like this morning when B.J. witnessed a beautiful sunrise. If it hadn't been for the need to get to the quilt class, he would have gathered up all his art supplies and headed to the beach to capture more clearly the morning's rosy dawn on canvas.

Ironically, B.J.'s favorite song from when he and Judy had dated was playing on the radio this morning. Even after all these years, he hadn't forgotten a single word of those lyrics. Were these little signs of awareness a clue that his death was closer than he thought? It just couldn't be. Not yet, anyway. B.J. needed more time. He had to say good-bye to his daughters, and he really wanted to find his son.

"I'm sorry to hear about your illness," Lamar said, moving across the room and placing his hands on B.J.'s shoulders. "We had no idea you were dealing with health issues, but now that we know, we will certainly be praying for you."

Emma bobbed her head in agreement, obviously left speechless with this news about one of her quilters.

"If you knew you were sick, how come you left your home in Chicago and came to Florida?" Mike questioned.

"It was on my bucket list," B.J. replied. "And when I got here and found out about the quilt class, I decided I'd like to make a wall hanging to give my only granddaughter. Hopefully, it'll be something she can remember me by."

"I'm surprised your daughters didn't talk you out of coming," Kim commented. "If I'd been sick when I left home, my parents would have pitched a fit."

B.J. drew in a couple of shallow breaths. "Neither of my girls knows that my cancer is terminal. When I left home, they thought I was doing better—that my cancer was in remission."

"So you lied to them, huh?" The blunt question came from Erika, who as usual, had kept pretty quiet during the first half of the class.

B.J. shook his head. "I didn't actually lie. Just didn't tell them the whole truth."

"My dad always says when you know something important but keep it from someone, it's the same as lying," Erika said.

"From your point of view, I can see that," B.J. responded, remembering when his daughters were Erika's age. "But from a parent's position, it's not so easy to reveal something this major to their kids. My daughters are very sensitive and even more so since their mother's death. As their father, it's only natural that I want to protect them from any kind of pain, especially news as serious as this."

"I can understand that," Jan interjected. "If I was in your position, I'd have a hard time tellin' Star about my illness."

B.J. sighed, picking up a pencil lying close by and tapping it on the table. While the room went quiet again, and B.J. thought about this a bit more, he realized what he must do and came to a final conclusion. "You know, Erika, maybe you're right. I probably should have told my children. No matter how you look at this, it'll be distressing all the way around. Some days I feel ready for the outcome of this, but when it comes to my children, I'm not ready to say good-bye. Even though I don't know how to easily handle it when I go home, I plan to break the news to my daughters."

"Psalm 46:1 says, 'God is our refuge and strength, a very present help in trouble,'" Emma said, her eyes tearing up. "He will give you the strength that you need to tell them, and we'll certainly be praying for you."

B.J. gave a slight nod. "Thanks, I appreciate what you said."

———

As Noreen sipped her tea, she reflected on all that B.J. had shared. Just because she felt vengeful, was it right to keep the truth from him about his and Judy's son? Was it fair to Todd not to let him know about his birth father and mother?

But if I tell B.J. or Todd, what good would it do? she wondered. *If B.J. really is dying, what's the point in revealing the truth? They would no more than get to know each other, and B.J. would be gone. Maybe it's better if I remain quiet about this.*

Noreen's gaze came to rest on the zippered pocket of her purse where she'd put her husband's ring. She couldn't help wishing Ben were here now to tell her what to do. He'd always had a way of knowing what was best and had set Noreen straight many times when her feelings ran amuck. But Ben wasn't here, and Noreen knew she had to make this decision on her own.

"B.J., do you feel up to continuing with the class today?" Emma asked. "You look awfully tired. Maybe you should go back to the place you've been renting and rest."

"Better yet," Lamar interjected, "you should go to the hospital or clinic and be checked out."

B.J. shook his head with a determined expression. "I came here to complete a wall hanging, and no matter how rotten I feel, I'm going to get it done."

That man is so stubborn, Noreen thought. *But then, I guess most men have a determined spirit when it comes to getting something done.* For a minute, when B.J. had first announced that he was ill, Noreen wanted to say that he deserved it. But her conscience quickly reminded her that it was wrong to think such thoughts, and pity for the man took over.

"If you need help with your quilting, I'm here to assist," Emma said, smiling at B.J. before she got up to open the curtains wider, letting more sunshine into the room.

"I appreciate that," he said with a nod.

Noreen could see by B.J.'s pained expression that he wasn't feeling well. *I think he's trying to put on a brave front, but B.J. shouldn't even be here today,* she thought. *I hope he goes home to his family so they can take care of him.*

Star felt relief when she pulled up to the Millers' house and saw no cars. She and Dad could take off on his bike and do something together. While she'd been driving around by herself, Star had discovered that Sarasota had a zoo. Thinking it would be something fun for her and Dad to do, she'd waited until shortly after noon, when she was pretty sure the quilters would be gone, to return to Emma and Lamar's.

After parking her dad's bike in the driveway, Star removed her helmet and sprinted up to the house. *Guess I'd better change into some shorts. Maybe I'll work on my tan while Dad and I are walking around at the zoo.*

When she stepped inside, Star found Emma and Lamar in the kitchen, eating lunch.

"You're just in time to join us. There's ham and cheese for a sandwich." Emma motioned to everything set on the table. "Let me get you a plate."

Star shook her head. "I appreciate the offer, but I'm hoping Dad and I can go to the zoo today, and I thought we'd catch a quick bite on the way. I just need to change into something a little cooler. It's really warming up out there."

"I'm sorry, Star, but your dad's not here," Emma said. "He and Kim decided to take her dog for a run on the beach."

"You're kidding, right?" Star mumbled. Then seeing their serious expressions, she realized that Emma was telling the truth. "That's just great! Dad didn't even have the decency to tell me he was going."

"Jan didn't know this morning," Lamar spoke up. "I heard him and Kim talking about it during class. Guess it was something they decided to do on the spur of the moment."

Star frowned. "Well, he could've at least called and let me know. Seems like he cares more about Kim than he does me."

Emma left her seat at the table and gave Star a hug. "I'm sure that's not true, dear. I know from the things Jan's said that he loves you very much. He's a different person now that you're back in his life."

"He has a funny way of showing it," Star said as she walked over to the window to look out. With her chin sticking out stubbornly, she turned back to the Millers and said, "Believe me, I get it. This change in Dad has nothing to do with me."

"I'm not making excuses for Jan," Lamar said, "but the two of you will be leaving soon, and he probably wants to spend as much time with Kim before then as he can."

"Whatever." Star turned away, struggling not to give in to the tears pushing at the back of her eyes. "That Kim!" she fumed. "She's ruining everything. I should have known better than to come here to Florida, thinking I'd have Dad all to myself."

"Aren't you going to join us for lunch?" Emma asked as Star moved toward the door.

Star shook her head. "No thanks. I've lost my appetite." Without saying anything more, she rushed out of the room. *For two cents I'd book a plane ticket today and head back to Indiana. What point is there in waiting to ride home with Dad, anyways?*

CHAPTER 35

J an laughed as Kim's dog darted into the surf, chasing a couple of seagulls. "I'll bet if my Brutus was here now, he'd be right in there with Maddie, havin' the time of his life."

"I'll bet, too," Kim said. "It would be fun to get our two dogs together sometime," she added.

Jan nodded. "Why don't we take a seat over there?" He motioned to the only wooden bench on this stretch of beach. "As long as Maddie doesn't stray too far, you should be able to keep an eye on her from there."

"Sounds like a plan." Kim followed Jan to the bench.

As soon as they sat down, he reached over and took Kim's hand. "I know it hasn't been that long since we first met, but I feel like I've known you for a long time."

She smiled. "Same here. I've felt it from that first day we ate lunch on the beach together."

Jan swiped at the sweat on the back of his neck, feeling nervous all of a sudden. "I really enjoy being with you, and I think if we had more time. . ." He stopped talking and drew her into his arms for a kiss that took his breath away. How was he ever going to say good-bye to this woman who had stolen his heart in such a short time? He couldn't ask Kim to give up her job and move to Shipshewana, and he couldn't give up his business and move here.

"Our friendship doesn't have to end after you leave," Kim said when the kiss ended. "We can keep in touch through phone calls, text messages, and e-mails."

"The phone calls I can do," Jan replied, "but I ain't that computer savvy, and my cell phone's just the basic kind, so I can't send text messages, either."

"After I've worked at the restaurant long enough to get some vacation time, maybe I can make a trip to Shipshewana to visit you," Kim said.

"I'd like that." Jan bobbed his head. "And I'll come back to Florida to see you again, too."

Who knows, he thought, *maybe after Kim visits Shipshewana she'll like it there well enough to stay. She could always get a job at one of the restaurants in the area.* Jan didn't voice his thoughts, though. He figured it would be better to wait until she visited and saw whether she liked it there or not. Maybe Kim was thinking the same thing and would suggest that he move to Florida.

It was hard not to let his thoughts run away with him, but he decided to keep these things to himself for now. Nonetheless, Jan couldn't stop himself from wondering what it would be like if he were married to Kim. Would she be okay with the small house he lived in? Would their dogs get along? Could Star accept Kim as her stepmother?

I wonder if my neighbor Selma would like Kim? Jan mused. Selma was hard to please, and it had taken him awhile to win over the elderly woman. But paying for her to take one of Emma's quilt classes had done the trick. Ever since then, she'd been sweet as cotton candy and had even brought Brutus a few doggie treats.

"Say, isn't that Erika Wilson over there?" Kim asked, breaking into Jan's thoughts.

He turned and looked in the direction she was pointing, where a teenage girl sat in a wheelchair with larger-than-normal wheels— apparently made for use on the beach. A man was crouched in the sand beside her. "I think you're right, Kim. That does look like Erika. I'm guessin' that's her dad with her."

Kim smiled. "I'm glad to see her here. From some of the things Erika has said during our quilting classes, it doesn't sound like she does much for fun."

———

"Now you'll have to admit," Dad said, grinning at Erika, "it feels pretty good to be here on the beach."

She grimaced. "Going to the beach might be fun if I had two good legs and could play in the water or run through the sand. Instead, I'm just sitting here wishing for something I can't have."

"While it's true that you can't run or walk anymore, you still have your senses of taste, smell, hearing, touch, and sight. Unlike that group of children over there," Dad said, gesturing to his right.

Erika turned her head and was surprised to see that the children Dad was referring to were holding on to a rope. "What are they doing?" she asked.

"Looks to me like those kids are blind. See that young man over there? He's leading them down the beach, using the rope so none of them wander off."

Erika's eyebrows shot up. "If they're blind, why would they come

WANDA E. BRUNSTETTER

to the beach? I mean, they can't see the color of the sand or watch the waves."

"That's true," Dad said, "but they can smell the sea air, hear the roar of the waves, and listen to the call of the gulls overhead. Those children can also feel the warmth of the sand beneath their feet, as well as the breeze coming off the gulf." Dad smiled. "Just listen to the sound of their laughter. It's obvious that they are having the time of their lives."

Erika reflected on that. She watched as one blond-haired little boy tugged on the rope to get everyone to stop. The child couldn't have been more than six or seven years old, yet he seemed thrilled to share with the others what he'd felt beneath his feet when he shouted, "The sand feels warm!" Then bending to pick something up, he turned the item over and over in his small hands.

From where Erika sat, she could see that it was a seashell. The young boy continued holding the shell and turning it every which way. He seemed to be using his fingers to touch each part of it. Then he said something to the little girl next to him and passed it over to her.

Erika watched as the girl, with dark hair full of curls, held the shell and became familiar with it, just as the young boy had done. She even held the shell up to her nose, apparently smelling it. Then she passed it on to the next child in line, and each one did the same, until all the children had taken a turn holding, touching, and smelling the shell. The last boy held the seashell up to his ear and said something to the rest. Then the children passed the shell around again, and this time, everyone held it to their ear.

Erika was impressed watching all of this and realized that if the sightless children could enjoy their time on the beach without seeing, than she could do the same without the use of her legs. "Guess maybe I need to appreciate things more and quit feeling sorry for myself," she murmured.

"At least I can see how beautiful it is here, where some of those poor kids may never have seen anything in their lives." Erika couldn't imagine what it must be like to have never experienced the gift of sight.

Dad took her hand and gave it a gentle squeeze. "Now that's the old Erika talking."

Erika glanced down and noticed something in the sand below her footrest. She repositioned the wheelchair and reached down to pull a seashell out of the sand. It reminded Erika of a snail-like creature she'd seen on a cartoon years ago. The dull white on the outside of the shell couldn't compare to its interior of smooth light pink. On one end were rows of little spikes that decreased to a smaller single point.

Erika ran her fingers over the surface, and then she held the shell up to her ear, just as the sightless children had done.

Dad looked at her and smiled.

She grinned back at him. "It's a great day to be alive and here on the beach."

———

"You look miserable, honey. Is there something I can do to make you more comfortable?" Randy asked as he and Jennifer sat on the couch watching TV.

"Not unless you can make the baby come early." She placed both hands on her stomach and leaned slightly forward. "I feel top heavy, and it's hard to find a comfortable position anymore. My back is just one big ache."

Randy rubbed the small of Jennifer's back. "Your due date's still two weeks away, so it's probably best if the baby doesn't come early."

She sighed deeply. "You're right; I'm just anxious for her to get here."

"So am I, Jen. And I'm thankful I have a job now, because I was beginning to think I would never find one."

263

"I knew you would, but I'll admit I was worried that we might go under financially. I was beginning to think we might have to move back home and live with one of our parents."

Randy shook his head vigorously. "I would have borrowed the money from my brother, Fred, before even considering moving into my parents' home. Dad's health isn't good, and the last thing they need are three more mouths to feed."

She nodded slowly. "My folks aren't much better off—not with having kids still living at home."

Randy clasped her hand. "We don't have to worry about that now. Thanks to an anonymous donor, our baby has everything she'll need." He realized now that his pride had gotten in the way when he'd first lost his job, but the evening they'd had the Millers for supper had made him see things in a different light. Talking with Lamar had helped Randy's attitude improve, and now that he had a job, things looked more hopeful for him and Jennifer than they had in a long time.

"Yes, we have much to be grateful for. I just hope and pray that when our little girl is born she'll be healthy and that the delivery will go smoothly."

"Don't be nervous," Randy said, hoping to relieve her anxiety. "I'll be with you through the whole process."

"I'm thankful for that, because I don't think I could do it without you." Jennifer paused and tipped her head. "What was that?"

"What was what? I didn't hear anything."

"It sounded like someone stepped onto our front porch."

Randy listened intently. Sure enough, there was a thump, followed by the sound of footsteps.

"Guess I'd better go see who it is," he said, rising from the couch.

Randy opened the door just in time to see a young Amish woman running away from the house. He glanced down and noticed a box of food on the porch. Cupping his hands around his mouth, he hollered, "Hey, did you leave this box on our porch?"

The young woman kept going, until she climbed into the passenger's side of a car parked down the street.

Randy squinted. She looked familiar—like one of the Amish waitresses he'd seen at work. But if it was her, why would she leave a box of food on their doorstep?

He bent down, picked up the box, and stepped back into the house. If he saw the Amish waitress at the restaurant when he went to work on Monday, he would ask if she was the one who'd left the food.

CHAPTER 36

B.J. yawned as he lay curled up on the couch. Today had been tiring, and he'd done nothing but rest since he got home from the quilting class this afternoon. Exhausted as he was, B.J. felt somewhat relieved that he'd let slip to the other quilters how cancer was slowly robbing his life. He hadn't felt that way at first, but after thinking things through, he'd come to realize that keeping his illness to himself had done him no good. Telling the quilters about it had sort of prepared him for giving the news to Robyn and Jill.

B.J. had left the Millers' today without saying anything more to Noreen and had given up asking her anything about his and Judy's son. She either didn't know the whereabouts of the boy or didn't want to tell him. As difficult as it was, he had to accept her choice.

Guess it shouldn't really matter, he told himself. *With the way my health is failing, even if I did know my son's whereabouts, I doubt I'd have the energy to go see him. It'll take all my strength just to get on a plane and return to Chicago, where my daughters are waiting. Maybe I should ask one of them to come down here and accompany me home. It'd be easier than trying to make it on my own.*

B.J. rolled from his side onto his back and stared at the ceiling. He'd had a good life with Brenda, raising their two beautiful daughters, and he was grateful for that. He'd also been blessed with grandchildren. Why then, did he feel the need to meet the young man who might never have been told about his biological father?

"I need to let this go," B.J. murmured. "Even if I did get to meet my son, I don't have enough time left to really get to know him."

B.J. squeezed his eyes tightly shut. *God, if You're real, please give me a sense of peace about this.*

"It's good to see you," Noreen's friend and fellow teacher Ruth Bates said when Noreen neared the entrance of the high school gymnasium.

"It's good to see you, too." Noreen gave her friend a hug. Still feeling a bit self-conscious about her hair, she said, "I almost didn't come to this reunion, but I'm glad I did."

Ruth looked at Noreen strangely. "Why wouldn't you come?"

Noreen explained about the hair color she'd put on, then quickly added, "I guess that's what I get for not looking at the color on the box closely enough."

Ruth laughed. "Things like that have happened to the best of us. You look fine, Noreen, so I wouldn't worry about it."

Noreen relaxed a bit. "I appreciate the affirmation, because this has been kind of a trying week for me."

"I'm sorry to hear that. If you'd like to talk about it, I have a listening ear."

Noreen shook her head. "It's a personal matter, and nothing I can discuss right now, but your prayers would be appreciated."

"I can certainly do that." Ruth gave Noreen's arm a gentle squeeze.

As they made their way into the gym, which had been decorated with colored balloons and streamers, a young woman came up to Noreen. "So glad you could be here tonight, Mrs. Webber."

Noreen thought the woman looked familiar, but she couldn't quite place her.

"You don't recognize me, do you?" the woman said, as a few other students joined her. "I'm Karen Rasmussen, the girl who spent more time in the principal's office than she did in your class."

Noreen recalled that Karen had been one of her most challenging students, always talking when she should have been listening, and making wisecracks about what some of the other girls in class wore. Back then, Karen ran with a rowdy group that thought nothing of skipping school or cutting up in class. To look at the young woman now, one would never know she'd been a wild child during her high school years.

"If it weren't for your patience and persistence, I probably would have flunked English and might never have graduated high school and gone to college," Karen said, resting her hand on Noreen's arm.

Noreen smiled. "People change, and if I had even the slightest bit of influence on any of my students, then I'm grateful."

"We are the ones who should be grateful," a well-groomed, auburn-haired man spoke up. "You were one of the best teachers at this school, and you always treated everyone with fairness."

Noreen swallowed hard, fighting the urge to give in to tears. Until this moment, she'd never realized that she had impacted any of her students' lives. Hearing their praise and seeing how well these two young people had obviously turned out lifted Noreen's spirits. For the first time since she'd found out who B.J. was, Noreen felt a sense of joy in her heart and maybe even hope for the future.

———

Jan whistled as he stepped onto the Millers' front porch that evening. Kim had just dropped him off after they'd spent most of the day together, and he was in an exceptionally good mood. He knew for certain that Kim's feelings about their relationship matched his.

Jan noticed his motorcycle parked in the driveway, so that meant Star must be here. Maybe the two of them could go out for a late bite to eat.

Stepping into the house, Jan spotted Emma and Lamar sitting in the living room with grim expressions.

"What's up?" Jan asked. "You two look like you've lost your best friend."

"Star's gone," Emma said, slowly shaking her head.

Jan's forehead wrinkled. "What do you mean she's gone? Where'd she go?"

"She left you a note," Lamar said. "It's on the kitchen table."

Jan hesitated, then took off for the kitchen. He scooped up Star's note from the table and read it silently.

Dad,

Since you would obviously rather be with Kim than me, I decided to go home. I was able to get a flight this afternoon, and one of Emma and Lamar's English friends is taking me to the airport. There's no need to try and stop me, because by the time you read this, I'll be on a plane heading for the airport in South Bend, Indiana.

Star

Stunned by his daughter's words, Jan rushed back to the living room. Waving Star's note in the air, he stepped in front of Emma and Lamar. "Do either of you know anything about this?" he asked. "Did Star say anything to you before she left?"

"Star is upset about Kim," Emma said. "We tried to talk her out of going, but she's convinced that Kim is coming between you two."

"How so?"

Emma sighed. "Think about it, Jan. Since Star got here, how much time have you actually spent with her?"

He shrugged. "Not a whole lot, I guess."

"Remember, Jan," Emma said, "for a good many years, Star was cheated out of having a father, and then just when you were developing a solid relationship with her, along comes Kim. Now, Star feels threatened."

Jan sank into the chair across from them. "She oughta know I love her and that Kim's not tryin' to come between us."

"I'm sure Kim isn't doing it intentionally," Lamar said, "but Star isn't ready to share you with anyone. Not this soon anyway. And if you want my opinion, things are moving pretty fast with you and Kim."

Jan rubbed his temples as he contemplated their words. He felt like he was being forced to choose between Star and Kim. "I can't lose the relationship I've established with my daughter," he said. "Guess the only thing I can do right now is break things off with Kim. If it's meant to be, then maybe somewhere down the road things will work out for Kim and me. Right now, though, I need to think of what's best for Star."

"We understand, and we'll be praying for your situation," Lamar said.

Emma nodded in agreement.

Jan was tempted to call Kim and talk to her about this, but decided it would be best if he discussed things face-to-face. Rising from his chair, he turned to the Millers and said, "Guess I'd better head over to Kim's house right now, 'cause there's no point in putting this off. Then tomorrow morning, I'll be heading for home so I can set things straight with Star."

Kim had just brought Maddie inside for the night and was thinking of going to bed, when she heard the unmistakable roar of a motorcycle pull up out front. A few minutes later, there was a knock on the door.

Woof! Woof! Maddie's tail wagged when Kim opened the door and Jan stepped into the house. Kim smiled, thinking she wasn't the only one happy to see Jan.

"This is an unexpected surprise. Did you forget something in my car, Jan?"

He shook his head. "We need to talk."

"You so look serious," Kim said, noting the deep wrinkles in Jan's forehead. "Is something wrong?"

"Yeah, I'm afraid there is."

With a sense of apprehension creeping up her spine, Kim motioned to the couch. "Let's have a seat and you can tell me about it."

"While we were at the beach today, my daughter got a plane ticket and flew back to Indiana." Jan sank to the couch, scrubbing a hand over his bearded face. "She thinks I don't care about her anymore."

"Is it because of me?" Kim asked, dreading the answer.

He gave a quick nod. "Star's jealous of our relationship, and I guess that's my fault. I really blew it, 'cause I haven't paid her enough attention since she came down here to join me for what was supposed to be our vacation together."

Kim placed her hand on his arm. "I'm sorry, Jan. I shouldn't have taken up so much of your time."

"It ain't your fault," he was quick to say. "I'm the one who messed things up with Star." Jan leaned forward, with his elbows on his knees. "There's no easy way to say this, Kim, but I think it'd be best if you and I break things off before we get too serious about each other."

It's too late for that, Kim thought. She knew it was probably too soon, but she'd foolishly allowed herself to become serious about Jan and had even fantasized about having a permanent relationship with him.

Deciding that it would be best not to let Jan know how crushed she was by this, Kim forced a smile, sat straight up, and said, "I understand. Your relationship with your daughter should come first, and I wish you both well."

"This ain't easy for me, you know," Jan said, "because I really do care about you." He leaned over and kissed Kim's cheek. "Maybe someday, when Star's more secure in our relationship. . ."

Kim held up her hand. "It's okay. You don't have to make any promises that you may not be able to keep."

Jan didn't say anything as he stood and moved toward the door. He'd barely grasped the knob, when he turned back around. "It's been great getting to know you, Kim, and no matter what happens in the future, I want you to know that I'll never forget you or the time we've spent together."

Barely able to speak because of her swollen throat, all Kim could do was give him her bravest smile and whisper, "Same here. Take care."

Jan bent to pet Maddie, as she had followed him to the door. "Take good care of Kim, now, you hear?"

As though understanding what he'd said, Maddie licked his hand, while her tail wagged furiously. When Jan went out the door, the dog slunk to the corner of the room, plopped down, and let out a pathetic whimper.

Tears streaming down her hot cheeks, Kim buried her face and sobbed, soaking the pillow she held. Like most dogs when they sensed things about people, Maddie got up and came to rest her head on Kim's knee.

"Just when I thought I'd found the perfect guy, all my hopes and dreams have been dashed," Kim cried. "Maybe I am destined to live with a broken heart." She got down on the floor and, holding her dog tightly, continued to sob.

CHAPTER 37

On Monday, after Mike fixed himself a high-protein drink as a mid-morning snack, he received a phone call telling him his boat was ready.

Mike smiled. His boat could finally be put back in the water. That meant he could start taking calls from people who wanted to hire him to take them fishing.

For the past several weeks he'd had to turn everyone away. He'd not only missed the cash flow but time spent on the water. Even sitting out on the deck of their house where he had a nice view of the bay gave Mike a sense of yearning to be on his boat.

Think I was born to be on the water, he mused. But the example of his brother's situation had made Mike realize that he couldn't be on the water all the time just to make money. A lot of things in his life were going to change.

Glancing at his watch, Mike realized it was almost time to head to the airport so he could pick up Phyllis. She'd called Saturday evening to give him her flight details.

"Sure can't wait to see her," Mike said before hurriedly finishing his protein drink.

———

Kim's hand shook as she turned in another customer's lunch order. She hadn't slept well over the weekend, and really wasn't up to working today. But it wouldn't be right to call the restaurant this morning and give them that excuse. She needed to save her sick-time benefits for when she was really ill, and not for jangled nerves, which she hoped to get under control. Besides, working and being around people might help take her mind off Jan and the fact that he'd left for Shipshewana yesterday morning. Kim knew that unless Star gave her blessing, there was no chance of her and Jan ever having a permanent relationship.

"Are you okay?" Anna Lambright asked as she joined Kim near the breakfast buffet. "I couldn't help but notice that you dropped a bowl of soup awhile ago, and then soon afterward you spilled coffee on the floor."

"Don't remind me. I've been a ball of nerves all day, and I also messed up someone's order and forgot to take 'em the beverage they wanted. In trying to make it right, I offered them a free dessert." Kim sighed, bringing her hands to her forehead. "I was doing better, but now I fear that if I keep doing things like that, I really could lose my job."

"What's wrong? Just having an off day, or did something happen over the weekend to upset you?" Anna questioned.

"I can't take the time to go into details right now," Kim whispered, "but the bottom line is this: Jan and I won't be seeing each other anymore."

"How come?"

"His daughter flew back to Indiana on Saturday, and Jan headed out on his motorcycle Sunday morning. He's probably getting close to home by now."

"I'm sorry to hear that," Anna said, giving Kim's arm a little squeeze. "You seemed so happy when you started seeing Jan."

"I was, but I guess it wasn't meant to be. I'll be fine, though. You needn't worry about me." *Yeah, right. Who am I kidding?* Kim asked herself. She knew in her heart that losing Jan was not going to be an easy thing. With Jan, it was different from any of her other failed relationships. She guessed she'd just have to take one day at a time and try to make the best of her situation.

Anna looked like she was about to say more, when the new cook, Randy, stepped up to them. He stared at Anna with a peculiar expression. "Mind if I speak to you for a minute?"

Anna squirmed nervously but slowly nodded.

"I'll see you later," Kim said to Anna, before heading for the kitchen. *I wonder why Randy wants to talk to Anna. Could she have messed up someone's order?*

"Uh, unless it's something important, I really don't have time to talk," Anna said, taking a few steps away from Randy, then glancing at one of her customers, who was obviously trying to get her attention.

Randy held his ground. The customer could wait a minute. "It is important. Someone's been leaving things on our front porch. And the other day I found a box of food there, and someone who looked like you was running down the sidewalk and getting into a car. Was it you, Anna? Are you the one who's been leaving things on our porch?"

Anna lowered her head. "Yes," she quietly said.

"Really? How come?"

"Because I knew you'd been out of work, and I wanted to help out," she explained, lifting her gaze to meet his. "I'd hoped that when I left them there, you'd either be gone or wouldn't hear me step onto the porch."

"But how did you know about our situation? I never met you till I came to work here."

"I met your wife several weeks ago, when we were waiting to catch a bus. We started a conversation, and she ended up telling me about your job loss. She also mentioned that she'd wanted to take Emma's quilting class but couldn't afford it."

Randy's eyebrows shot up. "You paid for Jennifer's quilting classes, too?"

Anna nodded.

"But why? You didn't even know my wife."

"That's true, but when I lived in Indiana, I took Emma's class, and it helped me in so many ways. I was hoping that if Jennifer took the class she would also benefit from it."

"So you know Emma and Lamar Miller?"

"Yes."

"Do they know about the things you've done for us?"

"Not everything. Emma knows I paid for Jennifer's quilting classes. I wanted all the other things I've done to be anonymous."

"How'd you get our address?"

"When I met Jennifer the day we were waiting for the bus, she pointed to your house, so I memorized the address and put the quilt class ticket in the mail, marked 'Dear Friend.' Then whenever I stopped to see the Millers, Emma kept me informed on how you and Jennifer were doing."

"I see." Randy scratched the side of his head. "I still don't get why

277

a complete stranger would spend their hard-earned money on people they don't even know. Was it you, by chance, who got us those baby things? If it was, all that stuff must have cost you a fortune."

"Not really. I entered a drawing at a store here in Sarasota, with the idea that if I won I would give the baby things to you and Jennifer." Anna smiled. "I've never won anything before, so I was surprised when the store called and said my name had been drawn. Since I had no way of delivering the baby things myself, I asked a friend who has a truck to drop them off."

Randy wasn't sure what to say. He'd never had anyone who was almost a complete stranger do something so nice. "Thank you, Anna. I appreciate everything you did," he said, blinking rapidly as his eyes grew misty. "But now I'm wondering, did you have something to do with me getting the job here, too?"

Anna shook her head. "Kim is the one who found out that they needed a cook, and I believe she told Jennifer about it during one of the quilting classes."

"Then I guess I have her to thank, too, and I'll do it right now." Randy turned aside, feeling eternally grateful. It was nice to know there were still some people who cared about others and wanted to help out. Someday, when he got the chance, he would return the favor—if not to Anna or Kim, then to someone else who had a need.

"Are you sure you don't want to go over to Pinecraft Park and watch me play shuffleboard with some of the men?" Lamar asked as Emma threaded her sewing machine.

"No thanks," she said. "I want to get some sewing done this afternoon, but you go ahead."

He bent to give her a peck on the check. "Okay. I'll see you later then."

Several minutes after Lamar left, a knock sounded on the front door. Emma set her sewing aside and went to answer it. She was surprised to see Noreen on the porch.

"It's good to see you. Please, come in." Emma opened the door wider.

"I hope I'm not interrupting anything," Noreen said. "But if you're not too busy, I need to talk."

"I was sewing, but I'm never too busy to visit." Emma led the way to the living room and invited Noreen to take a seat.

"Thank you." Noreen held something out for Emma. "I went to Lido Beach this morning, to do a little soul searching, and found this pretty seashell while I was there. I thought maybe you'd like to have it."

"Oh, that's a nice one." Emma took the pretty salmon-colored shell. "They call these conch shells, right?"

"That's correct. This one I believe is a horse conch, and it's actually Florida's state shell."

"That's interesting. I didn't realize Florida had a state shell," Emma said, walking over to the built-in shelf in the corner of the room. "Think I'll put it right here."

"Those are the types of seashells you'll see kids holding up to their ears," Noreen said. "In fact, I do it, too."

Emma smiled and took a seat beside Noreen on the couch. "I have a hunch that many other adults do, as well."

"When I was a girl, my family lived in Columbus, Ohio, and one summer our parents took Judy and me on vacation, here in Sarasota. We had so much fun that week, especially since it was the first time we'd seen the Gulf of Mexico." Noreen stared off into space, as though reliving the past. "We loved jumping the waves, and every morning we'd head for the beach to look for seashells. One day Judy found a shell similar to the one I gave you, only bigger. Daddy told us if we held the shell to our ear we could hear the ocean inside." Noreen looked back at Emma and said tearfully, "I still have Judy's seashell sitting on the coffee table in my living room."

"That's a pleasant memory," Emma said, feeling touched that Noreen had opened up to her like that. "I'm glad you shared it with me, and I can see that it's still very special to you."

"Yes, I guess it is," Noreen answered, straightening her shoulders. "Talking about seashells isn't why I came here today, though."

"Why did you come?" Emma asked.

"I needed to talk to you about something quite serious."

"Oh?"

"I did a lot of thinking over the weekend—about B.J."

Emma sighed deeply. "I felt sad hearing about his cancer. It must have been difficult for him to take the quilting classes when he'd been feeling so poorly."

Noreen gave a nod. "I feel the same way. He must have great inner strength to complete the wall hanging for his granddaughter. It sort of made me see B.J. in a different light." Noreen paused, took a deep breath, and looked straight into Emma's eyes. "I haven't been completely honest with B.J. about his and my sister's baby."

"Oh?" Emma folded her hands and waited for Noreen to continue. She could tell by the woman's pinched expression that this was a difficult subject to talk about.

"I do know where B.J.'s son is living, but I didn't want B.J. to know because I was angry with him for breaking up with Judy. It devastated my sister, and I didn't think B.J. deserved to know the truth because he'd hurt Judy so bad. I also blamed him for her death, because she died giving birth to his baby." Noreen's voice faltered, and she squeezed her eyes shut.

"And now?" Emma coaxed.

"After thinking things through, and realizing that B.J. doesn't have long to live, I'm wondering if it would best to let B.J. meet his son."

"Would that be possible?" Emma questioned. "Do you know where the young man lives, and have you spoken with him about this?"

Noreen drew in a long breath and released it in one quick puff. "B.J.'s son is named Todd. He's my adopted son."

"The son you said lives in Texas?" Emma asked in surprise.

"Yes, but Todd and his wife are coming to see me. They'll arrive this Wednesday." Noreen paused again and dabbed at the tears rolling down her cheeks. "Do you think I'd be doing the right thing if I told Todd about his biological father, and then let him decide whether or not he wants to meet B.J.?"

Emma mulled things over. Then she finally nodded and said, "Yes, I think that's the wise thing to do."

CHAPTER 38

Goshen

When Jan approached Star's house on Wednesday morning, he was relieved to see that both her motorcycle and car were parked in the driveway. That meant she must be here. When he'd arrived home late Monday night he'd called and left her a message, but she hadn't responded. He'd called again on Tuesday, but still no reply. Could her voice mail be full? Was the battery dead on her cell phone? Or was his daughter ignoring his calls on purpose? He hoped that wasn't the case.

Figuring that Wednesday was usually one of Star's days off, he'd taken the chance and driven to Goshen to talk to her face-to-face. That would be better than a phone call anyhow.

Jan parked his truck, got out, and glanced up at the stately old house. Star had inherited the place when her grandma died and her mom got married and moved to Ft. Wayne. He was glad Star had ended up with the house. She'd had a rough childhood and deserved a cozy place to call her own. Even though Star had been fortunate enough to have a couple of her song lyrics published and had even been offered the chance to move to Nashville, she'd decided to stay here, to be close to Jan.

How could I even think of establishing a permanent relationship with Kim if Star's not on board? Jan thought. *My daughter comes first, no matter what.*

He took the stairs two at a time and rapped on the door. Several minutes went by, then Star, holding her guitar, finally answered.

"Dad! I'm surprised to see you. Figured you'd still be in Sarasota."

"Headed for home after I got your note." Jan's lips compressed. "In case you've forgotten, you were supposed to be with me on the trip home."

"Yeah, that was the plan all right, but that was before I realized you'd rather be with Kim than me," she said, frowning deeply.

"Didn't you get my phone messages?" he asked.

She shook her head. "Turned the volume down when I went to see a movie the other night. Guess I forget to turn it back up."

"I left you a message saying I'd broken things off with Kim, and that I didn't want things to change between you and me."

Star's eyes widened. "Really?"

"Yeah, and I'm sorry for messin' up our vacation, Star." Jan turned his head to glance at the rain that had begun to fall. "Can I come in, before I get wet?"

"Yeah, sure." Star opened the door wider and Jan stepped into the house.

As Jan wiped his feet on the doormat, Star propped her guitar in the corner of the living room. "Would you like some coffee?" she asked. "I don't have any made right now, but it won't take long to fix."

"Sure, that would taste good," he responded. "But none of that flavored kind."

Star smirked and went to the kitchen, while Jan took a seat on the couch. She returned a short time later with two steaming cups of coffee.

"Boy that was quick! My coffeemaker takes forever to make a pot of brew. How'd you make this so fast?" Jan asked as he blew on his cup and took a tentative sip. "I know this isn't instant coffee; it's good and strong, just the way I like it."

"I got a new coffee machine that uses the pods. You can make a single cup of coffee in seconds." Star sipped some from her own mug. "Vanilla's my favorite flavor, but I bought a box of the bold coffee, since I knew that's what you like best."

"Well now, don't that beat all?" Jan said, shaking his head. "Never knew any coffeemaker could work that fast."

"You can even get hot chocolate and tea in the pods. And apple cider," Star added as she seated herself beside him.

Jan drank a little more coffee, then he turned to her and said, "You know how much I love you, don't you, Star?"

"I love you, too, Dad, but I was afraid if you kept seeing Kim that you might end up moving to Florida."

He shook his head. "Not a chance. My business is here, and so are you." Jan hoped his tone sounded upbeat so Star wouldn't think he had any regrets. Truth was, he didn't regret his decision to stay in Indiana; what he felt bad about was breaking things off with Kim.

Sarasota

"I know it's none of my business, but I feel like calling Star and talking to her about Jan and Kim," Emma said as she and Lamar sat in their backyard watching several wild parrots eat at the feeders Lamar had put up. They were such colorful birds and fun to observe. One was even hanging upside-down, as if showing off to the others.

Lamar touched Emma's arm. "I'm not sure it would do any good to talk to Star about Kim. Besides, it's up to Jan to work things out with his daughter, don't you think?"

Emma sighed. "I suppose, but I feel sorry for Kim. When we were at the restaurant for supper last night and she waited on us, couldn't you see how upset she was?"

"She got our order confused with someone else's. Is that what you mean?"

"It did show that she had her mind somewhere else," Emma said, "but there was a look of sadness in Kim's eyes that wasn't there before. I think she misses Jan a lot and is disappointed that he went home a week earlier than he'd planned."

Lamar reached for the glass of lemonade Emma had placed on the table between them and took a drink. When he finished, he turned to Emma and said, "Why don't we pray about it for now? Then in a week or so, if you feel the Lord is telling you to talk to Star, you can give her a call."

Emma smiled as she gave a nod. "As usual, you're full of *gscheidheit*."

"My wisdom comes from God," Lamar said, after taking another drink from his glass. "And I'm not the only wise person in this house. You have given godly counsel to many of your students since you began teaching quilting."

Emma pursed her lips. "That may be true for some in this group of quilters, but I don't feel like I've helped them resolve any of their problems. Some, at least, seem to be solving them on their own."

"Maybe that's a good thing, Emma," Lamar said. "I like seeing people realize they might be wrong about something or working to change their ways. People influence people all the time, not just by what they say, but by example." He patted her arm. "You know what, Emma?"

285

"What's that?"

"I'm thinking our students have been influenced in many ways by your example and how you get along with everyone."

She smiled and clasped his hand. "I am trying to be a Christian example in all that I do and say, but I admit that sometimes I fall short."

"We all do, Emma. That's because we're human. Guess the main thing to remember is to commit our life to Christ and ask Him to guide us in all we say and do."

Emma pinched the bridge of her nose. "Oh Lamar, there are so many people in our world, and those He's brought to our class are but a few. How I hope He will heal their hurts and touch their lives in some special way."

"He will, Emma, if they're open to it." Lamar took Emma's hand. "Now, let's pray."

———

"It sure is good to be home," Phyllis told Mike as they sat together on the deck, watching the boats in the bay. "I'm not used to that bitter North Dakota winter weather. I thought I was going to freeze to death when I took Penny's dog out to do his business during the blizzard. Thank goodness the dog didn't waste any time."

"When you told me about it, I worried about you and felt guilty for being here where I could enjoy the sun," Mike replied. "More than once I thought I should have gone with you."

Phyllis shook her head. "I managed fine helping my sister, and she's well-equipped for handling weather-related emergencies. I was glad you were here so you could take the quilt class in my place." She reached for his hand. "I'm looking forward to going to the last class with you this Saturday and can't wait to see how your wall hanging turned out."

"Well, don't expect too much," Mike said. "I'm all thumbs when it comes to a needle and thread. Even with Emma's help, my quilted project doesn't look nearly as good as it would if you had made it."

"That doesn't matter." Phyllis squeezed his fingers. "The important thing is that you were willing to take the class in my place and did your best."

Mike's cell phone rang, interrupting their conversation. "I'd better get this, honey. It could be a work-related call."

"That's fine," she said. "And while you're doing that, I'll go inside and fix our lunch."

When Mike answered the phone, a man came on, asking if Mike could take him and two other men fishing on Saturday. Mike was on the urge of saying yes when he remembered his promise to go to the quilt class with Phyllis. "Sorry," he said, "but I can't take you out on Saturday. If you can wait till Monday morning, I'll be free then."

"That won't work," the man said. "Saturday's the only day the three of us can all go. If you can't do it then, we'll call another charter boat service."

"I understand." Mike hung up the phone, struggling with mixed emotions. It had been hard saying no—especially when he really wanted to go out on his boat—but he knew it wouldn't be right to let Phyllis down. Besides, he'd promised himself that he would spend more time with her and less time on the boat and that he'd limit his work to just five days a week.

Guess learning not to be such a workaholic is gonna take some time, Mike thought as he leaned back in his chair. *But if spending more time with Phyllis will strengthen my marriage, then it'll be worth every minute.*

———

Noreen had just checked the roast warming in the oven, knowing Todd and Kara would arrive soon, when she heard a car pull up. Peeking out the window, her heartbeat picked up speed when she saw that it was them. Any other time, Noreen would have been full of excitement having her son and his wife come for a visit. But today she felt a bit rattled and full of apprehension. *Please let this all work out,* she prayed as she removed her apron and stopped by the hallway mirror to take a quick look at her reflection.

"It's sure good to see you, Mom," Todd said when he and Kara entered the house a few minutes later.

Noreen hugged them both. "It's good to see you, too. How are the children?"

"Doing well," Kara replied. "Since the boys are in school right now, they're staying with friends while we're gone."

"I'll look forward to seeing them the next time," Noreen said.

Todd, looking more handsome than ever with his dark hair and brown eyes, looked at Noreen and blinked. "What'd you do to your hair? It's darker than I've ever seen it before."

Noreen's face heated. "It's a long story, and I'll explain later. Right now, let's get your things brought into the house, and we can visit while we eat supper. You haven't eaten yet, I hope."

"We knew it was getting close to supper, and Todd said he was sure you'd have something waiting for us." Kara pushed a strand of her shoulder-length blond hair behind her ear and smiled.

"From what I can smell, I'm sure it's gonna be good," Todd said, sniffing toward the kitchen. "My mouth's watering already, Mom."

While Todd brought in their suitcases, Kara and Noreen set the table. When Todd returned, and they were all seated around the dining-room table, Noreen offered thanks for their meal, and for Todd and Kara's safe travels. Then she passed the food.

"If this roast is half as good as it smells, I'm definitely having seconds." Todd winked at Noreen.

"The potatoes and carrots look yummy, too," Kara commented. "You shouldn't have gone to so much trouble, Noreen."

"It was nothing, really," Noreen said, almost dropping the basket of rolls as she handed it to Kara. "Cooking a roast in the oven with potatoes and carrots doesn't take much effort, but it's one of my favorite supper dishes. Of course, I don't have it much anymore," she added. "Cooking for one isn't much fun, so I either eat something simple like salad, soup, or a sandwich, or I sometimes go out for a meal."

"It has to be lonely for you living here by yourself," Todd said. "Why don't you reconsider and move to Texas so you can be closer to us?"

Noreen shook her head. "We've had this discussion before, Son. Sarasota is my home, and I'm not ready to leave it right now. Maybe someday. We'll see."

"Okay, Mom, I understand." Todd reached for the salt shaker. "Just remember, you're welcome to come visit us anytime."

"Yes, and I will."

As they continued their meal, they talked about other things—the weather, politics, and what Todd and Kara wanted to do while they were visiting Sarasota.

When everyone was done, Noreen got up from the table to clear the dishes, but Kara said she would take care of that so Noreen could visit with Todd while they enjoyed some coffee.

"What's new in your life these days, Mom?" Todd asked, before taking a sip of his coffee.

Noreen shifted uneasily in her chair. Was this a good time to tell Todd about B.J., or should she wait a few days?

"Is something wrong? You're squirming around like you're nervous, Mom."

Noreen drew in a deep breath, unsure of how to begin. "There's something I need to tell you, Todd."

"What's that?"

She moistened her lips with the tip of her tongue. "You've known you were adopted ever since you were a boy. Your dad and I never kept that from you."

"Right. You both said you thought I ought to know."

Noreen grabbed a napkin and balled it up in her hands, damp with perspiration. This was much harder than she'd thought it would be. "There's. . .um. . .something else that you don't know."

He leaned slightly forward. "What's that?"

"Your birth mother, whose name was Judy, died giving birth to you, and. . .well. . .Judy was my sister."

Todd's forehead wrinkled. "My birth mother was your sister?"

Noreen nodded slowly.

The room became deathly quiet. Kara stopped doing the dishes and moved closer to the table. "So you're actually Todd's aunt?" she asked Noreen.

"Yes, that's right."

"Why didn't you tell me this before?" Todd's voice sounded strained, and a vein on the side of his neck bulged. "Did you think I couldn't handle it?"

"It wasn't that. I was afraid if I revealed the truth that your father might somehow find out."

"Dad didn't know who my birth mother was?" Todd's eyebrows drew together.

"Oh, he knew alright. It was your flesh-and-blood father I didn't want to know about you."

"I'm confused, Mom. Who is my real father, and why didn't you want him to know about me?"

Noreen squirmed under Todd's scrutiny as she explained about B.J. "And now, after all these years, B.J., whose real name is Bruce Jensen, made a sudden appearance. He's been attending the quilting classes with me, but I didn't know it was him at first. The truth of his identity came out later on."

"Does he know about me?" Todd asked, sitting back in his chair, while Kara came and stood behind him, placing her hands on his shoulders. They were obviously quite shocked by this unexpected news.

"He didn't know Judy was pregnant or that she'd given birth to a son until I let it slip during one of our quilting classes." Noreen drew in a deep breath to help steady her nerves. "The thing is, B.J. has cancer, and according to him, he doesn't have long to live. So I was wondering if. . . Would you be willing to meet B.J. after the quilt class this Saturday?"

Todd sat several seconds, reaching back and touching his wife's hands. "I—I don't know. I'll have to think about it."

CHAPTER 39

When the quilting students arrived on Saturday morning, Emma was happy to see that, with the exception of B.J., they'd all finished with the quilted part of their wall hangings and were ready to put the bindings on. She was also pleased that Mike's wife was with him.

"It's good to have you back with us, Phyllis," Emma said.

Phyllis smiled. "I'm glad I could be here for the last class. From what Mike has said, he's enjoyed getting to know all of you and has learned a lot while taking the classes."

Emma felt relieved because at first Mike hadn't seemed comfortable.

She glanced at Erika and noticed that the young woman wore a genuine smile this morning. Apparently, she was happy to be here as well.

Maybe Lamar and I have done some good while teaching this class, Emma thought as she placed several pairs of scissors on the table, along with the material each person would use for their binding. At least everyone had learned the basics of quilting, and they all seemed to have enjoyed the class.

Emma looked at Kim, who was chatting with Jennifer. She was probably still hurting over her breakup with Jan, yet she tried to remain cheerful and interested in what the others were saying.

What a shame, Emma thought. *I had hoped things would work out for her and Jan. I wish Star would have given herself the chance to get to know Kim better. I'm sure she would have realized what a sweet person she is.*

"Emma, did you hear what I said?"

Emma jumped at the sound of Lamar's voice, close to her ear.

"Uh. . .what was that?"

"I asked if you were going to explain to the students how to put their bindings on, or would you rather that I do it?"

"Oh, I was just going to do that," Emma replied, feeling a bit flustered. She knew better than to let her mind wander like that—especially during one of their quilting classes. It was important to stay focused, and for the rest of the class, that's what she planned to do.

First Emma explained how to cut, pin, and sew the binding to the edge of the wall hangings. Then, since B.J. had fallen behind last week because he wasn't feeling well, Emma offered to help him finish his quilting, while the others took turns using the sewing machines to put their bindings on.

B.J. smiled, although it appeared to be strained. He was obviously not feeling well again this morning, and Emma's heart went out to him. She knew that illness, injuries, financial problems, and many other painful things were a part of life, but it was hard to see people suffer, and she wished there was something she could do to make things better for B.J. She hoped, too, that as soon as today's class was over, the poor man would make plans to return to Chicago to be with his daughters. He really needed their support during a time such as this. His illness was not something he should have to face alone.

———

Noreen worked quietly at one of the sewing machines, every once in a while glancing at her watch and wondering if Todd would show up. This morning he'd agreed to see B.J., so she'd given him Emma and Lamar's address and said he should come by at the end of class. She didn't want to interrupt their final lesson, and knew that Todd meeting B.J. could end up to be quite an emotional experience.

Maybe it would have been better if I'd suggested some other place for Todd and B.J. to meet, she thought. She'd chosen the Millers' home because she knew they were good people and would have wise counsel to offer should things get sticky or too emotionally charged.

How different things would have been for me and Ben if Judy had married Bruce Jensen and they'd raised Todd themselves, Noreen continued to muse. *Judy and Bruce were really young back then, so marriage and raising a child would have been a struggle for them, but Ben and I would have helped in any way we could.*

Noreen had always wondered why things happened the way they did. Was there some big master plan for everyone's life? It was true Judy would have struggled even if B.J. hadn't been informed and she'd tried to raise the baby alone. Noreen knew that she and Ben would have given Judy a home and helped to make things easier for her and the baby.

But Noreen was certain of one thing: she had no regrets about raising Todd. She and Ben had been able to give their son a stable home. And if they hadn't adopted Judy's son, they would have missed out on the privilege and joy of raising him.

She lifted her gaze from the strip of material she'd been sewing and looked at B.J., who sat at the table beside Emma. She was pinning B.J.'s binding in place while he watched. Lines of fatigue etched his forehead, and the sparkle that had been in his eyes during the first quilt class was gone. The poor man probably wasn't feeling well and wished he was home in bed.

Should I say something to B.J.? Noreen wondered. *Maybe give him a heads-up that his son will be coming to meet him? Or would it better to wait and let him be surprised?*

Noreen's thoughts were halted when Jennifer, sitting at the sewing machine next to hers, groaned. Feeling concern, Noreen pivoted in her seat and said, "Are you okay?"

Jennifer rubbed the small of her back. "My lower back hurts this morning, and I'm having a hard time finding a comfortable position."

"I'm almost done with my binding now," Noreen said. "Would you like me to finish yours so you can sit on the couch and rest?"

Jennifer shook her head. "I appreciate the offer, but I'll be okay."

———

The truth was, Jennifer wasn't okay. She'd been having sharp pains in her back since she got up this morning, and they seemed to be getting worse, no matter what position she was in. Could these pains mean she was in labor? Oh, surely not. Contractions were supposed to be felt in the stomach, not the back. Then again, as she recalled during one of her childbirth classes, their instructor had mentioned that some women had back pain during labor.

I'm sure I'm not one of them, though, she thought. *My back just hurts because I'm so top-heavy up front.*

"If everyone's ready for a break, I'll bring some snacks in now," Emma said, rising from her seat at the table.

"I'll help you," Jennifer volunteered. She hoped that standing and moving around for a while might ease the pain in her back.

When they entered the kitchen, Emma placed a container filled with cookies on the table, and also a tray. "If you'd like to put the cookies on the tray," she told Jennifer, "I'll cut up some cheese and apple slices. Those will be better for Mike than cookies."

Jennifer nodded. "Oh, and Emma, I wanted to tell you that Randy and I found out who left the things on our porch," Jennifer said as she placed several cookies on the tray.

Emma's eyes widened. "Oh?"

"She's a young Amish woman who works as a waitress at the restaurant where Randy works now. Her name is Anna Lambright. Randy said you know her, right?"

Emma's cheeks colored. "As a matter of fact, I do. Anna used to live in Middlebury, Indiana, and she was a student in one of my quilting classes."

"Did you know she was secretly helping us?" Jennifer questioned further.

"I knew she'd paid for your classes, but she asked me not say anything." Emma put the cheese she'd cut on a second platter. "Anna went through some problems with her folks before she moved to Sarasota, and because of it, she's become sensitive to other people's needs," Emma explained. "I hope you and Randy were able to accept her gifts without reservation."

"We both felt funny about it at first, like we did when you and Lamar gave us food," Jennifer admitted. "But after thinking things through, we realized that we needed to appreciate what had been done for us and not let our pride stand in the way."

Emma began cutting the apples. "We all tend to be prideful at times, but God teaches us about the importance of humility. I believe that includes being willing to accept help from others."

"I agree." Jennifer picked up the tray of cookies. "Should I take these into the other room now?"

Emma nodded. "I'll follow as soon as I'm finished with the apples."

Jennifer had just entered the living room, when a sharp pain stabbed her lower back, this time, radiating around to her stomach. *So much for feeling better when I'm on my feet*, she thought, wincing.

———

"How did everyone's week go?" Lamar asked as they all sat around the table eating their snacks.

"Mine was good," Erika spoke up. "Last Saturday after class, Dad and I went to the beach. While we were there, we saw a group of sightless children being led on a rope." Erika's dimples deepened when she smiled. "Then one of their helpers, who I know from high school, came over and talked to me. After we visited awhile, I found out that they're in need of volunteers at the blind school, so I offered to tutor a few kids who are having trouble in math."

Emma left her seat and stood behind Erika. "I'm pleased to hear that, and I'm sure your help will be greatly appreciated," she said, placing her hands on Erika's shoulders. It did Emma's heart good to hear the enthusiasm in the young woman's voice and see the look of joy on her face. While she knew she couldn't take any credit for this, Emma was glad Erika had made a turnaround from her negative attitude and found some purpose for her life. She prayed that God would guide and direct Erika in the years ahead to do His will and make the best of her situation. If there was one thing Emma had learned over the years, it was that most people, including those who were faced with physical limitations, had the ability to do something positive with their lives.

Emma noticed that Jennifer's face was screwed up as though she were in pain. "What's wrong, Jennifer?" she asked with concern.

Jennifer took a deep breath and placed her hands against her back.

"I—I think I'm in labor."

Just then, there was a knock on the front door. Emma hurried to answer it, and as she was about to ask the tall dark-haired young man who stood on her porch if she could help him, he said in a deep voice, "Is Bruce Jensen here? I was told that he's my father, and I need to speak to him."

CHAPTER 40

Goshen

Star had just come out of the grocery store, when she spotted Ruby Lee Williams in the parking lot. Ruby Lee had taken the same quilting class as Star, and they'd gotten to know each other quite well. Ruby Lee's husband, Gene, was a minister, and Star attended his church whenever she could, along with her dad.

"Hey, how's it going?" Star asked, joining Ruby Lee at the trunk of her car, where she was loading several sacks of groceries.

Ruby Lee turned and smiled. "It's going well, Star. How are things with you?"

"Okay, I guess."

"I heard you and your dad went to Florida. How was your trip? Did you have a good time?"

Star shrugged her shoulders. "The beaches were nice, and the weather was warm, but Dad and I didn't spend much time together."

Ruby Lee's dark eyebrows lifted slightly. "Really? How come?

I thought the reason for the trip was so you two could spend some quality time together."

"That's what I thought, too, but Dad had other ideas."

"Such as?"

Star folded her arms. "Dad met this woman named Kim, and he spent most of his time with her instead of me. You should have seen 'em, Ruby Lee. They acted like a couple of lovesick teenagers." Star stuck her finger in her mouth and made a gagging sound. "It was just plain sickening."

Ruby Lee's surprised expression turned to one of joy. "So Jan has a girlfriend now? I think that's wonderful, don't you?"

A cold wind blew across the parking lot, causing Star to shiver. "Not really. I told Dad in a note how upset I was because he seemed to care more about Kim than me."

"What'd he say about that?"

"Said it wasn't true, and that he didn't want anything to get in the way of our father-daughter relationship, so he broke things off with Kim."

Ruby Lee tipped her head. "And you're okay with that?"

"Sure, why not? I mean, Kim lives in Sarasota, and Dad lives here, so a long-distance relationship would have been dumb."

Stopping to make more room in the trunk, Ruby Lee removed the last sack of groceries from her cart. After slamming the lid shut, she clasped Star's arm, looking her right in the eyes. "I can understand the way you feel to a point, but don't you think you're being rather selfish trying to keep your dad from falling in love and making a life with the woman he loves?"

Star rubbed the back of her neck, where the frigid wind seemed to have settled. "He loved my mom once, but when she walked out of his life he got over it."

"That's not the point, Star," Ruby Lee said gently. "I think I know Jan pretty well, and I don't believe for one minute that he would push you out of his life if he fell in love and got married. There's room enough in that big heart of his to love more than one person, and I personally think you ought to give him the freedom to date and fall in love with whomever he chooses."

Star dropped her gaze to the ground, suddenly feeling like a heel. "I know Dad's been miserable since he got home, and I suppose it's my fault. Guess maybe I oughta do something to make it right. I just hope it won't backfire in my face."

Sarasota

Emma had just called the restaurant to let Randy know that Jennifer was in labor and had no more than hung up the telephone when it rang, startling her. Too much was happening too fast here today, and her stomach quivered from all the excitement. First, Jennifer going into labor, and then the young man showing up, proclaiming to be B.J.'s son. It was a bit overwhelming.

"Emma, aren't you going to answer that?" Lamar asked, gesturing to the phone, still ringing.

"Jah, of course." Emma picked up the phone and was surprised to hear Star on the other end.

"I hope I'm not calling at a bad time," Star said, "but I was wondering if you had Kim's phone number. I need to talk to her about something."

"I do have her number, but Kim is here at the house right now, so would you like me to put her on?" Emma asked.

"Sure, that'd be great."

Emma called Kim to the phone, and after Kim had taken the receiver, Emma moved back to the living room where Noreen, B.J., and the young dark-haired man stood near the door. She glanced quickly at Jennifer, now lying on the couch, waiting for Randy to come. Mike's wife, Phyllis, sat nearby, offering encouraging words to the expectant mother, while Erika and Mike looked on with concerned expressions.

"What's this about you being my son?" B.J. asked, stepping up to the young man who had shown up a few minutes ago. Could it be possible, or was this some kind of a hoax?

"This is my adopted son, and he's yours and Judy's boy," Noreen spoke up.

B.J.'s throat constricted as he stared at Todd, noting that the young man had some of his own characteristics—thick dark hair, like he'd once had, oval face, and slender build. However, he had Judy's dark brown eyes and dimples.

"I'm happy to meet you," B.J. said, extending his trembling hand to Todd. Then he turned back to face Noreen. "I thought you didn't know where my son was."

"I—I'm sorry, and I'm ashamed of myself, but I lied."

"Why'd you keep it from me?" B.J. rasped, feeling weak and shaky.

"I didn't think you had the right to know because I blamed you for Judy's death."

"And now?"

"After I learned of your illness, and thought things through, I changed my mind." Tears welled in Noreen's eyes. "God spoke to my heart, and I realized it wasn't right to keep the truth from you any longer."

B.J. swallowed hard, barely able to keep his own tears from falling. He looked back at Todd and said, "If I'd known about you, I never would have broken up with your mother or gone off to another state to attend college. I would have stayed in Columbus and done the right thing by Judy."

"When Mom and Dad found out Judy was pregnant, they sent her to me and Ben, since we lived here in Sarasota by then, and they knew that nobody in Columbus would be any the wiser," Noreen interjected.

"Did you plan to adopt me from the very beginning?" Todd asked, turning to face Noreen.

She shook her head. "But after Judy died, we knew adoption was the best thing for you, as well as us, since we truly wanted you, Son." Noreen touched Todd's arm. "We never regretted it, either. You were a blessing to both Ben and me. We loved you as if you were our flesh-and-blood son."

"Todd, I'm sorry I didn't have the opportunity to know you during your growing-up years," B.J. said, barely able to speak around the lump in his throat. "I have many regrets, but so little time. If only we had more opportunity to get to know each other. I'd like you to meet your half sisters, too."

"My wife and I will be here visiting Mom for another week," Todd said. "I think we should spend that time getting to know each other, don't you?"

B.J. bobbed his head. "I'd like that, too. I had planned to return to Chicago early next week, but it can wait a few more days. Getting acquainted with my son takes priority over everything else right now."

After a slight hesitation, Todd took his father into his arms. To B.J., nothing had ever felt better. His son's strength was just what he needed as he stood enveloped in the young man's arms, and Noreen stood by, her cheeks damp with tears.

———

Emma, seeing that things seemed to be working out between B.J., Noreen, and Todd, moved back to the couch to see how Jennifer was doing.

"I hope Randy gets here soon," Jennifer said, looking up at Emma with wrinkled brows. "I'm a little scared."

Pulling a chair over to be near Jennifer, Emma sat down and held Jennifer's hand. "Having a baby for the first time is always a bit frightening since you're not completely sure of what all to expect. But once that little girl is in your arms, you'll forget everything else and concentrate fully on her."

"Thank you, Emma," Jennifer said, squeezing Emma's fingers when another pain started. "They told us the same thing during the birthing classes."

A few minutes later, Randy burst into the room. Emma hadn't heard him enter the house but figured Lamar must have let him in.

"I came as soon as I got the call," Randy said, dropping to his knees in front of the couch. Taking his wife's other hand, he asked, "How far apart are the pains?"

"Kim was timing them for me before she went to the kitchen to take a phone call, and they were about six minutes apart." Jennifer clenched her teeth. "It feels like the pains might be coming even closer now."

"Time to go the hospital." Randy helped Jennifer to her feet and led her toward the door.

"Please call and let us know once the baby is born," Emma called after them.

"Will do!" Randy said over his shoulder as he steadied Jennifer, going out the door.

A short time later, Kim returned from the kitchen, wearing a huge smile. "You'll never guess what Star said. She apologized for causing the breakup between me and her dad and said that after talking with her pastor's wife she realized it wasn't right to stand in the way of Jan's happiness. She also said she was sorry for not getting to know me or even giving me a chance to be her friend."

"I'm pleased to hear that," Emma said.

"And so am I," Lamar agreed.

"Star also said that if her dad was going to have a special person in his life, she was glad it was someone like me," Kim added, squeezing her hands together.

Emma smiled. "That's wonderful. I was hoping Star would realize that Jan having a relationship with you wouldn't affect the way he feels about her."

"And you know what else?"

"What's that?"

"Star invited me to come visit them, and as soon as I get some time off, I'm going to do just that." Kim eyes brightened. "When I get home this afternoon I'm going to give Jan a call. I'm just so happy I could burst!"

"*Ach,* my!" Emma exclaimed, looking at Lamar. "Such excitement we've had here today."

———⚬———

That evening while Emma was preparing supper, the telephone rang. Lamar stepped into the kitchen to answer it.

Trying not to eavesdrop, Emma kept stirring the kettle of chicken-corn soup.

A few minutes later, Lamar hung up the phone and joined Emma at the stove. "That was Randy. Jennifer had the baby, and they named her Anna." He grinned. "I think they chose that name because Anna Lambright was their secret gift-giver."

"That's *wunderbaar!*" Emma drew in a deep breath and released it slowly.

"It seems they made it to the hospital in time, because little Anna was born a few hours later," Lamar added. "Randy said she weighed almost seven pounds and is nineteen inches long."

"Randy and Jennifer have been blessed in so many ways. And now, they've received the biggest blessing of all—a precious baby girl." Emma remembered the joy she'd felt when her own children were born. "How grateful I am that we've had the privilege of not only teaching, but getting to know so many of our students. I pray that God will bless this group of quilters in very special ways."

EPILOGUE

Shipshewana
Six months later

Think I'll meander down to the mailbox and see if the mail's come yet," Lamar said as he and Emma sat on their front porch, watching their goats frolic in the pen.

"That's a good idea," Emma said. "I'm hoping to hear something from my sister in Oregon, letting us know if she's feeling up to us coming for another visit later this fall. They'd visited Betty in the spring, and Emma had been pleased to see how well she was doing. It was hard to believe that just a year ago, her dear sister had been so ill she barely recognized anyone. *The power of love can work miracles*, Emma thought.

Lamar patted Emma's arm. "I'll be back soon with the mail."

Emma watched as he made his way down the driveway, walking easily and without a limp. They'd had a good time in Florida, but she was glad they were home now, close to their family and friends. Being in the warmer weather all winter had helped the symptoms of Lamar's arthritis, but of course, the weather was warm here in Indiana now, too.

But, in a few months when it turned cold again, they would catch the Pioneer Trails bus and head for their Florida home.

Emma leaned her head against the back of her chair and listened to the twitter of the birds, while a slight breeze tickled her nose. *God has surely blessed us,* she thought.

When Lamar returned with a handful of mail, as well as a large package the mailman had left in the phone shack, he handed the envelopes to Emma and set the package on the porch. "Looks like there's a letter from Noreen Webber and one from your sister's daughter, too."

"Oh, that's good." Emma took the mail and eagerly opened the first letter. "We've been invited for a family get-together next month in Portland," she said after she'd read her niece's letter. "Do you think we can go, Lamar?"

He gave a nod. "Don't see why not. Cheryl and Terry's and Jan and Kim's double wedding is in two weeks, so it won't interfere." He grinned. "I'm almost sure that some of our earlier quilting students will be at the wedding, too."

"I wouldn't be surprised."

Lamar gave Emma the other letter. "Guess you'd better see what Noreen has to say."

Emma tore open the envelope and tears pooled in her eyes as she read it aloud:

"Dear Emma and Lamar,

"It's with sadness that I'm writing to tell you of B.J.'s passing. His funeral was last week, and Todd and I went to Chicago for the service. It was a sad time for all, but Todd had the chance to get to know his half sisters, and they plan to stay in touch.

"I've kept in contact with the others from our quilting class.

Mike and Phyllis recently returned from a trip to Hawaii.
Jennifer and Randy are doing well, and their
sweet little girl is growing like a weed. Kim, as I'm sure
you know, will be getting married soon. Oh, and I saw Erika the
other day at the children's hospital, where I volunteer. In addition
to doing some tutoring at the blind school, Erika has been making
cloth dolls to give to the children at the hospital.

"As for myself, I'm keeping busy with my volunteer work, and
more recently, I've gotten involved with a seniors' group and have
even gone on a few dates with a very nice man.

"I feel, as I'm sure the others who attended our class do, grateful
to you and Lamar for your kindness, patience, and the Christian
example you showed each of us during our quilting classes. I can
honestly say that I learned a lot more than quilting while attending
your classes. I've been able to let go of the anger I felt all those years
towards B.J., and it feels as if a great weight has been lifted from
my shoulders.

> *"Many blessings to you and yours,*
> *"Noreen*

"P.S. Almost forgot to mention that before I left Illinois, B.J.'s
daughter Jill gave me a picture of a seascape her father had started
painting while he was in Florida. He finished it after he returned
to Chicago, but due to his weakened condition, he never got it
mailed. Jill said her dad wanted you folks to have it and asked that
I get it to you. It should be arriving at your place soon."

"I wonder if that's what's in there," Emma said, gesturing to the package.

"Well, let's take a look." Lamar opened the box and removed some wrapping paper. Then he lifted the most beautiful painting out for

Emma to see.

"Ach, my! It's just lovely," Emma gasped as her eyes focused on the seascape, to which had been added a quilt similar to one that Lamar had designed and showed the class. It was spread out on the beach, and the colors from the setting sun cast a rosy appearance across the quilt. At the top of the picture, engraved in the frame were the words: THE HEALING QUILT.

Tears welled in Emma's eyes and she sniffed deeply. "Oh Lamar, even in B.J.'s darkest hour, he remembered us. Wasn't that thoughtful of him?"

"Jah, it certainly was," Lamar agreed.

Emma clasped her hands lightly together, gazing at the painting through watery eyes. "I'm looking forward to the days ahead, knowing that with God at the center of our lives, we will continue to be blessed, as we allow the Lord to help us bless others."

Emma's Raisin Molasses Cookies

2 cups raisins

1 cup shortening

½ cup sugar

2 eggs

1½ cups molasses

4 cups flour

3 teaspoons baking powder

½ teaspoon baking soda

1 teaspoon salt

2 teaspoons cinnamon

2 teaspoons ginger

Preheat oven to 350 degrees. Rinse and drain raisins. In a mixing bowl, cream shortening and sugar. Add eggs and beat well. Blend in molasses. Sift flour with baking powder, baking soda, salt, cinnamon, and ginger. Blend into creamed mixture. Stir in raisins. Drop by teaspoons onto greased cookie sheet and bake for 15 to 18 minutes. Yields about 6 dozen cookies.

Discussion Questions

1. Emma agreed to spend the winter in Florida because of Lamar's arthritis, but she missed her family in Indiana and soon became bored. What are some ways we can deal with being separated from family and friends?

2. B.J. hid his health issues from his family, wanting to spare them the truth for as long as possible. Is there ever a time when it's right for someone to keep something like that from their family?

3. Since losing the ability to walk, Erika Wilson had no confidence in herself and felt as if she was worthless. Have you or someone you know ever felt that way? What are some ways we can offer encouragement to a person with a disability?

4. Noreen struggled to forgive B.J. for hurting her sister in the past. Was Noreen justified in feeling bitter toward B.J.? What does the Bible say about forgiveness?

5. Star, having been reunited with her father two years ago, felt jealous when he showed an interest in Kim. What are some ways an adult child can deal with their parents' desire to date again?

6. Mike Barstow was a workaholic and wanted to be on his boat all the time. Do you or someone you know tend to work too much, neglecting your personal relationships in exchange for your job? What are some things we can do to curb the desire to work all the time? How can we find more time to spend with our family and friends?

7. When Kim felt nervous, she was a bit klutzy, which often resulted in minor accidents on the job. Yet because of her friendliness, Kim's customers liked her and didn't complain to her boss. Has a waitress ever given you the wrong order or spilled something on you or the table? How did you handle the situation?

8. Noreen had a secret she was keeping about her sister's child. Do you think an adopted child has the right to meet his birth parents if possible? How should an adoptive parent respond when their child wants to look for their birth parents?

9. Erika took a risk the day she had the diving accident. After doing several previous dives, she was tired, yet chose to do one more dive to show off for her friends. Erika's father urged her to get out of the pool, but when Erika did the dive anyway, it ended in a serious accident that changed her life. Would you take a chance, of any sort, doing something risky that could possibly cause permanent injury to yourself?

10. Kyle didn't try to stop his daughter from doing one more dive, even though he knew she was tired. After the accident that left Erika paralyzed from the waist down, he felt guilty. As a parent, do you find it hard to allow your children, especially as teenagers, to make their own decisions, even though you feel their decisions are wrong or risky? When should a parent step in and say no to what their child wants to do?

11. Jennifer's husband, Randy, was discouraged when he couldn't find a job. What are some ways we can help someone who is unemployed,

yet actively looking for work, without making them feel inadequate or indebted to us?

12. Jennifer and Randy were being helped by a stranger. Would you be able to accept such generous gifts from someone you didn't know? If you had been Jennifer, would you have been able to take the quilting class, knowing someone had paid for your class, while the rest of the quilters had to pay for their own?

13. This story was set in the small community known as Pinecraft, which is part of Sarasota, Florida. What differences did you see in the way the Amish live there, from other Amish communities in different parts of the country?

14. Emma sometimes quoted different Bible verses to her students. Were there any verses of scripture in the book that spoke to your heart? If so, in what way?

About the Author

New York Times bestselling author, Wanda E. Brunstetter became fascinated with the Amish way of life when she first visited her husband's Mennonite relatives living in Pennsylvania. Wanda and her husband, Richard, live in Washington State but take every opportunity to visit Amish settlements throughout the States, where they have many Amish friends.

Wanda and Richard have been blessed with two grown children, six grandchildren, and one great-grandson. In her spare time, Wanda enjoys beachcombing, ventriloquism, gardening, photography, knitting, and having fun with her family.

To learn more about Wanda, visit her website at www.wandabrunstetter.com.

Other Books by Wanda E. Brunstetter:

Adult Fiction

The Half-Stitched Amish Quilting Club
The Tattered Quilt

The Discovery Saga
Goodbye to Yesterday
The Silence of Winter
The Hope of Spring
The Pieces of Summer
A Revelation in Autumn
A Vow for Always

Kentucky Brothers Series
The Journey
The Healing
The Struggle

Brides of Lehigh Canal Series
Kelly's Chance
Betsy's Return
Sarah's Choice

Indiana Cousins Series
A Cousin's Promise
A Cousin's Prayer
A Cousin's Challenge

Sisters of Holmes County Series
A Sister's Secret
A Sister's Test
A Sister's Hope

Brides of Webster County Series
Going Home
Dear to Me
On Her Own
Allison's Journey

Let's Keep In Touch!

Want to know what Wanda's up to and be the first to hear about new releases, specials, the latest news, and more? Like Wanda on Facebook!

 Visit facebook.com/WandaBrunstetterFans